T0243283

ANTONIO RAMON

A TINY RIPPLE OF HOPE

First Edition, 2023.

ISBN: 979-8-35093-428-1 (print)
ISBN: 979-8-35093-429-8 (eBook)

1

The sirens blare just a few blocks away, and I freeze up. But it's not the whirling up-tempo shrill, the pulsing rush of some high-speed chase, that chills me. No. It's the sound of *arrival.* The way the noise caves suddenly, the notes dying off at the end, sinking five octaves into oblivion, as I imagine LAPD squad cars slow, then stop. What's the opposite of crescendo? *De-scendo?* I have this obsession where I try to be precise with my words, ever since one of my doctors suggested I take up journaling as a proper outlet for my emotions. And sometimes, I accidentally make up words that don't exist, but I think they should, and so I go on and use them anyway. *De-scendo* – I'll look it up later.

Next comes the bustle of people, the murmur of a swelling crowd, and though I can't see any of it, maybe that's what makes it even scarier. I rush off, away from the commotion, my fast-twitch muscles pumping my arms and legs like some Olympic racewalker. Besides, whenever I sense the presence of police, I usually just turn and hustle in the other direction. I've got a history with them, and it's nothing good.

I'm cool with crowds, though. Actually, it's that density of people and the energy it brings that attracted me to Koreatown in the first place. L.A. is sprawling, running on for miles and miles in all directions, and with few exceptions, there aren't many skyscrapers; the city being built *out*, not up. And that's a shame because it has all the big-city issues but none of that dynamic, big-city feel. But I once researched how K-town was the most densely populated area in Los Angeles, and so I thought this would be the perfect place for me. I'd never ventured here before, having grown up in the Valley and then spending a short stint in Santa Monica before the ugly Cup O' Joe's incident. But K-town clicked right away because, though it was still L.A., it felt as though I were in another country—a sense of adventure, something new and different—and with so many people out and about, it just felt good to be out in the middle of crowds and activity because it made me feel as though I were a part of something.

My grandmother once told me the appeal of bookstores is their infinite possibilities. With each book, there's the chance of something larger, an opportunity to learn something new or evoke some new emotion, or change and become a different person—hopefully, a better one—and all the wonderful things a new book can do. And I love reading—though it doesn't always work for me because it's, by nature, slow, and I often can't downshift my mind to that pace. Still, it's about the *possibilities*, except instead of books, it's people, which is what big cities and crowds and K-town do for me too. Yeah, many keep their heads low and plug ahead, looking down at the soft-gray sidewalks, maybe listening to music through earphones, or just being lost in their thoughts, and with their lack of smiles, maybe they have some big worries, but all of that is okay—the humanity, the sheer numbers, give me hope. A lot of lonely people are still a lot of people, and if maybe one or a few are open to connecting, then we can all be a little less lonely.

The sun dips below the skyline, and everything's splashed in a dull amber shade. I've walked a long way, but now I've got to head back since I'll be meeting Ray for dinner at his favorite Mexican restaurant on Olympic—the one with the name I can never pronounce. I take long walks through Koreatown every day. It's all the energy—way, way too much—that I need to quell—that's a good word—and so I need to move, need to walk. In the months I've lived here, I've walked just about every street in K-town. Still, it's never dull. There are countless strip malls, clearly built around the 1960s and never modernized since then, but they hold a certain charm because the small shops that make up each of these malls hold endless surprises, like sections within a bookstore. I've stumbled into herb shops that sold me bizarre pills, and some may have improved my health, while others I'd swear nearly killed me, Pilates classes where the instructors and the middle-aged Korean women pushed me into joining them for a trial class, and then I signed up for six more given how limber and loose I felt after just the one; the pastry shops I can never resist; the countless mysterious storefronts with signs in Korean or Spanish; or the shop on Eighth painted all in black and going through constant renovation with scaffolding covering the entrance beyond which I could never possibly guess what goes on . . . *Endless surprises.*

I turn a corner and slow, inching forward, realizing I've arrived at a street where I can now clearly see in the distance the crime scene that wailed out to me before. I stop hard when I see the police tape stretched taut across a fence just outside an old apartment building, forcing the large huddle of people clustered on the sidewalk to spill onto the street. There are cops everywhere—several LAPD units with lights twirling, a black van that must be some sort of forensics unit. But I'd never seen police tape before. The sting of bright yellow, the hard boundary of some serious event.

I spin around, but as soon as I try to walk off, I feel something hard pushing back against my chest. There's nothing there, in front of me; nothing I can see anyway. And yet, I can't move forward. I back off, looking around, searching for anything that might be the cause, searching for an explanation. But there's nothing there. I step forward, but, again, I'm held back, like hitting some invisible wall. But it's not flat like a wall. There are two pressure points, as if two unseen hands lean on my themed T-shirt—one right on top of the word *Yell* and the other covering *Care.* I wave my arms wildly in front of me, trying to break this force, and though I'm not hitting anything, this pressure continues to keep me back. I stop when I see a young Mexican mother coming down the sidewalk toward me, her two small children tugging her forward to see what all the police commotion is about. Her eyes are on me, the weight of fear and curiosity—the way people look at the homeless here when one suddenly bursts into a crazy, arm-swinging rant. I let them pass.

Relax, Cole. Please, just relax.

I exhale, then try again slowly but forcefully to push ahead. But it's still no good. I don't know what's happening. My breathing accelerates and I rake my fingers through my hair hard and fast, pulling my big, brown waves up and back. I try again, but it's the *same damn thing*. I then take slow, small steps backward, giving up. Dazed. It's clear: the only way is to go back in the opposite direction, past the crime scene.

I walk toward the mass of people gathered on the street just beyond the sidewalk, cordoned off by that tape. Though I haven't encountered too many police in my life, the few times I have did not turn out good, and though I'm slowing, I do not stop, walking with a steady, deliberate step. But I really start to drag when I see the worried expressions on the faces of everyone standing behind the line. Most of the faces are Hispanic, which used to strike me as odd since it's Koreatown, but that's L.A. Some poke their heads above the others to get a better look, while others turn away, head in their hands. Some are crying. This can't be some minor incident—a petty theft or a homeless guy loitering—or something like campus police escorting my naked body off the cold lawn and handing me a blanket, which I twist around me like a poorly wrapped toga, but that's another story. These faces all look scared.

The police come in and out of the apartment building, through a door on the first floor, some in uniform and others in crime lab smocks, though not as many as I would have expected for some gruesome crime. Still, I want to keep moving—moving on, moving away from here—but I stay. I reach out to touch the police tape, feeling the crisp plastic in my fingers. It reads: *Departamento De Policia De Los Angeles—Linea De Policia—Por Favor No Cruzar*. The English translation follows, then back to Spanish, then again English, and it goes on. . .

"What happened?" I finally ask an elderly lady next to me, her face scrunched up, a pained look, to the point it's hard to tell if she's Hispanic or maybe Asian. Her eyes are swollen with tears.

"The boy," she says, shaking her head.

"The boy?"

"Someone has taken the little boy."

I jump back, my eyes darting all around, the shuffling of the crowd, the police line, the metallic screen door swinging open and closed as police come and go, a gloved hand dusting the window sill for fingerprints, crying and wailing coming from inside the apartment. Though K-town isn't considered the safest part of L.A., its crimes are usually tied to the night and drunkenness. Something like *this*, I only hear about these crimes on the news, which, along with gang shootings in South Central or suicide bombings in the Middle East, are just some of the reasons I never watch the news except for occasions when I feel I've been disconnected a little too long with what's been happening in the world, combined with a need to see the beautiful morning reporter on the local news station, but the worst stories are about the kids, and I beat my forehead with my fists as I try to force the thoughts out of my mind, practically running from the crime scene now, the things that should never happen to kids in this world, like the little girl dying of leukemia at City of Hope, or the baby left in the car when it's ninety degrees out, or the high school kid who gets gunned down by a gangbanger's stray bullet, or the eighth grader who kills himself because he was bullied at school, or the little boy taken from his K-town apartment, or the kid that gets yelled at in the middle of the night because he's not good enough.

2

I'm walking down Normandie now, an unlit cigarette dangling from my lips, as always. But I sense a shake there, a quiver, and so I push the cigarette in deeper so that it doesn't slip. If I keep the brisk pace, I won't be too late, and it's only Ray, so he won't mind because he doesn't have anywhere to be later, just like me. I scratch at my unshaven face, and my big hair is a mess, junked up by nervous hands and frayed nerves. I can't stop the images from the crime scene from replaying in my mind.

I try to focus on the pedestrians passing me on the sidewalk. The many people who just put their heads down and push on remind me I need to look up. I am more manic than depressive—along with extra servings of some attention-hyperactive-deficit-whatever-disorder-syndrome—but when I do get down, it is way down, *scary* down. So it's a good thing that I'm mostly positive, and as I walk, I try to appreciate the great weather and the shorter skirts the girls wear on warm May afternoons like today. The only diagnosis of all of them—and I think I have four or five—that makes me sort of proud is ODD. That's short for Oppositional Defiant Disorder, though I like to refer to it as just ODD. I like this one because it helped explain how rebellious I was as a kid, although I wish I was a bit more rebellious now. But when I think back to that day when the doctor told me and my parents about it, I felt good not only because it wasn't going to require more meds but mostly because, when you shorten it, it's not even like you're sick or anything. You're just *ODD*.

I step into the Mexican restaurant, which is Ray's favorite place. Ray is easy to spot, even if he weren't waving me down like a cab, sitting there in the same fashion he always sports—a tan fedora, a bowling shirt, and of course, the Ray-Ban Wayfarer sunglasses he always wears outside and typically sports indoors too if it's a hip place, a place where he might be seen.

"S'up, Cole?" he says just before slamming a tequila shot.

"Hey, aren't you working later tonight?"

"Done! I was hustling all day. Man, business has picked up. I think I've hit that tipping point where the word is out on me, my ride, and I'm big with the old ladies; they love me! They're calling now for all their short trips to the market or the beauty salon, and I think they like me because I'm young and compliment them, give them a little flirting action, make them smile. . ."

Ray is Korean and drives an illegal taxi, one of many drivers in K-town that specialize in Korean customers, many whom don't speak much English or just appreciate the dirt-cheap fares, so low that it's worth it to quickly call a ride and have a driver take you a few city blocks rather than walk it yourself. They try to crack down on these illegal cabs now and then, but according to Ray, it's impossible. It's all some foreign-language black market that's tough to bust because all sides of the economic equation are winning.

The waitress—a slim, full-figured Mexican girl—stops at the table, hands me a menu, and doesn't say anything, but gives me a smile, and holds that smile for just a millisecond too long, making it just a little strange. It makes me wonder if there isn't something more there. Does the smile mean something?

"Hey, drink with me," Ray says.

"No, thanks."

"We can just do the tequila. We don't have to go mezcal like last time, even though this place has the best damn mezcal in L.A. Look, I'm just hitting the Don Julio."

I don't want to get into talking about my meds and how I'm not supposed to mix them with drinks. Besides, I've already told him before about how I'm trying to not drink anymore, either liquor or caffeine, because I'm trying to find the right . . . balance. That's the best I can explain it—the equilibrium where my body and mind feel just right.

"No, really, I'm out," I say.

"Are you ready to order?" the beautiful Mexican waitress asks, smiling first at Ray, and I notice it's the same smile she gave me, so there is, in the end, nothing special there. She just happens to be a friendly waitress.

"First, let's switch it up to my usual mezcal. I'll also take the chicken enchiladas—and to start with—hah, hah, hah. . .!" Ray says, turning to me and laughing, "a small order of *chapulines*!"

The waitress giggles as I shake my head.

"We can make it a large order to share; what do you say?" Ray asks me.

"No."

"They're really very good. . ." the beautiful waitress says, and I'm not sure I ever had any chance with her, but now, with my cowardice fully exposed, I was done.

"Oh, and no smoking in here," she tells me.

"It's not lit."

She bunches up her face, struggling to think through the rule and whether the cigarette being unlit is a good enough excuse. But I suppose in the end, she figures the law is No *Smoking,* and in order for someone to smoke, the cigarette has to be lit, and therefore, I'm good. Or she just doesn't care that much because I point to the quesadilla on the menu, and she turns and walks away.

Chapulines are grasshoppers, toasted in lime juice and garlic, brown, and about an inch in length, but they still maintain the shape and look of a small grasshopper. They are, according to Ray, crunchy, and wth a spicy flavor, and whenever he suggests we meet here, I know he'll have the *chapulines* and taunt me for not even trying them.

"Hey, that's a great T-shirt," he says, words garbled by a mouthful of tortilla chips.

I nod but don't respond. I have serious issues with this shirt. I had pulled it this morning and almost vetoed the selection. It is a black shirt with bold-faced white print, reading *I YELL BECAUSE I CARE.* I have a daily ritual of selecting a shirt from my big collection of themed T-shirts, and then honing in on the shirt's message and graphics to see how it applies to my life that day. This often helps my mind to slow down and focus—a small meditation for the day. Otherwise, my mind shoots off into God-knows-where, and I need to bring it back and keep it here, because that will help me cut through all the noise. But I had just pulled the shirt yesterday and had vetoed it then, and so it defies all logic and odds—with four hundred fifty-three shirts hanging in my closet—that I would pull the same one again the next day.

"No, really," he says. "It's the perfect attitude girls go for. I mean, 'I Yell' is by itself pretty badass, but then there's the 'I Care' part, which is just enough to show you have a sensitive side. I bet the girls are all over you when you rock that shirt."

I lift my hands to my chest, brushing the fabric, remembering the strange force that held me back—*What the hell was that?*—and I really want to tell Ray about it and ask if there's something I'm missing, some possible phenomenon of nature that I haven't considered that might explain that mystical power, but I also *don't* want to tell Ray because I have too few friends as it is, and I don't need him thinking I'm crazy.

"Hey, I forgot to tell you," Ray says. "I mentioned your whole weird, ritual shirt thing to my sister, and she thinks it's great. She told me it's the greatest thing she's ever heard of."

"Really?"

"Yeah, she's very Buddhist, very Zen, and she said monks used to be given little sayings—*Koans*, she called them—to stop their minds from wandering."

I break a chip into the bottom of the salsa cup and stop dead.

"You okay?" Ray asks.

"Huh? Yeah. Listen, can I meet your sister?"

"Hey, man, you can't date my sister. We'd have to stop being friends and —"

"No, no, I just want to talk to her and ask her about the monks."

"Sorry, man. She just took off for Europe for the summer. That's what all them UCLA kids do."

I make a face, then take out my phone and make a note to myself to ask again in the Fall when she's back.

The waitress returns with Ray's food, sets it on the table, then steps back and actually waits there for a moment, watching Ray.

He takes a few of the *chapulines* in the fingertips of his left hand, raising the cup of mezcal in his right. He tilts his head back and lowers the bugs into his mouth. He chews them for a moment, grinning all the time at the waitress, who returns a satisfied look. Then he pounds the mezcal and gives her a wink.

She lowers her head, smiling shyly, then turns.

I watch her walk away, a little dance to her small steps as they shake the bright red and green skirt from side to side. I then study Ray, his mouth full and stretched to a wide grin, and all I can think is how I would love to have some of *that*, just a little, that essence that would let me chew on *chapulines* and down mezcal and have it be so second nature—so, *nothing*—that I could smile and wink as I'm doing it.

3

It's night. 3:45 a.m. I'm alone in bed. It's the time when I'm most alone. It's the same for everyone. Even the guy with the huge social network, running his own company, a steady girlfriend, a rave warehouse full of friends . . . at night, is alone. Even if he, or anyone else, has someone to hold in bed, he's *still* alone. That's because, at night, there is no noise. Not the outside world kind of noise that keeps you busy or distracted during the day. No. Here, there is only the noise in your head. This is when your darkest thoughts come out—when who you *really* are comes out. Because I battle this noise all the time, none of this is a surprise to me. I'd like to sleep, but when those black thoughts attack, there's no hope. Night is when the monsters come out. Memories of being a kid again and my father entering my room after I've been singing loudly or trying to tell myself stories for bedtime, also at a high volume, and him yelling as loudly as he can for me to stop. And I can still smell the alcohol. *Even now.* But I don't stop. I really can't. I'm *ODD*. But he yells louder, saying, why do I have to be this way and how I embarrass him all the time and why can't I be normal like everyone else? And he doesn't stop. I don't know how to be anyone but me, but he doesn't want that. And so, I wish I could be someone else, but I don't know how to change. I yell, saying it's not my fault. He screams and tells me it's all my fault, and we go at it—him bigger, his voice louder. He yells that he's trying to help me because he loves me, and he really cares, and other such things. Why can't I try? he asks, telling me to try to be more normal. To be still. He's trying to help me. He *cares*. Sometimes, my mother comes into my room and tells my father he's not helping and to leave me be, and it usually doesn't stop until she pulls him away by the arm. He yells as he's being pulled out the door, *You're a freak!*

Then I'm alone, and I go quiet. But I don't fall asleep. Just like tonight. I don't sleep. Instead, I cry but try to silence it, which I suppose makes it more like sobbing. I want to be precise—I'll look it up tomorrow. And I wish I could just cry myself to sleep, but that doesn't happen. Too much energy still. Maybe when I focus and think about something, my mind won't let it go, and something like sleep isn't possible. Or maybe I can't doze off, tired as I am, my voice gone, throat sore, body sweating from all the energy and convulsions of the argument, eyes red and swollen from the crying, because of who I am. But I can't be me. *I have to be better.*

4

I TAP THE TV REMOTE CONTROL ON MY SMALL, GLASS COFFEE table—a chiming echo of a tap—at least thirty times before turning the set on. There is a strange push-pull inside of me—the need to know more about the kidnapped boy against not wanting to know. I switch to the morning news just to see if there's any information. Hopefully they found him, you know, and it was all one big misunderstanding. The uncle took him to the Dodger game, and the family forgot that it was yesterday and not next week. But I know these stories almost never turn out that way.

They show the entire morning team in a wide shot, and the beautiful blonde morning anchor must be off today, so I'm even less inspired to keep watching. But I sit through stories of a young woman training to swim the English Channel, a '70's rock band I'm not familiar with coming to L.A. next year as part of their farewell tour, and a Filipino cultural festival this weekend at Griffith Park with dancing and food. The fluffiness of all these stories is just nauseating, which I know seems like a contradiction since I also hate the stories of all the meanness in the world. But how can the morning crew laugh and be so upbeat while there is still a kid missing in the city?

I realize I've joined the telecast too late, and a story like the missing boy would've been at the top of the show. I can't explain it, but I'm actually relieved. I close my eyes, and I'm there again—the sirens, twirling police lights, and crisp yellow tape.

Outside my window, I can see the Griffith Park Observatory and the Hollywood sign on the distant hills. But I think what stands out most about Central L.A. are the palm trees lining the sidewalks of the endless city blocks, some as tall as my window, and gently swaying if there's a breeze. A beautiful reminder that this isn't Manhattan or Paris or just about anywhere else. And there are so many homes, apartments, places to hide—or to hide someone.

Up high, what really hits me this morning is the rich blue of the sky—that postcard azure blue—a blue that gets tourists just rising in their hotel rooms to snap dozens of pictures to send back home to their friends to show them what Southern California is all about. I can feel something stirring now, my engine beginning to rev on high. Just about anything can set me off, but today, it's that sky, and in my psyche, that blue stings like ice water. I worry that next will be the barrage of thoughts coming out of nowhere but coming hard at me—then through me—like a quadrillion shooting stars, leaving my mind a completely pure, brilliant white.

Quadrillion is my second favorite word.

It's almost time to select my shirt, a ceremony I perform daily, but there's one more thing on my apartment that may not be important, but I'd like to think *is* important because it's at least a little different, and it matters to a guy like me because I'm truly a *spirit* guy, and it makes me question my spirit and the state of the soul. Maybe I'm not making sense, so I'll just tell you the previous tenant died here in the apartment, shotgun barrel to his head, the trigger cocked then hammered forward, and the gray matter and blood blasted to all the walls, and I'm not trying to be melodramatic, *really*, but I think the way you check out of this world says something about who you are—*were*, whatever—and so, this has to say a lot about him, though I never knew him, but I have given serious thought to researching him and his life to determine not only what caused him to end it all but also why by *that* means. I mean, it's so over-the-top when you could just take an overdose of pills or use a small handgun. And to make such an unbelievable mess means he really must have had it in for cleaning people, but the most important thing about all of this is that this apartment is in the heart of Koreatown, and Asians are superstitious about such things as living in a home where someone has died, and then along comes a Caucasian guy like me who is seriously working on his spirit. However, I'm more concerned at this stage with my spirit in *this* life, or better yet, my spirit for this *day*, and I can't be too burdened with afterlife issues. So, after weeks of having an apartment sit empty, the desperate Chinese landlord, hating Mexicans who he will never rent to but who actually make up a big part of the K-town population, finds me, and I get the apartment for half price. *Score.*

I head to the bathroom, and now I just need to take my pills and get that over with. I never take my full dosage of meds. In fact, I usually just take half or less. I'm fully aware of the risk and the trade-off because, at half strength, the medicine may not be effective when I need it most. The pills are supposed to make me feel a lot better and calmer—and the doctors have been saying that all my life since I was a kid—but a full dose makes me feel a numbness, and not just in my body and my mind, which most people might relate to as the way cold medicine dulls your mind, but deeper still. It's as if my spirit, something inside that makes me who I am, is stunted just a bit, a feeling like I'm halfway to morphing into a mannequin.

5

I WAS HOPING FOR A SHIRT TODAY THAT'S UPBEAT AND POSITIVE, but instead I chose one that is exactly neutral. I had bought the shirt at the Los Angeles County Museum of Art just down Wilshire when they had a special exhibit on science-related art, and I laughed out loud as soon as I saw it hanging there in the museum store, which drew some looks, but I'm used to that. The shirt has the internet symbol—the letter *i*—speaking to a pi symbol. *i* says, *Be Rational.* Pi responds, *Get Real.* It clicked with me right away, but I think a lot of people probably won't get it. The challenge for me today as I think about the shirt is to discover what it really means on a deeper level and how, maybe, it applies to me and my life and the potential for something new.

I'm excited and committed to being out all day—no playing Minecraft on my laptop, watching Euro soccer on TV, or reading in my apartment. Yes, that's where big things happen—out in the city. I put on my latest anti-aging cream with SPF 30, but I'm not sure I'll stick with it because there's something in the SPF, I think, that seems to bother my skin. I'm not breaking out or anything, but at the end of the day, my eyes feel just a little puffy, and so if it's a slight allergy, maybe I should consider trying something new. The nice saleslady at Beverly Center always has something new for me to try because there are a thousand different skin creams, and yes, I know she's on commission, but I really think she's trying, and I know I'm not the easiest customer. Still, it's important because I spent so much time in the sun as a kid, swimming in our backyard pool or going to the beach in Malibu, and then swimming on a team all those years with daily workouts, lap after lap, with the sun reflecting off the water. So, I need to protect myself even though I'm only twenty-one and have no wrinkles—yet.

I head over to a cafe just two blocks away, cutting through the morning haze, the mysterious May gray. On the walk over, I keep patting my chest, then reaching out in front of me to see if there is any hint of that mysterious pressure that pushed me back yesterday. Thankfully, I feel nothing there.

I slip into a corner booth and order some toast, slightly buttered, and orange juice diluted with water.

"Is that all, honey?" says the waitress, a thin Latina, maybe in her mid-thirties, with her hair up to reveal the nicest slender brown neck. "That's not going to give you enough energy for the day."

"Just not a breakfast guy," I say, "and I never have problems with energy."

"I like your shirt." She smiles, and as always, I'm checking to see if it's just a smile or if it means something more.

"Most people don't get it," I say, then stop myself, on the chance that she's open to connecting and so as not to mess it up so quickly by talking excessively about virtual reality or rational numbers. *No*, I have stated my simple and direct, true statement, and now the Defense rests.

"I used to like science and math so much," she says. "Back in school. . ." Then the smile fades. "And then I got married early, and then the kids, and no more school. . ."

She shrugs and then tries to bring back a smile to her lips, but it only gets halfway there.

"And now, here . . ." She shrugs again. "That's life."

That's life—the ultimate conversation-ending cliché. But here, I feel sad for her because, although typically I think the throwaway phrase could translate as a shortened version of *That's the way life goes*, I'm worried that, for her, it's worse. What she's really saying is that's all there is to her life and that essentially it's over, which would make me feel really sad for her because, even though mid-thirties is pretty old, I would hate for anyone to think she still couldn't change her life. I suddenly think about where I might be and what I might be doing when I'm thirty-five or so, and I get scared because I have no idea—and I mean literally no thought as to what my calling, my true purpose in this life might be because, as of today, this very moment, 9:42 in the morning of a gray, L.A. day, I'm not on any path.

Terrified, I throw down a few bills for the breakfast and rush out.

I walk and am especially focused on keeping a brisk pace. Even though I've walked just about every street of K-town, I never get tired of it. Beyond the anticipation of new encounters, the strip malls, the palm trees, there's also my innate desire to roam. I'm not in school now, things having not turned out too well at Columbia the one semester, despite the hope of a new beginning. Nor am I working right now, and it all suits me just fine because I can walk and walk for miles each day.

It's a little past 4:30 p.m. when I step into the ping pong hall at The Royal hotel in Downtown L.A. I'm a little late, unnerved, and I can't explain it. My palms are clammy, and I'm jittery. It's the kind of feeling I have when I sneak some caffeine, but I almost never do that anymore because of exactly this.

"S'up, 51-50?" Jamal says, strutting in. Jamal doesn't walk; he struts, with a second step lagging just a beat slower than the first and with a slight drag. He's Black, and he's got his fro puffed out big today. His jeans are spotted with paint, so I know he must have just come from work, freelancing as an artist, mostly painting murals on commission. He's the only other friend I've made since moving to this part of the city.

I should probably qualify the use of the term *friend* as it applies to Jamal, or Ray, for that matter. They're really more like character actors in the *Life of Cole Reeves* show—a sometimes comedy, often tragedy. On the other hand, my cousin Robbie—who lives in San Diego but visits once in a while and always leaves me with a fresh perspective on life—would be more of a cameo appearance, because my father once explained to me that a cameo is an actor of distinction or fame and carries greater importance than character actors, even though neither will have as much screen time as the stars. My father would know, because he was never a star but was a steady working character actor whose face would prompt people to say, *Oh yeah,* that *guy—what's his name?—I loved him as the nosy neighbor in that romantic comedy film a couple of summers ago, or the detective on that crime show that lasted just three seasons,* or maybe any number of other commercials or daytime dramas where he just passed through and they would say, *Oh yeah,* that *guy, I* know *that guy*. Well, they didn't really know that guy, and I was just his only son, and, of course, they never knew me at all. Still, he left me with a not-so-huge but comfortable Trust when he passed away after years of working in Hollywood. The money is nice, but what I really could use are a few stars.

"Hey," I reply, and we fist bump as a waitress pauses to give me a questioning look before moving on.

"Say, I been fixin' to ask you'bout that cigarette thing. . ." Jamal says.

My back stiffens.

"If it's okay with you," he goes on, "I was thinking of doing that too, you know, just having it hang there but not lighting it."

I shrug. It truly doesn't matter to me.

"I know you won't tell me what it means, but I really like the attitude. I think it's like you're saying *I am in control.* I can either smoke or not. I'm not hooked, addicted. The cigarette doesn't own me."

"But you smoke a pack a day."

"Stay with me on this—it's about the attitude."

"Just saying. . ."

"*Attitude*, man. I seen you with waitresses who tried to get you to put it away because it's a law against smoking in the bar here, but you turn it back on them."

I rub at my temples, both hands stroking.

"Listen, I won't do it when I'm around you, when we're together," he says. "It wouldn't look right, a bit too much."

"Whatever. I don't hold any trademarks or patents on this thing."

I pick my battles carefully with Jamal, and I worry about him because he's always angry and threatening violence, though I think that's all talk. I often see him tell people off with *Yo Mama*, and though I think that's dated, he seems to pull it off because whatever he says comes out sounding smooth and cool.

51-50 is police code for a crazy person, and the other thing about him is that he's got his own language, knows things like police code, and has this aura of walking on the edge of the dark side, so I like him and let him call me 51-50.

"Game on, homes," he says. "'Bout to take you down."

The Royal has a second level that is solely a bar and two massive rooms of ping-pong tables, soaked in blue neon, and a chill vibe that makes it one of our favorite places to hang—this ain't no neighbor's garage ping-pong here. He orders a beer, and I get a Sprite—fresh, lem-on-lime taste, and no caffeine—and then we play, as we have regularly since I moved to this side of town. We actually met here and were two of the fiercest competitors in the bar, and still are to this day, and if you were to watch us playing, you'd think you were watching the finals of the Chinese national championships—except Jamal is black and I'm white—the way we squat down in a ready position for our serves, and then smash the ball at blinding speed and contort our bodies into crazy positions as we paddle the ball back and forth, usually for long rallies with onlookers gathering around and applauding.

We're going at it, and I play my best ping-pong since I've known him—even since my freshman year at Columbia, where they call it Table Tennis and where I played a lot, didn't talk much, and afterward drank a lot of beer. Since most freshmen were a little off, me being just a little

51-50 didn't hurt me much, until finally it did, and I had to leave. But now, I'm not coming out of my zone—my effortless, mindless zone—and I'm winning point after point in a performance that's almost mystical. I remember thinking how much I wanted to be a guy who could tap into more than just ten percent of his mind, because that's what I've heard: that we humans use only about ten percent. I thought if I could just up that a little more, then I could improve myself, and maybe it would make up for other shortcomings I have, but as I stand here now, I'm thinking, *Maybe it's not just about the mind, and there's something deeper that I, or we, need to connect to.* Something else that can take me to another level. It's that something else I need to figure out.

I end up winning, but Jamal is off the hook for beers because I don't drink anymore, not to excess anyway, and I'm trying, really trying, to cut it out altogether. I take some mineral water and lime instead of more Sprite, which has a lot of sugar.

He asks what I've been up to, and I just shrug. He stays silent, which is unusual for him, and he's got this concerned look on his face. He then starts telling me about the march he walked at City Hall yesterday with about a thousand others, which I think is a good number because if you get numbers like that, you're sure to make the News, but I don't watch the news anyway, and he goes on and on, and I can feel his anger building up about how the protesters wanted a higher minimum wage even though the state just increased it, and I can see his eyes bulging, and so I have to stop him.

"What did you chant?" I ask. I couldn't think of anything else to say.

"Say what?"

"What did you chant? You know, as you were marching and holding your signs?"

"We yelled, 'What do we want? A Living Wage! When do we want it? Now!'"

He stops and looks at me to see if that satisfies my curiosity.

"That's pretty lame," I say.

"Yeah, well. . ."

We sit there quietly and I think maybe I hurt his feelings or something, but Jamal attends every protest in town, and they usually use this or some other equally lame chant and then I remember the story from history class where marchers, including Martin Luther King Jr. supported the Memphis sanitation workers in their strike for better wages and working conditions after two workers were killed on the job, crushed to death in the compactor of a trash truck. The rules didn't allow a black man to take shelter in a rain storm anywhere but in the back of the trucks, and in this life-and-death cause, where they had to crystallize what this was really all about and what they stood for, you know what they came up with as they marched? *I Am A Man.* If you think about it, that is about as on-point as you can get, so much so that it's almost like an epiphany. But most of the time, I sense Jamal's heart isn't fully into it, and maybe that's why they wind up with cheesy slogans. But when your heart is in it and it's your passion and your life, so much a part of you that you would die for it, then that's when you find your precise voice and a blue flame of truth ignites. *I Am A Man.*

"So what about you?" he says. "What's been going on? What did *you* do yesterday?"

"Nothing."

"No, really. You always say that. *Nothing*. But what did *you* do yesterday?"

"Had dinner with Ray."

"What about before that? During the day?"

I don't want to think about the crime scene, so I don't go there. But it hits me that I can't remember much of anything before that. Where was I? I didn't do any shopping. There were no good soccer matches on

TV. I can't recall picking out a book and spending time reading at a cafe, as I often do. I think I may have stopped at a pastry shop.

"I-I walked around for a while," I say.

"What else? What did you see? Who did you talk to? Help a brutha out here."

I go silent, struggling to remember where I'd been. But I can't bring it back.

"Well?" he presses.

"I-I can't remember."

"What about today?"

My memory here isn't much better. I know there was the breakfast with the pretty Latina waitress. I walked for a long time afterward, I know, but no specifics are jumping out. There's a big hole, and I met Jamal at four—

"Man, please tell me yo brain ain't so whacked you don't even—"

"I said, I can't remember!"

6

As I drive back to K-town, I worry that something's off, maybe seriously off. I wonder whether I should've vetoed the selection of this shirt, although there really was no reason to. In the years since I started my daily ritual—four years ago, and I'm now twenty-one—I have only used the veto three times. But say, for example, I wake up in a bad mood because of nightmares or a hangover – I'm not sure I could manage a Free Hugs or classic 70's yellow Happy Face T-shirt on a day like that.

I feel I need to take a step sideways here and mention that, although I want one, more than I could possibly ever want any other shirt in this life, I do not own a bright yellow Happy Face T-shirt. I've never believed it was right to just go online or actively search in some way for a certain shirt, a certain message, feeling that the beauty to any of this is in the magic of discovering in a natural way something new, a new message that comes to me through a gift or my stumbling into a store and seeing a lonely shirt cast off to the side on the discount rack that happens to catch my eye. Yeah, that's the way it should be. But I would love to land that Happy Face shirt, as dated and cheesy as it may be, given the hipper, more insightful messages dreamed up by the pop-culture geniuses of today. Honestly, could there ever be a greater shirt?

I decide to head over to Yellow House Cafe, which is one of my favorite places in the neighborhood because they have a homey backyard patio with tall, tan umbrellas that provide a little shade, and rich greenery with string-lighting that gives the place a romantic charm at night. It's a relaxing oasis, where I usually settle in during the afternoons for a waffle, or on a hot day, I could go for a shaved ice.

As I pull into the last open spot in their small parking lot, I can still hear Jamal's voice in my head. *Please tell me yo brain ain't so whacked. . .* It's about *Time*. Where does it go, and why doesn't it stick with me?

I snatch my cellphone, then quickly scroll through the Notes app. My journal is really my phone. The process of writing helps me to slow down and be precise in my words, and focus—which can be hard sometimes—and strive for structure, and so I put it all in here. This might offend some people who think journaling is something that should be done at the end of the day, in quiet reflection over a cup of hot tea, with a Montblanc pen in a nice leather-bound book. Well, I tried all that, and it never worked because by the end of the day, though I definitely had more than enough energy, I couldn't remember all the thoughts and observations and things I wanted to say; there were just so many that had passed through the freeway of my mind. So, no more of that. Now, I have my phone with me all the time, and I write with immediacy and in the present tense and as soon as something hits me, because that something may be helpful, a clue to help me get better or at least get through the day. The beauty of this is no one suspects what I'm doing. They might think I'm getting off an important text or email to that serious person to *Make sure you close that deal* or maybe to a honey to tell her, *Running late—just finishing up my workout*. But, of course, I don't have someone to get a serious message to or a honey to text, and so I'm just putting down what's inside of me.

My heart sinks as I have no entries for the last couple of days, and so I don't know exactly how I spent the hours. This is bizarre in itself because I never go that long without an entry.

I tug at my hair, then quickly pull a book from my glove compartment, *The Sun also Rises* by Ernest Hemingway—a gift from my grandmother—then head inside. The book is one of my favorites, the tale of American expatriates living in Paris, disillusioned with life, following the horrors of the First World War. Though I've never come close to seeing war, or running with the bulls in Spain, or any of the other experiences of the novel's characters, I seem to have an affinity—one of my top ten words—with them. They have been described as a Lost Generation. I've reread the book at least a dozen times, more than any other.

I wave to the waiter who always seems to be working, no matter what time or day, but I can never recall his name. I order a sweet potato waffle and an Italian soda. I watch the people, looking for familiar faces, or faces open to connecting. There are some families with children, and I think about what it must be like for the missing boy, torn away from his family. I read snatches of the book, but raise my eyes often to study the faces.

After a while, it starts to get dark and my mood sours. I've got a case of nerves and agitation shooting through me, and I don't know what's driving it, so I decide to head home. Realizing I can't wait until the morning news for an update on the missing kid, I turn on the evening news, maybe even take a sip of the Don Julio I have resting on top of the fridge, although I know that's a horrible idea. Still, I feel I need a crutch, something to get me through the newscast.

I flip the channels to the local independent station. Sure enough, at the top of the show, they break to a reporter standing outside the boy's apartment building. It's not the beautiful Shawna Cleary, but I wouldn't have expected her to be there since she must have to wake up early to be on the set, in time for the morning show, so I'm sure she's just catching an early dinner now before calling it a night, maybe with a friend or even a boyfriend. I don't know, but I know she's not married because she doesn't wear a ring. This reporter is Jose Ortiz, and he looks to be just a little older than me, and I wonder how he got his job, but I imagine he went to college, maybe a good journalism school, and I know Columbia has a great journalism department, and I had even thought about taking a class. But I never made it to the second semester. So now, Jose is saying that essentially, there are no new leads or developments in the story, and the police are asking the public for their help. And then, they flash the photo of the boy on the screen.

When I see his face, I take two slow steps back, my hand shaking, reaching back to make sure the sofa is there, and I don't somehow hit the floor, then ease down onto the soft leather.

I know this kid.

His face rises from the TV screen—black hair and pale complexion, eyes squinting in a smile so big, it is actually a laugh, and that's how I recognize and know him, by that horrible, hideous hyena laugh. I grab the remote, turn off the set, and slam it back down onto the coffee table.

It took me a long time to get his face out of my head after I came across him, one dull Friday afternoon, about three months ago at the Tofu House on Wilshire. And now, he's back, reaching out from my TV screen to taunt me again.

I don't know how to feel. At this precise moment, I have no fix on my thoughts or emotions, and I get very scared when this happens because it's one thing to have feelings I recognize but don't like, because at least I know what I'm dealing with and can reach back into my memory and process how I should react based on my past experience. I am, I suppose, shocked that someone I know is actually on the news for some terrible crime, being kidnapped from his home, and I know this person! On the other hand, this is a child I *hated.*

It happened at about 2:30 on a Friday afternoon, and I remember the time because it was a late lunch and I needed to eat healthy because I don't always do that living by myself and not being a good cook, and I had looked to my watch because I was thinking I could still get over to Yellow House for a sweet snack, now that I had done my duty with a healthy serving of vegetables. As I was settling the bill, the boy walked right up to my table and stopped to stare at me.

I tried not to make eye contact because I'm not good at that sort of thing but I glanced up, then back down, then continued to see him out of the corner of my eye until I finally looked up and locked in on him.

He pointed directly at me. And laughed. It was loud and annoying and like I said before, it was like a hyena, although I've never heard a hyena laugh in person, so maybe I shouldn't use that description, but it was wild and relentless, and he kept pointing at me, and his finger was shaking as he was laughing so hard, and I looked around because I didn't understand why he was laughing, even if there was some small thing I had said or done, how anyone, even a ten-year-old kid, could be so rude as to point a finger in my face and laugh, laugh as if I was the most ridiculous person on earth, laugh as though I was some hideous, less-than-human creature that deserved to be pointed out and laughed at, just like it was in the first grade or again in the fourth grade or again in middle school or again in high school or again in my first semester at Columbia, where some frat guys pretended to be my friends and invited me for drinks and I went along, even though I wasn't sure the drinking was a good idea, thinking maybe I had turned a corner and it was a new page in my life where college kids, especially at Columbia, were more mature and open, open to befriending a guy like me, but in the end their goal was to get me as drunk as possible and, when I couldn't even stand, drag me back to the grass courtyard outside Butler library, take all my clothes, and leave me completely naked, knowing I wouldn't have frozen because it was just before dawn and someone would find me soon and, as they would explain to me later—not in front of the counselors, but only just to me as some form of weak apology—they had heard the best cure for a hangover was to go outside and roll around in the wet grass naked, and so they wanted to test it on me, and in the end, I was just their lab rat, and it was all just a big laugh, even when I was expelled for it because that, on top of other concerns the school administrators had had about me, led to the decision I had to go and so, in the end, this little lost, kidnapped boy was no different than any of them.

I breathe hard, realizing I'm hyperventilating, my face flush with anger, and I jump up and begin to pace the apartment, and then I realize the meds aren't working, at least not anymore, and I am on fire and can feel my pulse racing, and I don't know what to do.

I go outside and walk, and walk. I want to talk to someone, but there really isn't anyone, not *really*, that I can share something like this with—not mother or Robbie or Ray or Jamal, and they couldn't possibly help anyway. How could they ever tell me how to feel? I want to hate the boy, but now he's gone, and would that be right? Is it right to hate someone who's now probably suffering something worse than he ever did to me, as bad as that was? It's like talking bad about someone who has just died. You know, he could have wronged me in the worst way, but if he's dead now, hey, better to just be quiet and let it go or else I'll seem petty and small.

I stop walking, realizing I'm at the corner of Wilshire and Vermont and that I have already been here, I don't know, maybe an hour ago, and whenever I'm doubling back on turf I've already covered, I decide it's time to do something else, but this time, I don't know what because I still have too much energy to just go back and sit in my apartment to read or watch TV.

The only thing that comes to me is to dance. That almost doesn't feel right—a bit absurd—but there's too much inside of me, and it just won't fade, and so there's only one thing to do and that's to dance.

After a quick change at the apartment I'm heading downtown, trying very hard not to speed. Ray and Jamal like to go to Hollywood but I hate that because they always seem to go to clubs where there's a long line and the bouncers pick out the beautiful people they want to allow in and that just seems so elitist, and for what? – to dance or hit on girls or get drunk – you need to be a good-looking elite to do that? Plus, I think those guys only know where to score ecstasy in Hollywood and just don't have the connections downtown, but I like downtown because some of those clubs are massive, and getting lost in a sea of people makes me feel more alive than anything else.

I check in to an illegal rave raging in an abandoned warehouse near the Garment District. As I walk in I'm greeted by a flashing array of lights – green and red lasers – shot from one end of the massive hall to the other, up and down, side to side, then twisting in rubbery swirls on themselves as the music blasts pure EDM—Electronic Dance Music. I *live* for EDM, the loud, pounding beat of bass and synthesizers and the songs blending one into the other. Its beat keeps in perfect sync with the light show as the flashes seem to tear into everything, the stone walls, jade necklaces, broad smiles, tall cool drinks. I throw my head back, losing myself inside this shredding kaleidoscope. Then I hit the floor and dance. I become one with the beat and the lasers as my eyes focus on nothing yet take in all the faces that seem to mutate into bizarre space aliens by the lighting effects, the green blindness as I look up into the lights, and I dance forever, by myself, yet in a crowd so large and tight upon me, the jeans brushing up against me, that we move as if we are one. Though I can't really showcase my best moves like I did during that one week when I twirled a banner ad on the sidewalk down near Beverly and cars would honk in support as I jumped and danced and spun with boundless energy, it's okay because here, now, I'm not noticed and no one cares I'm here. I am just like everyone else and no one is laughing at me.

7

I AM SLOW TO RISE THIS MORNING AFTER GETTING BACK LATE LAST night. I feel compelled to watch the morning news show. I can tolerate the morning news better than the later broadcasts because the morning team tries to keep it light and funny, and they have great banter—a very cool word—and often make me laugh. Besides, they're always breaking for weather and traffic, and I don't care about either of those.

The first time I saw Shawna Cleary on the morning show, I thought she would be the one for me. I know that sounds ridiculous now, but at the time, I was wearing a new shirt that said, *Everything is easier said than done—except Talking. That's pretty much the same*, and I made the association with the news because my father would always say talk is cheap when he would rail against film critics and the news media, saying all they do is talk. They don't really *do* anything, create anything, or contribute in any real way. Though he was always highly regarded and respected for his professionalism and the quality of his work, I feel certain there must have been a bad review somewhere along the way that left him bitter. *The media, they just talk*, he would say, which is *easy*.

Shawna is all-American, girl-next-door beautiful—not flashy-anorexic-model sexy, but just that natural beauty who is smart and has the kind of laugh that warms your heart. She's probably naturally funny herself, or at least she always gets the better of Stan when they go at it on set. She looks great right now in the white blouse she seems to wear often, probably on the advice of some fashion consultant who noticed, as I did, that a simple bright color best reflects her personality and contrasts nicely with her ever-tan skin. *Perfect.*

It's been a long time since I've seen her, but as I turn on the show, she happens to be saying to Stan, "Well, I hope your wife doesn't know about that," and the entire news team, Stan included, laughs, and Stan, shaking his head, laughing, says, "No comment, no comment."

She then turns serious and covers the story of the missing boy. But there's nothing new to report. The police are asking for leads. Teams of neighborhood volunteers are scouring the nearby alleys and *dumpsters*. I cringe when I hear this. There's a tone in her voice that goes a bit beyond one of concern. The way she emphasizes the word Please, as in, *If you have any, any information at all, Pleeeze don't hesitate to call the police*. She gives their phone number. Twice.

The boy is apparently low-functioning autistic. His name is Juan Machado. I repeat the name several times aloud. Names are funny. They're really just labels. They don't mean anything, and yet, we often say he looks like a Steve, or a Jocelyn, or Bella is such a beautiful name and it fits her perfectly. But there is also some magic to a name—the label. Knowing now that it's not just some kid who once laughed at me and lives in the neighborhood and is mentally impaired who is missing. No, he's more than that. He is Juan Machado.

I sense the faintest whiff of smoke in the air, like residue from a smoker who had left a while ago. I remember having the same sense yesterday but had quickly let it go. It doesn't make any sense since I don't light up, and the smell is so vague that I wonder if it may be something else I'm picking up on, but it still leaves me with a darkness that fills my lungs, a smoke of death, memories of my father, lung cancer, and the rotting weight loss and the slipping away of life, and I'm scared because I don't like the thoughts I have when this darkness seeps in. Or maybe it's the boy; maybe I'm feeling like it may be too late for him; or maybe it's the spirit of the suicide who lived here before me, because I felt this same way the morning after I moved in, and I thought for sure it must be him, welcoming me in his own way.

Whenever I think of death, I either walk down to Robert F. Kennedy Inspiration Park, not too far from here, a memorial to the late political leader, or I drive to Green Hills Memorial Park down in the South Bay and talk to my father, who is buried there. I decide I'm not in the mood for a forty-five-minute drive, and so I will select a shirt, take my meds, then go down to RFK.

My shirt today is a monogrammed *Angels* T-shirt. I pause, given that it was an *Angels* shirt that first started my whole collection. My father had given it to me when I was a kid. I thought, at first, it was because he wanted me to be more of an athlete, a jock, like he was when he was young. But he explained that I need to be a part of something bigger, and maybe, dedicating myself to following a baseball team would be good. Because Robbie grew up in Newport Beach, he's a huge fan, and I always sensed my dad wanted me to be closer to him, like some of his confident swagger would rub off on me. I don't know. Robbie is now a wild man, living at San Diego State, but he's always been smart—test scores right up there with mine—and what really makes him stand out is that he is the most intuitive person I've ever met, so I liked getting closer to Robbie and going to Angels' games. I also couldn't disagree with Dad because I did need to be part of something bigger.

I arrive at Robert F. Kennedy Inspiration Park, right on Wilshire, which is really a small plaza with stone benches and eight-foot-tall granite walls etched with quotes by Kennedy. In the center is a metallic wall with cutouts of what look like ripples of water when something lands in the middle of a pool, and the small waves reach outward. The words on this center wall talk about how few of us will ever have the chance to bend history in a big way, but each of us has the power to work small change in our lives, and the total of all these good acts will build into a force that can change the world. This happens each time a person acts out on a positive ideal, or seeks to help others, or fights against injustice, and when this happens, he says, it sends forth a tiny ripple of hope, and crossing each other from a million different centers of energy and daring, those ripples build a current that can sweep down the mightiest walls of oppression and resistance.

I smile, close my eyes, and envision millions of small waves of energy, tiny acts of goodness, connecting, spilling over on each other, and flowing, ever flowing. . .

I pull out my cell phone from my back pocket, which is important because you never want to leave it in your front pocket because the electromagnetic waves or whatever is emitting from the phone will seriously decrease a guy's chances of ever having kids, and while, in my case, that feels like a long shot anyway, I'm trying to stay optimistic. And now it's out of my pocket and in my hands, and I open the Notes app, where I type furiously into my journal, head down, thumbs flying. I want to hold on to this image. Millions of flowing waves. . .

Sparse trees provide a little shade for the homeless here, and there are always a few loitering in the plaza, which shook me a little the first time I came here because I was looking for a small piece of greenery, a Zen retreat within the concrete and glass of K-town, and with a name that includes the word *Inspiration.* I was certain it would be the perfect place for when I was tired from my walks and wanted to just meditate on my shirts or catch up on my journal notes. The homeless never seem to bother me, although they occasionally ask for money, and mostly they just lie there on benches, maybe sleeping, I don't know, or sitting and muttering to themselves, beneath the etched words on the metallic wall that speak of hope. My grandfather used to call him Bobby Kennedy, and I don't know what Bobby would think of the scene here today.

I've read a little about Kennedy because I have a fascination with the 1960s. It's strange, I think, the way some people get hooked on a certain period of time and can't get enough of it. Like Robbie reading countless books on World War II or Dad dressing up in a Civil War uniform and re-enacting battles with a hundred other grown men with the same obsession. For me, it's the'60s, and if one of my doctors were psychoanalyzing me, he'd say it probably had to do with the aura of rebellion and passionate—though sometimes over-the-top—desire to change the world for the better. But it was my grandfather who really liked Bobby Kennedy and told me several times how if he had been elected president, he would have been the best president we ever had, and the first time he told me that, I asked him how he could know. He listed some qualities like being tough on crime and the mob and fighting for the little guy, and since I was young at the time, I asked, *Then why did someone kill him?* He thought about that for a good while, then said it's because the special people, like Bobby, who are not just satisfied with being a decent person, really put themselves out there in a big way—way out there on a lonely limb where they're fighting against great forces of evil—and if you ever put yourself out there like that, there are going to be people who hate you. But you *have* to do it, he said. If you have the chance, you have to have the courage to do exactly that.

I decide to go over to The Line hotel for lunch because they have chic circular booths in their lobby arranged at angles to ensure privacy, and you can order a sandwich, read and relax, or just think. As I pass a street light on the way, I see a poster plastered to the pole with the face of the little boy and the word MISSING written across the top. The boy has a wild and strange smile in the photo—no, it's not a smile, really. It's that hideous laugh he had the day he saw me, the pointing, shaking-finger hyena laugh, and I feel a heavy weight of déjà vu that I just can't take, so I quickly walk ahead.

As I enter the lobby, I see a kid over by the check-in counter, and he's pulling his sister's hair while his dad is trying to haggle a room upgrade or something, and Mom is texting furiously. The girl screams while Mom just shooshes them, never looking up, and Dad never loses focus on the check-in clerk, maybe because she's a young, pretty Korean girl or maybe because he's close to closing the deal on the upgrade because he sure is smiling now, though not as big as the smile the boy wears as he's getting away with torturing his sister, and I think about whether we are born evil. Maybe we are born good—we certainly seem innocent in the beginning—and it's the world and our influences that make us evil. But then again, it might be our natural spirit to be evil, or, if that's too strong a word, to be cruel or selfish. Every kid, early on, thinks the world revolves around him and there's no way that can jibe with empathy or compassion, so perhaps that's our true nature, and it's only when we are taught—actually *taught*—through repeated instruction and sometimes punishment that we can't just do whatever we want that we finally understand we must respect others and abide by rules. I wonder if we all wouldn't pull our sister's hair if no one is watching, and those that don't get the proper instruction wind up sociopaths like the guy at Cup O' Joe's.

I rub at my temples again and feel overwhelmed, and so I leave. I look at the pedestrians as they rush by outside, and though I never really want to just walk right up and talk to them, I desperately want to talk to someone now. Even the homeless are sleeping or resting in such a way as to say, *Don't bother me,* but I've got to move, or talk, or focus on my *Angels* shirt. I need to stop at a corner for a red light, and my lips tremble so my unlit cigarette falls to the ground, and I can hear a man right next to me saying, "Hombre, you okay?" but I'm not okay because it's all getting darker in my mind. I realize I don't know where I am. The neighborhood doesn't look much different from K-town; I mean, it's not like I totally got lost in my thoughts and walked for miles down Wilshire and ended up in flashy Westwood.

I'm tired. I look for a place to sit, but there's nothing—not even a convenient coffeehouse—to stumble into and grab a sparkling water. I lean against a light pole. The street signs say I'm at Normandie and Pico. I close my eyes, and the inside of my eyelids glow a hazy orange from the burning dusk sky beyond. I breathe slowly now. I don't know what's happening or why I'm so tired. I usually don't tire from just long walks. I'm used to it and do it easily most days. No, it's something else. I think about Julie, who works over at Q Bar and is not only beautiful but also the most sympathetic listener I know, and I want so much to see her tonight, but feeling the way I do now, I'm not so sure. I feel like I need sleep, and yet it's so early. The orange beneath my eyelids feels warm. I barely open my eyes, and the burning sky is a blur. I sense there are two figures there, up in that brilliant sky, and they look like they have wings. They are together, long and soft-pastel in color, just there together, not moving, and one seems to have his arm around the other.

"Angels," I say softly.

I allow my eyes to open more and realize that I'm facing a tall building that stands across the street. There is a massive mural painted on the side of the building, and for a moment, I think of Jamal and wonder if he had a part in this one, but I don't think so, as his work tends to be stark and bold. This is a pastel, soft, almost impressionistic painting of peach, white, and soft-gray shades—a perfect blend into the glowing sky—of two people. They look just like ordinary people, though faceless, but they have wings. Actually, as I study the mural a bit longer, I realize that each of the figures is missing a wing.

Across the top of the mural, it reads, *We are each of us angels with one wing. We can only fly embracing each other.*

I read it again, slowly, mouthing each word. I stare. I wonder if it could be true. *We are each of us angels with one wing*. . . can that be? What about the guy you see in the bar with his arm around his beautiful model girlfriend, and she has all her beautiful friends there as well, and his buddies are there too, and they compliment his slim European-cut shirt and sport coat, and he shrugs it off like it's nothing but knows he looks sharp as he tells jokes that everyone laughs at and not just out of courtesy—no, he is truly funny, and he makes them all laugh as they pat him on the shoulder, shaking their heads in laughter, refusing to let him buy drinks because this round, the next round, and the one after that are on them. Does that guy have one wing or forty-five?

But looking at it, I realize it's the most beautiful painting I've ever seen. There is something rising in me. It's not elation, but something close. It's just a small current of something that I start to feel but realize is incomplete. It's not there, not just yet. But I believe it's true: we all are angels, with so few exceptions that it doesn't even measure on any kind of scale, because there is something good there, maybe deep inside us—so deep that we may have felt it was lost forever. And we all do have just one wing, and those who appear to have more, well, that's an illusion, or maybe for the briefest moments in our lives, we do sprout a second one—or, *or*, maybe, just maybe, there are moments when things are lining up and going just right, and we have, in fact, learned to fly with just one wing! I'm laughing out loud now. It's as if a bolt of energy is now passing through me, and I don't know if it's what Zen monks would call enlightenment, but there is a truly deep and good understanding that warms me.

We all have just one wing.

I do.

The little missing boy does too.

8

"HERE YOU GO," A YOUNG GUY SAYS, HANDING ME A FLIER. HE'S GOT a scraggly beard, wears glasses, and wears a blue baseball cap that's flipped backward. As I study him for a second, he pushes the paper forward.

"Wha . . .?" I ask.

"We're looking for this kid," he says. "He was snatched from his home. Everyone's trying to help find him."

"Okay, sure," I say, taking the flier from him.

He walks off, and I can see that he's part of a group of about ten people, all with fliers in their hands. They look all around, poking their heads into the alcoves of buildings they pass, cupping their hands as they press their faces close to the windows of empty shops that have gone out of business. One points to his left and veers off to check a small alley. Another follows.

Without thinking, I march in their direction, following them, I suppose. I watch them closely and connect that they are one of the groups mentioned in the news broadcast. But something's not right, and I run to catch up with the guy who gave me the flier.

"Hey, I need some of those," I tell him.

"Sure, here you go. We're always looking for more helpers."

"You're missing something," I say.

With this, I can feel the eyes of the group on me. They've stopped, I'm sure to see what I'm up to.

I hustle back and give a flier to every homeless person they've passed on this block. It's a big boulevard, and there were maybe ten that had been missed. I explain to them that they really need to watch for this boy.

"He's lost," I tell them, "and he needs help. He may be with an adult, but please remember his smile. He's supposed to be with his family, not an adult. And he's a little sick, so he may not be as tough as other kids to fight and get away. You really have to remember this face. This smile."

I meet back up with the volunteers.

"You need to talk to the homeless," I say. "They're here every day, and they usually don't wander too far. *They* might see things. But everybody else is distracted. Everybody else is rushing off because they're late to work, or their minds are filled with lists of things they've got to do, or their eyes are stuck staring down at their phones, watching some videos of kittens playing with yarn or photos their friends sent them of avocado toast. Here you go."

I try to hand the fliers back to the guy, but he just stares down at them.

"Why don't you join us?" he asks.

I hesitate. It feels like forever, and so the guy starts to ask again, but I interrupt.

"I'm not looking in any dumpsters!" I say, a bit too loudly.

We walk on with our search, with me taking the lead in approaching any homeless person, as I seem to have less fear than the others when it comes to this.

"You know, I think I can sense why you don't like the search in dumpsters," a man says to me. He's wearing a Polo windbreaker and is middle-aged with salt-and-pepper hair. He's got a pleasant smile, but it's a little too pleasant, a little too broad. It's a fake smile, and I'm the leading expert on smiles among everyone I know.

"You see," and he starts to talk softly now, "it's not that we're just presuming he's dead, and we're looking for a body. I mean, maybe he's hiding or playing hide-and-seek!"

This doesn't feel right to me, but I just nod.

"My name's Roger," he says, extending his hand.

"Cole," I say, and we shake.

He's got a firm grip, authoritarian, and walks so upright it wouldn't surprise me if he had a two-by-four strapped to his back. And he starts asking me questions—a *lot* of questions. They start off friendly enough, but he just keeps talking, and it feels like he wants to know everything about me and seems more focused on me than the search. He's barely doing any searching. And then I latch onto something that bothers me. He's asked me several times why I'm doing this. But he asks it in slightly different ways, and it reminds me of a psychological test I took years ago with one of my doctors, and they did the same thing. I remember researching this later, and it had to do with something like getting to the *real* truth, because if you ask just once, the respondent might give the answer that he thinks the questioner wants to hear, but if the questioner asks again in different ways, he can determine if the answers line up and it's actually the truth.

"How would you be spending today if you weren't with us?" He now asks, which I think is another variation on *why are you doing this*?

I really can't take this anymore, and I just remind him I was minding my own business until someone put the flier in front of me and, so, I thought I might help. That's all. There's nothing more to it. *That's all.*

"Sure, sure, that's fine. Sorry. It's just that you were just standing there, staring at that mural for a while. It didn't seem like you were doing anything or were on your way to—"

"It's a beautiful mural," I say, "with a beautiful message. I like murals. My friend paints murals. That's all."

I rub at my temples. The clanging sound of metal causes me to look up as I see two of the volunteers have thrown back the lid of a large blue dumpster and climbed the sides to peer inside.

No. This is all wrong.

I shove the fliers I'm holding back into the hands of the guy who first gave them to me, and then I dash, running hard. It's strange, but I can hear the sound of someone running behind me, and has started to chase me, but then decides against it.

When I run—or even walk—as fast as I can—*escaping* is what you might call it—I sometimes go into a zone, a mental state where I almost don't know what's happening. And when I stop, I sometimes forget the running or walking experience itself and am aware only of the point where I've arrived and the place I was when I started. The world around me disappears.

I arrive at a shop with large Korean alphabet characters at its entrance that, of course, I can't read but recognize as old Mrs. Kim's shop. As I walk inside, a fat, tabby cat lying on the counter lazily lifts her head to watch me, then cradles it back down into her curled napping position. There are large jars filled with what look like huge slices of mushrooms soaking in water that sit on shelves, filling an entire back wall. The first time I visited the shop, Mrs. Kim explained that the jars are filled with deer antler velvet.

"Deer antler velvet?" I asked.

"Yes."

I thought about this for a moment.

"Why?" I asked.

"Vitality," she answered, clenching her fists before her.

"Oh."

"Energy," she said, shaking her fists.

"Huh."

"Healing," she said, with a look of deep relaxation as she let out a slow exhale and released her fingers, extending her hands out slowly, palms down.

"Wow. How much for one of those big slices?"

She laughed.

"No, no, no," she said. "That is raw. We make into pills."

Though the shop's specialty is deer antler velvet, Mrs. Kim carries other herbs and nutritional pills as well. These are neatly organized in a hundred small wooden drawers with Korean characters written in black, sitting behind the counter. But what really sets Mrs. Kim apart is her mystic sense of the world and people, and I enjoy our talks because her perspectives are always different from anyone else's. And she is *always* right. I especially like when we discuss my shirts and their many possible meanings and levels of understanding. But what I'll never understand is how she can almost immediately tell what my shirt says or represents, which is the most miraculous thing I've ever come across in my pretty boring daily life because Mrs. Kim is blind.

The only way to explain it, I think, is that Mrs. Kim is a shaman. A *Manshin*, to be specific, is what she calls herself. The first time she told me she was a shaman, I really didn't understand what it meant, and so I looked it up on my laptop later. But it turns out shamanism believes the world is full of unseen spirits who play important roles in our daily lives. Shamans are mediators, gifted with a calling that enables them to connect us with the spirit world. This immediately impressed me because it means that Mrs. Kim is on another level, like Da Vinci or other gifted souls who can somehow reach beyond the ten percent the rest of us are tapping into of our full abilities.

"Polar Bear!" she exclaims as I enter. Again, I have no idea how she knows it's me. Even if, let's say, she wasn't completely blind—which she is—and could make out light or shapes and figures, I'm still too far away for her to be able to make out that it's me. She calls me Polar Bear because of my long, long daily walks, which I had explained to her is just like what polar bears do.

As she approaches me, her smile turns to a look of concern.

"You are troubled, Polar Bear," she says. Again, I have no idea how she could know this. I suppose it's because I'm panting from the long run, and I may sound tired. Maybe there was something in my voice when I greeted her.

"Come to the back," she says. "I will make tea."

I pass a cute but bored-looking young lady at the cash register who I recognize from before. She was her daughter. She helps with the family business from time to time but doesn't look happy to be here, and I wonder if she perhaps once had dreams of being a mathematician, or a beautician, or something else but instead wound up here because, after all, *that's life*.

The back room is part office, part bedroom, part storage, and it's impressive as it is, inch for inch, the single *messiest* space on this earth. It even tops my studio apartment. But there is beauty here too, as the wall boasts colored robes of blue and white hanging brightly, along with more colorful banners with long strips of cloth, which I'm pretty sure she uses for her shaman rituals.

"Tell me," she says, handing me a cup of green tea. She has added ice and some honey for a little sweetness.

"There's a little boy from the neighborhood who's missing," I say.

"So I have heard."

"I'm going to find him."

She takes a long sip of her tea, then turns her head up to the ceiling with a pensive expression.

"This will be a difficult task," she finally says.

"I understand."

"Though a noble one."

"Sure."

"How will you do this?"

I gulp down some tea and just stare down at the cup, having no real answer.

She reaches over to touch my shirt at the chest, as she often does. Today's shirt is easy even for a blind woman to make out, as the letters are embroidered and raised.

"You will need angels," she sighs. "And with angels, anything is possible."

I don't understand this, and as I sit here still struggling with the *how will you do this?* question, I sense something from the shirt, as if the thin cotton fibers tingle.

"Cole, I must tell you something." My focus shifts like a laser beam on her because she never calls me Cole except when she's beyond serious, like when I told her the full story of what happened at Cup O' Joe's, which no one else knows about except for my mother, but as she listened to me telling her that day, Mrs. Kim said something in Korean, like a chant, and then said to me, "Cole, you will find peace."

"As I said, I believe it is possible for you to find this child. But there are two things you must understand. And these are very serious things. First, your search may be successful, but it may also be late. If so, you must know this will weigh on your heart for a long time."

I know she's telling me the boy may be dead, but I don't want to hear that. I don't want to believe this kid I know will wind up just like any other horror story I hear about on the news.

"Second, if you are not late and you find him, you are likely first to find the person who took him..." She shakes her head. "A person who does such a thing . . ." she shakes her head again. "This journey will be a great danger to you."

I nod.

She then grabs both my arms and says loudly, in a tone of despair, "I fear for you, young Cole!"

For a moment, I can't speak, and I'm really glad she's blind so she can't see the shocked expression on my face. When she lets go, her body just slumps forward, as if she'd heard the saddest news ever and can't even think of anything more to say.

By the time I arrive at my apartment late at night, I consider how many miles I may have walked during the afternoon. The long walks. It's more than just about burning nervous energy. No—there's something else.

I once tried to research what it must be like for animals caged at the zoo. How do they cope? The limitations of interactions to just a few others, the cramped quarters compared to the vast African Serengeti. Though I never found something that hit the mark exactly, I did find an article about whether animals had better lives in zoos or in the wild. Did these animals appreciate being caged? Were they even aware of it? And if so, were they better off? The article said, well, it depends, because if you're an antelope or a zebra and spend most of your waking moments just trying not to be somebody else's lunch, then the zoo works out for you because now you're safe, you can just relax and savor your own meals, and your blood pressure is lower. You can ponder the deeper philosophical questions of life—well, the part about blood pressure and philosophical questions wasn't actually mentioned in the article, but I think they're a natural extension of the article's intent. But—*but*—it's not that way for all the animals. The one that has it the worst, likely, is the polar bear, because it's used to roaming miles and miles every single day, and no exhibit could ever replicate that, and though the article went on about how it needs to continually hunt for food, or stretch its muscles, or befriend other bears, or some other excuse, I really feel—*really*—that the point is about the freedom and the discovery, and there must be something there I'm looking for too because I roam every day like the polar bear.

9

Only Ray knows about my T-shirt selection ceremony, and no one else. I don't know why *him*, except maybe because once we were stuck in a neighborhood bar on a rainy night and I'd had too much *soju*—a sweet Korean liqueur—and when I get a little relaxed, I sometimes share too much. He laughed, of course, but I feel okay about that now because his Zen sister seems like she might appreciate the ritual, and I can't wait to meet her when she's back from Europe. Maybe, finally, someone who understands.

But right now, this is all I've got. It really feels like that, and so I've absolutely got to focus.

When I say selecting a T-shirt is a ceremony, it really is just that. It makes me think of the Japanese tea ceremony, which you wouldn't think of as a ceremony in the Western sense because it's so subtle and nuanced—the focused bowing, endless cleaning of the cups and utensils, and then the slow pouring of the tea with compassion and a sense of giving. The beauty of it is in the spirit of the gestures—the symbolism of something greater happening—and maybe that too is happening with the selection of my shirt.

I walk over to the closet, a walk-in closet, which is strangely configured to be much too big for my Mid-Wilshire studio apartment. This is where I enshrine my four hundred and fifty-three carefully selected themed T-shirts. They're not valuable in the monetary sense, but in the sense of truly guiding me through existence each day. I'm not joking or exaggerating their importance, and yeah, I know that when they were created, they were just the superficial, easy idea of some marketing guy out to make a dollar, but I know little things in life can sometimes mean something deeper.

I begin now to consciously slow my breathing to try to calm myself and my mind, and I do this by focusing on the exhale. Slow. Exhale. I'm sometimes amazed by this—the way I can actually control it if I really want to. The problem is that it takes a lot of time to get there, and, of course, I can't walk around doing this all day because people will think I'm crazy. I once witnessed an actual Japanese tea ceremony at the Los Angeles County Museum of Art, not far from here, where they have a special pavilion on Japan. At that tea ceremony, they explained the purpose is to focus on harmony, purity, and tranquility, and while I could certainly use all of them, the one I desperately need is tranquility. And so, as I slow my breathing, my mind says over and over *tranquility*. I try to make the exhale long, and I do this by stretching the word *tran-quil-i-ty* to cover the entire breath. Slow. Exhale.

I bow before entering, then step inside onto the *tatami* mat I've placed there. The light off, I shut the door, and it is complete darkness. The shirts hang on individual hangers exactly one-inch apart, which is perfect for a light touch of the fingers across their shoulders while in total darkness. I just let my fingers roam gently until a magical energy pulses from the soul of the shirt to reach out to my fingers with a calling of *I am the one for you today*. I can't tell you what exactly causes me to stop at a particular shirt. I do feel something, and the best I can describe it is that it's a feeling like a slight breath on the back of your neck, except the sensation is on my fingers, rising up from the shirt. Sometimes, this process takes several minutes; sometimes, it's quick.

And then it happens.

I pull a shirt, and the energy begins to surge in me again. All tranquility is lost, now replaced by a rush of anticipation, like a kid anxious to open his birthday gift. My breathing becomes fast as I flip up the light switch.

The shirt I pull today has a depiction of a unicorn lying on a psychiatrist's couch, and the psychiatrist says to the unicorn, *You have to believe in yourself.* I laugh. The shirt is old—one of the oldest in my collection. An old girlfriend gave it to me, and when I received it, I really thought she cared about my struggles, and it was a message of strength and to, well, believe in myself. But it turns out she really just had a thing for unicorns. I mean, it was a little weird, the way she had unicorn stuffed animals in her room and some freakish 3D wall posters of unicorns—the kind of thing that fascinates a seven-year-old, not a seventeen-year-old. But it taught me something about the meanings of shirts: that they can have *many* meanings, and two people can see the same shirt and interpret it in completely different ways.

At the entrance to The Royal, Jamal is already there, and he's in a rage. I can tell by the look in his eyes. I know he's going to be angry at me because on his days off, he absolutely does not wake up until the crack of noon. He explained this to me once, but I told him on the call that I absolutely needed to meet him this morning, and that it was a matter of life and death. So he reluctantly agreed.

"Inside!" he says, pointing to the hotel lobby before storming off ahead of me.

He's walking fast, and as I follow him up the escalator, I'm looking up at a black hair pick with a clenched black power fist of a handle sticking up out of his fro. I say to him that I just want to talk. No ping-pong today.

"Cole, you just dragged me outta bed, and it ain't even ten o'clock. We're here, and I'm a-gonna whup yo crazy ass at pong!"

We arrive at the top of the escalator, and he stops cold. I stand way back because I don't want to hear his reaction when he realizes the hall is closed because it never opens until the afternoon.

"Let me buy you breakfast!" I say, quickly.

At the restaurant down on the first floor, he's calmer.

"You out dancin' all night?" he asks. "Dem is some big bags under yo eyes."

"Just doing research on the Internet, and I went late. Fell asleep on my laptop."

"Well, this better be damn good," he says. "What's going on where you all CIA and can't tell me what's up on the phone?"

The waitress stops by with water and hands us menus. I take several big gulps, chugging the water down hard.

"Gotta tell you something," I start.

"Hit me."

"I'm. . . " I take another swig of my water. "I'm gonna be working on something. May need your help."

Jamal looks at me sideways.

"Okay," he says. "What's the script?"

"You know that missing boy on the news?" I ask.

"Sho 'nuf. The one from K-town, right?"

"Yeah. Well, see, I'm going to set out to find him."

"You are?" he laughs. "Well, let me know how you do."

"No, man, I'm serious. I'm going to find this kid."

He takes a big hit of water and grimaces.

"So, Sherlock, how you plan on doing that?"

"I don't know. I mean, not yet. But I'm gonna figure it out."

"You are, huh?"

"Yeah, I just feel I need to be doing this. Like I'm *meant* to do this."

"Well, I seen on the news they got folks walkin' the hood and looking in dem big trash bins."

"No, I'm not talking about that. I mean, I'm going to figure it all out. I feel like there's something maybe I know, or can piece together the clues, and find the kid."

"51-50! You got heart, I'll give you that. But you got no sense. They got professionals—they's called Po-lice—who get paid to do that job, and they do a damn good job of it."

"They've got nothing. No clues."

"How do you know? And hey, don't be tellin' nobody I said the Police was good at they job or I'm feeling like some brutha's gonna cap me."

"Man, I just have this sense; I can't explain it—like I need to be doing this, like this is my place and time, and this is what I'm supposed to be doing."

"Huh."

We each take a drink and stare out at the space in front of us. I suppose I should have considered that he might be skeptical, but it's for the best cause I can think of, and I just wanted a little *Sho 'nuf brutha. I got yo back,* and now I can feel a pain in my chest and the lungs, like some air is escaping me, and I can't get it filled up again.

"So whatchu need from me?" he asks.

"Huh?"

"You said you may need my help."

"Yeah, I'm not sure, but, I may need some muscle."

"Some muscle? Listen to yo-self! Whatchu think, I'm like some Incredible Hulk bustin' through walls just to save yo ass? I thought you didn't watch no TV and no crime drama fiction—talkin' bout needing muscle." He shakes his head. "Sorry, homes, but I gotsta give it to you straight. I'll talk slow. First, your shirt blows."

"Huh? Why? I think it's pretty positive and . . ."

"It's positive in a superficial joke way. But the real joke's on the psychiatrist—and you—because unicorns don't exist. But you chasing dem just the same. This whole scheme to find a missing kid and you got no plan but yo heart is telling you it's the right thing to do, and so, I don't know if you got some hero complex or delusions of grandeur and envision yo-self like some Navy Seal storming a compound and putting a cap in Bin Laden, but this will not work. You are chasing unicorns, and they don't exist. You need to stay with me here, in the real world."

"But, but . . ."

He laughs. "Talkin' bout finding a missing kid . . . might as well find the next Dalai Lama."

He downs the rest of his water, checks his watch, and says he has to go. I say, "Sure," and tell him I just want to hang back a bit.

"Look, man," he hangs his head, "sorry if that came out harsh."

"No, no big deal."

"But you seemed to be feeling a bit too high, like, crazy high."

"Yeah. I was feeling . . ." and I don't say the next word because I'm not sure of the next word. Maybe. . .*happy*.

"But I seen you before when you get a little manic, and then when you crash later after it didn't turn out the way you hoped."

"Got it." And I really did get it. I was just hoping for something more—just a little something.

We fist bump, and he walks away. I stare at my empty glass, twirling it on the table. A moment later, I chase after him as he's ready to walk out to the parking lot.

"Hey!" I yell. "What's that about the Dalai Lama?"

He waves me over so as not to yell across the hotel lobby.

"You don't know how they find the next Dalai Lama?" he asks.

"No."

"Well, don't quote me on all the details, but after a Dalai Lama dies, some Tibetan monks set out on a search for the next one. Thing is, they're really looking for the *same* one."

"I don't understand."

"It takes a few years, but after waiting and seeking out some clues and whatnot, who they're really looking for is the reincarnation of the Dalai Lama who just kicked it."

"What?"

"Yeah, they follow clues until they find a boy who just may be the reincarnated soul of the dead Dalai Lama. They then show him some toys and trinkets, and most are just random, but a few are actual objects he owned in his prior life. If the boy picks those up, and *only* those, then they know they've found him."

"But how do they know where to look?" I ask. "I mean, how do they get started?"

"I think the monks go to some special lake in Tibet. Sacred place. At this lake, they have dreams or visions—maybe there are other clues—and they just go from there."

"Huh."

We stare at each other for a moment, and I think he can tell I'm *really* thinking hard about all this.

"So," he says, "what I'm saying, my good-hearted but naive 51-50 head case, is whatchu trying to do here—find the kid—you may as well try to find some soul across another lifetime. That's all."

He turns and walks, giving a big wave with his back turned to me.

He doesn't see my smile.

"But they always find him!" I yell. "The next Dalai Lama. They always find him!"

10

Jamal's gone, but I sit here in the hotel lobby area, on a cushy red Art Deco sofa, watching the cars pass on 6th Street. I'm one of those people who can't think too quick on his feet, but then as soon as a situation passes, I come up with all these great comebacks and things I should have said back in the moment when it would've counted for something. I'm thinking I should have explained to him about Bobby Kennedy and his belief in these infinite waves of positive energy and how, if enough of us put ourselves out there, then these waves can build a force against any oppression or wrong in the world, and we can really make a difference. I could have explained more about how really committed I am to this now and how I stayed up all night researching Kennedy, his life, and his speeches. Besides the tiny ripples of hope, he also said the greatest truth must be the recognition that, in every man and in every child, is the potential for greatness. I really liked that one. He talked about the violence of institutions, meaning indifference, inaction, and slow decay, and how this violence was just as deadly as a gunshot or bomb in the night.

But the one that really hit home was when he quoted a writer who said perhaps this world is a world in which children suffer. I gasped when I read that. *Perhaps this world is a world in which children suffer.* But Kennedy said we can lessen the number of suffering children, and "if you do not do this, then who will do this?"

I'm thinking hard about Jamal and the Dalai Lama search, and my spirits slowly rise, knowing there are people keen enough to find souls across lifetimes based on limited clues, not the hard facts or clues the police use with fingerprints, scientific forensic testing, and all the modern technology. No, these clues are more esoteric—I think that's the word—and more nuanced and connected to a great universal soul that we all tap into. That's how they can discover things in this life that are connected to the last. This is what I need to use because I don't have the experience or technical expertise of a detective. But I'm feeling frustrated because I can't figure out how to use this information or what my next steps should be.

I think a bit about the lake in Tibet. The only other international trip I've ever taken was the trip to Paris right after my father died. To this day, I can't even tell you exactly why I picked Paris. I mean, sure, it's a beautiful city and supposedly great for romantics, but I don't go for anything like that. I like museums, and I guess Europe has plenty of those. I just felt like I needed to get away. I stopped by Shakespeare & Co. because I heard that when Hemingway was poor and before he was famous, he was allowed to borrow books there, and that also was the place that first published *Ulysses* by James Joyce, which is supposed to be the greatest modern book ever, but I tried to read it twice, and I couldn't manage it. I didn't stake out any other Hemingway haunts, so I don't think it was some intense fascination with him that pulled me there.

I went on to have a nice little vacation in Paris and later to the Loire Valley, but I don't think the trip really changed me at all, even though maybe that's what I was hoping for, the same as a lot of people hope for when they do something like that: go far away to a foreign land to seek new experiences, to *find yourself.* I don't think it ever works. You're still you, and whatever's going on that makes you want to escape is probably going on inside of you, not outside, and so I didn't find myself in France, and I'm quickly realizing that I'm not going to find the boy by going to Tibet, so I cross out that idea.

I pull at my hair. Time passes.

I think about the web searches I did last night—innumerable variations of *how to find a missing person*. But they weren't much help; all of them stated pretty much the obvious. *Contact police. File a missing person report. Check with the hospitals in the area. Put up "Missing Person" fliers. Talk to friends and relatives.* This last one may prove helpful, and I'm thinking about contacting the boy's mother. Who knows? She might remember me from that day at Tofu House. Still, what could I possibly ask that the police haven't already? I groan.

It's afternoon now, and I decide to head back to my apartment, maybe check the news for any new developments with the boy, catch some dinner, and then figure out my next moves.

I'm stopped at a light near McArthur Park, and I think about my dad. I could never figure him out. I was never good enough for him, and I wanted so, so much to be good enough, and all he ever wanted out of me was to be good enough, and so it boggles my mind how two people who wanted exactly the same thing, the precise identical outcome, could have gone to war like we did.

"Cole," he would tell me. "You know how ironic life is? *You're* the one who has the movie star name. *Cole Reeves.*"

"You can have it, Dad. Really."

"No, it doesn't work that way."

"Yes, yes, it can. Just take it. And then, I can be Cole Jr."

"No, it's not possible," he would say, his voice rising. "Too many people already know my name, and so I can't just go and change it. I'm stuck. But I didn't realize it until I gave you the name, and then I understood what a grand name it was, and I wished it could have been mine."

"Just change it, Dad."

"No, damnit! Why aren't you listening? Why don't you understand such basic things even when I explain them to you slowly? If I say it can't happen, then it can't. Not everything can be changed. Life doesn't work that way."

I let it go. It seems like forever ago, that talk. All I wanted to be was Cole Jr.

I pass the park with all its bustle of people going for afternoon strolls around the lake. Everything is soaked in an orange glow from the sinking sun, and though I've passed the lake a hundred times on my way Downtown, I've never seen it in this light—an eerie, foreign landscape. I drive on, but there is something pulling me back to the lake, as if I need to explore it more or become one with the orange creatures strolling the shore. It hits me that I really need to be there.

I pull a U-turn and go back to park about a block away. A dull headache begins to throb, like a beating drum behind the eyes. The lake's fountain is gushing in the middle, blasting water fifty feet into the air. There are families and children with balls, baby strollers, couples holding hands, and countless others sitting on the grass along the shore. There are the homeless here on the grass too. I walk along the concrete pathway that lines the shores of the lake, watching the people, the water, and the nearby downtown skyline. Every few steps, I stop to squeeze my eyes shut, trying to push back the pain. I never get headaches, and I'm a little scared of what this might mean.

A little Asian girl and her brother run ahead of their family toward me, and as she comes right up to me, she stops.

"Unicorn!" she shouts.

"Yeah, that's right," I laugh. Why do girls love unicorns? I bend down to her eye level. "Do you like unicorns?" I ask stupidly.

"Yes!" Her smile is as big as the sky. There is so much joy there, on the inside, that I can almost feel it gushing out of her and extending beyond this park and city. It is the kind of smile that flows up from a spirit within and pushes out to splatter the faces of everyone, and it then seeps in to infect us all with that same spirit, and I can only hope it stays with her and keeps, so that in the future when a dark day comes, as it eventually comes for all of us, she still has that inside her, and it keeps the smiles going.

"How much do you like unicorns?" I ask even more stupidly. I've never had young nieces or nephews or other younger family members, and so I have no clue how to talk to kids.

"This much!" she says, and though I didn't think it was possible, her smile grows even bigger, and she throws her arms out wide as if she were about to give me a hug.

"When will you show me Pluto?" she asks.

"Huh?"

"You promised to show me Pluto!"

"What?!?!"

I hear yelling.

"Hey! Hey, hey! You stop!" An old man with an accent, maybe Russian, stands from behind a stone table up on an embankment where he has interrupted his chess game to yell in my direction.

I look around, but there's no one else close enough to us that he could be yelling at.

"Stop, I say! Get away from the girl!" he shouts.

I stand, shaking my head, palms up and open, as if to say *I'm not doing anything*. The girl, frightened, runs back to her parents. The old man glares at me, pointing as if challenging me. I watch him, then I turn slowly and start walking.

The thing is, in Los Angeles, there are as many insane people as there are sane ones. I use those terms loosely and would even put myself, sometimes, in the former category. So something like this incident with an old man yelling really should be something that I, or anyone else, should just shrug off with a good laugh. *Old kook*, I should say, probably had too much vodka for lunch, or maybe skipped his meds altogether today. Ha, ha. I've had enough similar experiences personally with the homeless in K-town.

But there's something different here. I look over my shoulder, and he's still standing there by his chess board, watching me. This bothers me, and I'm not sure why it does, but it just *does*. So I turn back.

As I get closer, his eyes grow wide, and he grabs a cane that is resting alongside the table with the chess board.

"Stop right there!" he yells, lifting his cane as if ready to swing. The other players stop their games and all turn to watch the showdown.

"No, I need to come closer," I say. "I just want to talk to you." I am still at least twenty feet away, and I don't want us shouting at each other.

"Stay right there!" he shouts.

I place my palm to the side of my head; the pounding is really hitting me hard now.

"I just want to talk," I say.

"About what, you sick pervert?"

"What are you talking about? I was just *talking* to the girl." I keep stepping closer.

"Just don't come back here. I know what you are!"

His chess opponent taps at his arm. "Alexei," he says. "Maybe that's not him?"

I step right up to the table.

The old Russian leans in and examines me closely. He has a perplexed look on his face.

"No," he says in a lower voice that still simmers. "I just saw you here earlier. We called the police, and you ran. You probably will again now. But do not ever, ever come back here again."

I turn and head for my car, a bit rattled that I look so similar to some child molester that a group of men have mistaken me for him. I try to find consolation, telling myself he's old and his eyesight can't be that good. Still, I notice I'm chewing on the end of my cigarette, something I do when my nerves are shot. I don't know what to do, and I feel like walking, but I can't leave my car here, and so, at my car, I just pace back and forth on the sidewalk, rubbing my eyes hard to quell the ache in my head, trying to decide what to do, and unable to decide, I ask myself why is this happening and why I was drawn to the lake. I think it must all mean something because, while there are certainly random happenings in this world, I've always held that the really important events have some meaning. After all, why did Jamal tell me about the Dalai Lama? How is that even possible, that of all the ridiculous things to talk about, he chose unicorns and the Dalai Lama and a sacred lake that pulled me to this lake where I'm being chased out for being some pedophile, even though I've never been here before? *And what about Pluto?* The girl asking me to show her Pluto—what the hell was that about? There has to be some reason for all of this, but after a lot of time passes, my head starts to hurt more, and I'm convinced that even if I spend my entire lifetime and the next, I still won't have figured it out.

11

My favorite bar in K-town is Q Bar because it plays EDM nonstop, with live DJs on weekend nights and a big screen behind the bar with taped footage constantly playing some wild EDM festival somewhere with thousands of young people dancing. The decor is that of a nice upscale nightclub, with tasteful neon—not overdone—and comfortable booths with privacy but still open enough to see who else is there. But my favorite part is the bar itself, because I can sit there and talk to the waitresses, who will even have drinks with me. It's actually part of their job to serve, to drink, and to chat with the customers because, hey, who doesn't want to talk and drink with a beautiful girl?

The girl I would most like to be with is Julie, who is Korean, petite, with black hair and the purest white skin I've ever seen. But what I love most about her are her eyes. I know a lot of guys say things like that to girls, but I really mean it, and I told her that the last time I saw her and also how they have this unusual quality of seeming both happy and sad at the same time. That stopped her, and she gave what I thought was a soft gasp, but of course it was so loud in there, I couldn't hear anything, and she stared at me for about a minute with a look that was one of . . . longing . . . or maybe I was just imagining it, but it really seemed to me that her eyes had a look of longing.

I know it's a good night to visit Julie because, after showering, I happen to select one of my favorite bad boy shirts that I love to wear whenever I'm in a situation where there might be beautiful girls involved. It reads, *I'm only here to establish an Alibi.* Another good sign is that Julie is actually at the bar tonight, which is always a hit-or-miss proposition because her schedule is so erratic. Julie's behind the bar, and I wave over to her as soon as I walk in, and though she notices me, she gives only a quick nod and an even quicker smile. She's talking to three Asian men, all in business suits, and I'm guessing they just finished up some important dinner or business deal and now want to spend the night bragging about their successes to young waitresses.

Though I always want to see Julie, I especially want to see her tonight. I couldn't figure out any angles on how to find Juan Machado. Plus, I'm feeling really out of it right now, discouraged at Jamal's put-down of my quest to find Juan and the bizarre incident at MacArthur Park Lake. I'm going to break down here, I know, and have a drink. Maybe a few. But I need to see Julie and maybe talk to her about all of this because I think she might understand or have some advice or words of encouragement.

As I take a seat, a thin Korean waitress who's cropped her hair short and dyed it blonde asks me what I'd like to drink. She's striking in that she's pretty, though not beautiful, but has these soft, blue-grey eyes, and combined with the hair, she would stand out even if she were across a crowded dance floor.

"I'll have a vodka cranberry," I say.

"Oooh. Good choice," she says with a wry, sexy look, her eyes dreamy and half-shut.

"Really?"

"Perfect for men."

I think for a second that she's making fun of me, like maybe the drink isn't manly enough since most of the Asian guys go hard on the whiskey, and the Mexicans like the tequila.

"It's good for you down there," she says, still holding that same dreamy look while pointing between her legs.

I give her a knowing nod but, of course, have no idea why a vodka cranberry would help me down there. I hate bar talk.

Three Korean girls enter and sit on the stools next to me, bouncing back and forth to the rhythm of the song the DJ's playing, which has a great beat, but I don't recognize it.

I watch Julie across the bar, still talking to the suits, and I want her to look over so much, but she's so focused on the men. She's laughing, and it crushes me because she's *really* laughing—not the fake courtesy laugh she will sometimes do but the kind she laughs when she's really having a good time, and I've been here enough times to tell the difference with her.

"So you like Julie?" My blond, blue-eyed Korean waitress says, smiling.

I give a noncommittal tilt of my head.

"Yeah, everybody does," she says.

The words sting, like getting a needle poke from an inexperienced nurse.

"I like your eyes," I say to her, just trying to make conversation.

"They're contacts."

"No! You're not supposed to tell me that. Just let me live the fantasy."

"Sorry," she says, "I always do that. I can never tell a lie. Just like Abraham Lincoln."

"I think you mean Washington. George Washington." I'm talking loudly now because the DJ has kicked up the volume as more and more people come noisily into the bar. I like this because it forces me to keep my sentences short, and there's less chance I will just run on and on, although it's not usually as bad at night unless I get really worked up over something, in which case it's bad anytime. I'm getting a little edgy because I can't talk to Julie, but I think the music and the vodka cranberry will keep me in check.

My waitress covers her mouth and giggles, then goes to the girls who have approached the bar next to me and takes their orders.

If she comes back, I'll probably need to buy her a drink. This place is legit, and so there's never any shady business like with working girls or anything like that, though I've heard that used to be the case here in K-town with a lot of so-called hostess bars, where the young ladies would accompany you to your table and drink with you and maybe go sing karaoke with you later as well, but there was always a chance with a little more money you could get a little more. I think something like that may still go on in some places because I know I've been to bars with Ray that are still open at four in the morning when they're supposed to shut down at two, and there are girls everywhere, and they seem cozy with the men. So if the bar is willing to violate the law over something like closing hour, then I'm sure they look the other way if working girls do their business there. Still, here it's all legit, the girls sit on their side of the bar while we patrons are on the other side, and while the waitresses do sit down and have a drink, the two sides never cross.

Julie finally glances over, gives me another smile as quick as the last, then turns back to the men before her. Still, I get a sensation running through me—a tiny pulse of positive energy—because she didn't have to do that, to acknowledge me. We have no ties together; we have no bond. There is nothing understood that if I show up here, she will be my waitress. Still, I've got to believe she must sense that I would prefer to have her over anyone else. If I'm lucky enough to sit at a stool where she happens to be stationed, then we talk and drink.

The girl next to me keeps accidentally bumping into my elbow, to the point where I'm not so sure it's an accident. Each time, she smiles broadly. She has a dark tan, not like she is a darker-skinned Asian, but more like she has spent some time in the sun or a tanning salon, and the blondish streaks in her hair, clearly dyed in, tell me the latter is probably the case. Still, she is pretty.

"Hi," she shouts above the din of the music.

"Hi," I say.

"So what's your crime?" she asks.

"Huh?"

"Your shirt. It's awesome. You're only here to establish an alibi. So if this is just your alibi, what's your crime?"

We look at each other for just a moment, but it feels like several minutes, and then I turn away. Julie is laughing harder than ever. I realize I should probably make conversation here since Julie may not come by for a while, and I want to talk to somebody, really talk, about what happened today and where I'm going with my new path, and I feel like Julie would understand because even if she didn't, even if she thought it was the craziest idea in the world to try to find a lost boy, I don't think she would ever say it. Though I don't know her very well, I can just sense this from the conversations I've had with her in the past about college and my father, even though I'm sure part of her job is to never laugh at people, to understand and be sympathetic when they're in a tight spot, to cheer them up when they're down, and so tonight, more than any other night, I really want to talk to her. I know I need to just be a little patient and reserved, but that's not me.

I watch her for a long time, but she doesn't turn. I then feel another bump on my elbow.

"I can't tell you the crime," I say, "because then I'd have to kill you. Can't leave witnesses."

"Oooooh."

"I'm Cole," I say.

"Oh no!" she says, slurring a little. "But I can warm you up." She puts her hand on my back and rubs it softly in circular motions.

"No, I'm not cold. My name is Cole." This actually happens quite a bit, especially in bars or on dance floors—the misunderstanding of my name, that is, not the offer to warm me up.

She laughs, and yet she doesn't remove her hand from my back.

"I'm Stefunny," she says, "with an F."

"With an F?"

"Sure. Ste-Funny. Get it? Isn't that cool?"

I smile, but I'm thinking it's actually the exact opposite of cool. Still, within any group of people, any small ecosystem of similar-thinking individuals, anything can be deemed cool. I decide not to tell her it's actually quite lame, and I feel that if the waitresses here never laugh at me, I should at least extend the same courtesy to someone who wants to get to know me.

"Don't you love this music?" she asks as she bobs from front to back, then side to side, and she's all over the place, and it is the exact opposite of the rhythm Julie and I have when we talk because Julie likes to shake her head from side to side while I bob my chin up and down, and yet, we are both in perfect sync.

I talk about my passion for EDM, and she tells me her girlfriends are all celebrating her birthday. Our conversation is like shattered glass, with bits and pieces of edges everywhere and no resemblance to anything that once connected. We drink hard, and though I know this is not a good idea—never a good idea—I do it anyway because, though her conversation is weak, her spirit, her bubbly enthusiasm, is something that brings me up since the experience at the lake and Jamal's negativity. The only problem is when I drink, I can sometimes be a little too open and truthful, like Abraham Lincoln, and not know where to stop or have the emotional awareness to understand my environment and the audience and act appropriately. I have a lifetime history of acting inappropriately.

"I'm on a new path," I tell Stefunny loudly.

"A new what?"

"A new path."

"What's that supposed to mean?"

"It means I have a new direction and a new purpose to my life."

"What is it?"

"I can't tell you. Somebody already laughed at me today, and so I don't want to have any more negative vibes about it."

"You're just teasing me, I know."

"No, I'm not; besides, it's not important that you know what my path is. I only told you because I thought it would be good for you to know that I'm growing and moving forward in my life."

"Look, guys hit on me all the time in bars, so I know you're just saying something like that to get my curiosity up and make me think you're some man of intrigue and mystery."

"No, that's not it."

"Just tell me."

"That's not what this is about."

"Whatever. Hey, do you have any Molly?"

"No. I have a buddy who likes that stuff. But shouldn't guys just call it Ecstasy? Isn't Molly what girls call it?"

"Is your friend coming by?"

"No."

"And you don't have any . . ."

"I can't do that." I feel myself taking quick breaths—the buildup to hyperventilation. "And I'm really not supposed to drink either," I blurt out. "See, I take some medicine, although I never take the amount the doctors want me to, so that I can calm down my energy level and slow my thoughts down because it all moves so fast. It usually works, and I stay pretty up but not too up or get too excited, though sometimes I do get down, but I'm doing better at recognizing that and controlling that—"

I see her sling her purse over her arm, then grab the shoulder of her friend and lean in to say something in her ear.

"No," I plead. "Wait. Don't go."

She begins to walk past me, so I grab her forearm.

"Listen," I say, "I'll tell you my new path. I'll . . ."

"Freak," she says blandly, not even turning to look at me.

I lean back, resting a hand on the bar for support. I watch her walk away, followed by her friends.

I sit down on the bar stool, dazed. Like a blunt strike at the back of my skull, I feel the pain of a short, piercing word. What stuns me most is how casually she said it—not as if she intended it to hurt, but more like she was just simply stating an obvious fact—something so blatantly obvious it didn't require the addition of an angry tone or even meeting my eyes—just a direct, declarative statement. *Freak.*

I feel dizzy, sitting there at the bar, with the alcohol, blue neon, thick bass beat, and, of course, her one word, one syllable, summation of my entire being, all swirling in my head.

Julie glances over, and that's all it is—just a glance, as quick as the others, but this time there is no smile.

What's my crime? Somebody, please tell me. *What's my crime?*

12

It's 8:45 in the morning. I'm awake but keep my eyes closed after a quick peek at the clock. I am late. For the first time ever, I am late for my morning ritual—my steady, daily repetitive motion of sanity. The shirts, my daily guide to focus, inspiration, and maybe even a little growth, can hang there in the big closet all day, every day. I won't need them anymore. I threw the alibi shirt in the trash last night when I stumbled in. I'll still wear the others for a short time, only because I don't want to walk around shirtless. But I think that if I do get out of bed today, I'll go over to the Beverly Center and ask the nice cosmetics lady who sells me all the skin care products to introduce me to a friend in the men's shop so I can buy polos or nice, plaid shirts with collars. It may change my whole look too, going with collars and all, and I don't know why I started to put so much value into T-shirts in the first place. It started with my dad and the Angels shirt, and I suppose there was something really special in that, like I wanted it to be a special connection with him. Maybe my grandpa had an influence because when I was much younger and would watch soccer games on TV with him, we would always root for Atlético Madrid because they were always the underdogs, especially to rival Real Madrid, and at the end when the players would exchange jerseys out of respect for their competitors and the hard-fought battle, we would do the same, except, of course, my grandpa and I—me being a kid—wore completely different sizes. My shirt was too small for him, and so he would just flip the shirt upside down and place the neck hole over his forehead, and I would do the same. We would laugh hard at our appearance. Everything was simpler then.

I'll also tell the cosmetics lady I won't need the creams, scrubs, sunscreen, masks, emulsions, lotions, gels, or anything else she has, and although this may disappoint her because I'm sure she's made serious commission off me constantly trying new products, I just don't care anymore. If my skin turns leathery and wrinkled like an eighty-year-old by the time I'm twenty-five, then that's okay, because none of that is important. The only truth I need to somehow learn to live with—and I mean to finally face the cold reality of—is that I am a *Freak*.

I open my eyes but stay in bed, just staring at the ceiling. I think about the man who died here not long before I took the apartment. *What was he like? Why did he do it?* I think about whether he lay in his bed just like me now, on his last day. *What was going through his head? What were those final, conclusive thoughts that told him the only logical course of action was to place the end of a shotgun to his head and pull the trigger?*

Sitting up, I see that the way the apartment is laid out, the floor plan of this small studio apartment mean that his bed had to be here, exactly where my bed is now. Did he kill himself here, in bed? Was it in this very same position that he thought it all through—his pain and worries—then sorted it all out and came to the conclusion that *I am a Freak*, then BANG?

The clock says 9:37 now, and I'm getting restless—not in that energetic way, where I feel I need to do something like roam K-town and meet new people or find new herbal medicine or pastry shops. I just feel like I need to move my body. I go over to the sofa and sit there for a bit, but I'm not in the mood to play Minecraft or watch Euro soccer. I feel hungry for some reason and decide to get dressed, go down to a cafe, and have a little snack. I pull some underwear from the drawer and a pair of jeans.

I plod over to the closet and decide not to turn on the light. I do not bow before entering. My hand glides over the shoulders of the shirts quickly, without trying to feel for any subtle vibration or pulse coming from them. I finally settle on one, then turn on the light.

At first, I'm jolted, as if someone has slapped me. I slowly return the shirt to hang it once again. Confused, I scan through my memory quickly to see when and where I would have gotten such a shirt. Terror rushes through me, and I jerk back out of the closet. *Nothing is making sense.* There is just no way. I rush to the bathroom cabinet and shove a full dose of medication in my mouth, then chug down a big glass of water. I turn on the faucet and run it as cold as I can, then splash the water on my face and continue until I'm drenched. I've made a mess with water all over the sink and floor. I've soaked the small mat that is just underneath my feet. I turn, and from the bathroom, I can still see the glow of the closet light seeping out onto the wood flooring.

I feel myself breathing fast and hard, and I tell myself that I need to control it. Maybe I was still dreaming, or the alcohol in my system has mixed with my emotions and the meds in my body. *Did I take a full dose yesterday or only half?* Maybe it all came together to put an image in my mind.

I walk slowly over to the closet, then tap the door open. With a high-pitched creak, the door opens to the sight of the same shirt. The shirt is real.

Rushing back away from the closet, I can feel a fear rising in me as I rake my fingers through my hair and hear myself saying, *No, no, this can't be*, and I need to do something, but there's nothing I can really do. Who could I possibly talk to? Who would ever understand, and more important than anything else, how can any of this even be happening?

I run to the nightstand, pick up my cellphone, and dial. There are four rings before she answers.

"Hello?" she says.

I stay quiet, wondering what to say and how much I should say, especially since she worries constantly and always overreacts to any little thing. Plus, I know she's going to give me her regular lecture on how I should get a job and make something of my life, which will lead to a burst of emotions and energy, and yet I had tried that already, the getting a job and trying to make something of myself, and though I'm sure I'll give it a shot again someday, I'm still reeling from that last stint as a barista at Cup O' Joe's on La Cienaga and the shocking combination of too much caffeine and my medication that I promise I will explain, but let me just say right here *I tried!* I really tried.

"Hello?" she says again.

I try to talk, but I'm just choking on words.

"Uggh," I hear her say, clearly frustrated by what she thinks must be a crank call, and I can feel her pulling the phone from her ear and moving to replace it on the hook when I shout.

"Wait!"

"Hello, who is this?"

"Mom."

"Cole?"

"Yeah, Mom. It's me. Sorry about that; I was just . . . I was just eating breakfast and had a mouthful of food, and for a split second, I thought something was starting to get lodged in my throat and that I might choke, so I just waited to let it pass."

"Oh, sweetheart, are you okay?"

"Yeah, sure. Sure, I'm okay."

"How is everything?"

"Well. . ."

"Cole, is something wrong? You sound funny."

"No, Mom. I just had some more cereal get stuck down there."

"Well, drink some water then. I'll wait."

I cover the mouthpiece with my hand for a moment, imagining myself and the time it might take to get some water.

"I'm back," I say. "Much better."

"How are you feeling these days?"

"Well, fine."

"Are you taking your medicine?"

"Sure."

"All of it?"

"Yes."

"You remember the last time you went off the dosage, that whole ugly coffee shop incident?"

"Mom, I know. You don't have to bring that up."

"And the way the police had to get involved. . ."

"Yeah, I'm doing okay. I'm doing the right thing now. But listen, I did want to ask you something—something about my past and all the problems I have."

"*Used* to have. You're perfectly fine as long as you take the full strength of medicine like Dr. Sanders prescribes."

"What I need to know is, with all the talk of bipolar, ADHD, ODD, and all the other stuff, did I . . . did I ever hallucinate?"

"Hallucinate?"

"Yeah, you know, see things that weren't there?"

"Oh my goodness, no! Cole, only crazy people do that. You just . . . you just had too much energy. That's all."

"That's all," I say, in a voice so low I'm sure she doesn't hear.

"What's happening, Cole? Do you need to see Dr. Sanders or one of the other doctors again?"

"No, no. Like I said, I'm fine."

"He's just over in Beverly Hills, and his office now has a concierge service, so they can just pick you up."

"No. I don't need Dr. Sanders."

"Are you having hallucinations now?"

"What? No, hey, only crazy people do that."

"You're sure?"

"Yeah, Mom, listen, I need to go. I need to meet someone. But I'll come by and see you next week."

She agrees, and I think we set a specific date, but I'm not sure, and I don't write it down or calendar it on my phone, so I'm sure I'll break it. I've broken dates with her before. She always seems to forgive me. My forgetfulness—just one of the many issues, one of the many disappointments—she has to accept.

I sit back down on the sofa. I stay here for a long time. I begin to feel that numbness of the soul that comes with the full dosage I've taken. I'm feeling slower. But it's more than that. There is an out-of-body sensation that brings with it so many things, including fear, I think. After a while longer, I rise and walk straight to the closet. After all, it's just a shirt. And maybe it's some sort of twisted joke, the irony and all.

The shirt still hangs there, and I am bold enough to touch it as if to make sure it's real. I then lift the hanger and carry it out of the closet, walk over to the bed, and gently lay it there, staring down at it.

I don't own many black shirts, and so it stands out for that alone. The brighter-colored shirts seem to align with my goal of lifting my spirits. But this shirt is black. And then, in even bolder white ink, written all in caps, are the words *I AM A MAN*.

I touch it again, and it's still real.

Removing it from the hanger, I hold it as if it were some ancient, fragile parchment—something historic. I hold it there for a long time. I'm not sure what to do, but eventually decide to put it on, slowly pulling it over my head, then extending each arm through the short sleeves.

Now there is a pulse, a tingle, and then a penetrating warmth. And then it's all gone, just like that. But I feel different. It's my breathing, slow and steady. And I don't feel quite so out of it.

I stand before the mirror, admiring the shirt and the way it fits and looks. I say out loud, "*I am a man.*"

Then I place both my hands on my chest and breathe in deeply, feeling the soul of this shirt. A shirt I have never seen before. A shirt I have never owned.

13

Mr. Li actually lives not too far from K-town. I could bike it if I really wanted to, but there is an urgency. I have to talk to him, so I decide to just drive over to Hancock Park and the nice estate he has there. We lived in a big home like his when my father had a recurring role on a network detective show as one of the rivals of the lead cop, the actor in the starring role. The facade of his house is mostly brick with bright white shutters and trim and ivy that runs up the walls in a way so as to give it a magazine-cover-home charm. They must trim the ivy to make it look this way.

I pay Mr. Li a visit in person every month to pay my rent, and while my father always taught me to do things in person whenever I can because it's that connection with people that will help me get somewhere in life, I think I just do it because I like Mr. Li. He gave me a big break with the apartment, and maybe on some subconscious level I don't want him to change his mind and raise my rent someday.

I knock on the door, and Mrs. Li answers, wearing a traditional black Chinese dress. She is very nice, shows me in, and invites me to have a seat. For some reason, she is really impressed that I always stop by with the check and often compliments me on being such a polite and quiet young man. I think that's just because I usually take all my meds before coming to see Mr. Li, so I can't possibly talk too much or act strange because I don't want any of that to happen in front of him. I love my apartment that much. But I'm not sure what to think of it now, after having sworn off my shirts for good earlier this morning only to find one that doesn't belong to me and for which I have no explanation of how it got there. I'm a little nervous and unsure of what exactly I might ask him or how this conversation might go.

"Good morning, Cole!" Mr. Li says, walking into the living room and coming over to shake my hand. My accountant, the one who manages my Trust and also gives me grief sometimes over my spending habits, also handles Mr. Li's finances. That's how we met. My first conversation with both of them had to do with my not understanding how the fixed money my father left could continue to support me for so long. Mr. Li explained the concept of compounding interest, saying, "Your money makes money. And the money that money makes, makes even more money." He told me that Albert Einstein called this principle the most powerful force in the universe, and that it will take care of me for the rest of my life.

Mr. Li has a genuine, firm handshake, and I feel he is always welcoming, although it does bother me that he doesn't like Mexicans. I think that's something he needs to work on.

"Good morning, Mr. Li."

"What brings you here, Cole? The rent isn't due yet."

"I just wanted to talk about something, if that's okay."

"Yes, of course. You are my best tenant!" He claps his hands once. "But I need to go to one of my properties later this morning to check on a drywall problem."

"Sure. This won't take long. I just wanted to ask if anyone, any prior tenant of my apartment, ever said anything about strange occurrences there."

"What kind of strange occurrences?" he asks, leaning in and studying me closely. When I see his serious demeanor, I regret asking the question so directly. I don't want him to be alarmed, and I backpedal fast.

"It's nothing, really," I say. "Nothing to be upset about. I just thought I heard some noises at night. But I was half-asleep, and I sometimes have problems with my hearing."

"Hmm."

"There's also been construction going on down the street, so maybe that's playing tricks on me. That must be it."

"Well, there has never been anything strange happening there. No one's ever said anything, anyway. Of course, just before you, as you know . . ."

I nod my head.

There is a silence now that begins to feel uncomfortable as we eye each other, then look away.

"Tell me about him," I finally say.

"Well..." he shrugs. "His name was Martin Conrad, and he lived in your apartment for many, many years. He was in his mid-forties. As quiet as can be. Very alone and quiet. I was astounded by his death."

"Huh."

"He was in the same business your father was in, but not as successful as your father."

My mind feels confused by the statement. I had never thought of my father as successful, and I think it's because he never saw it that way himself. But I start to reflect on the countless shows and movies he worked on—I mean, he was *always* working—and I'm suddenly struck at how I could have ever considered him *not* to be successful. There are so many people in this city that would die just to have landed one of his roles, but instead, they work as waiters, part-time teachers, or real estate salespeople while they wait for that break, which for most never comes. But my father never saw himself as successful, so I didn't either. It's because he wanted something more. He wanted to be the star. He could act better than any of the actors who landed the leading roles over him, he would tell me, but he didn't have that commercial look—that leading man look—and so he was always in supporting roles. Everyone wants something more.

When I turn my focus back to Mr. Li, he's clarifying that Martin Conrad was not an aspiring actor but an aspiring writer.

"He had one script he sold as a TV show," Mr. Li says. "It was a long, long time ago. I don't remember the name. But when the production company bought it, they didn't want him to be part of the team of writers. They only bought his original idea for that one show. I think that hurt him. He always had a pained look on his face when he talked about that, but he didn't really talk much. He was quiet, like I said."

"Was that it, that one show?"

"Yes. Sometimes I think that is the cruelest trick of life. To give you just a hint—a small taste of something that really isn't for you. And then, you spend the rest of your life wanting more. But there is no more there."

I hang my head and give a nod. There's no crueler trick I can think of.

"Why do you say that writing really wasn't for him?" I ask.

"Well, I'm not really saying that. It's just my impression."

"But why?"

"Well, it's just that he never seemed to be doing much writing. From time to time, I would stop by the building to fix things. Oh, my goodness, that cute girl who lives in the apartment just down the hall from yours, was always breaking something."

"There's a cute girl living down the hall from me?"

He gives me a stunned, *What? Are you deaf, dumb, and blind?* look.

"Really?" he asks, his eyes truly bearing in on me as if to say I must be a complete idiot.

"Uh, I think I know who you're talking about," I stammer. "It's just that I'm out a lot and don't spend much time there at the apartment."

"Just like Martin Conrad. He was always out. Drinking, I think. And when he was in, I would sometimes hear soft, classical music, or he would just be talking to himself. I would sometimes stand close to his door and try to hear what he was saying, but it was just gibberish. I think he talked more to himself than anyone else."

"That's not good."

"True. He was so quiet. But I think all of us have so much running through us—*noise* really—that doesn't make it to the surface. The more we keep it down, the more it comes out one day, in an explosive, uncontrolled way."

I cringe at the word *noise*, not wanting to think about how much runs through me every day that I don't let out.

"I used to think," I say, "about why he wouldn't just go quietly, with sleeping pills or something."

"Hmm. Maybe he was asleep his entire life. Maybe he wanted to be as awake as possible as he transitioned into whatever was next."

I'm not sure what to say here, so I shake my head. "I feel bad for him," I say.

"Don't!" Mr. Li snaps. "Listen, after his death, they found strange things of his. Bizarre writings. Talk of mass murder and shootings. Violent videos on his computer. This was a dark spirit. I don't know what made him this way, and maybe, early on, some of it wasn't his fault, but ultimately, we *do* have a say and a course of correction available to us. I really believe each of us has that available to us, but in the end, he chose a path. In the end, he chose to be a dark, dark spirit."

I nod my head; there was nothing else I could do. Mr. Li was so sure of his assessment of Martin Conrad, and I couldn't really disagree with anything he said. It was just shocking that a man's life, with all its complexity, depth, noise, and all, could be whittled down to two words. Dark spirit.

Mr. Li rises and extends his hand, ending our conversation.

"Never let us talk about this again," he says.

I don't know if I got anything, any real knowledge, from our talk. I feel bad that I'm not making any connection to how this ties to Juan Machado, and yet, in my core, I know that this has got to be connected somehow. These strange occurrences have got to mean something.

After a quick lunch at the bar down the block from the Wiltern Theater, I decided to walk the rest of the afternoon. I am going through the conversation with Mr. Li in my head just to see if there is something to glean from it, but my head is still in a fog. I decide to stop at Robert F. Kennedy Inspiration Park to write as much of the conversation as I can into my phone, and then maybe this evening, when my meds wear off and my mind starts to clear, I can make some sense of it.

The sky turns gray, and it looks like rain may be coming. I know I'm far enough away from the apartment that I'll get soaked if it really starts to pour. My entries into my phone are garbled, and so I put the phone away and sit on one of the benches, directly facing the iron gates that shield the massive school complex and the bygone Ambassador Hotel beyond. My grandpa said the hotel was an iconic Hollywood landmark that had hosted two Academy Award ceremonies, and countless movie stars from Hollywood's golden era had stayed in its rooms. He said it went downhill with the neighborhood in the seventies and eighties, and they couldn't revive interest in the hotel, which proved a little premature, I think, because while mid-Wilshire today is no Beverly Hills, I hear it's safer than it used to be. I guess the hotel would stand out nicely today. But there's nothing anyone can do about that now. I focus on the right side of the building complex because, on my first visit to this park, a homeless man told me that it would have been right about where Kennedy was killed, shot by an assassin in the pantry of the main kitchen.

I remember now the photo of Kennedy I saved on my laptop the other night when researching his life. Lying on the floor, dazed, his head held up by a lone busboy. The busboy said that while dying, Kennedy, with a pool of blood flowing beneath him, asked if everyone was okay. When the busboy assured him they were, Kennedy, with some of the last words he spoke on this earth, said lowly, "Everybody's going to be okay."

Bittersweet is my all-time favorite word. To capture two distinct but completely opposite sentiments in just one word, and yet, completely making sense, in one poetic pinpoint emotion. He cared about everyone else. And yet, he had to know. I mean, *he had to know* that it was going to be okay for everybody except *him*.

A light drizzle starts to fall, and though I'm partially shaded by the trees, I know this will get bad and start to come down hard. Still, I don't move. I can't move. There is something big here that I don't understand. Maybe no one can ever understand, not in this life anyway. Why a good man is killed. Why an innocent boy is taken. Any of it.

"Did you send me the shirt?" I say it out loud and unashamed, though I never would have dared to talk this way before, not before today. I notice none of the homeless look at me. I suppose because they talk to themselves all the time.

"If you did, just tell me. Or maybe give me a sign."

This is futile, I'm sure. I just thought, *Well, Kennedy knew Martin Luther King really well, and King really supported the sanitation workers' march in Memphis, where they first came up with the truly greatest protest chant of all time: I Am A Man.*

"Did you send me the shirt?" I call out again, a little louder. But still, no response. I don't know why I would have expected any. I have never heard any stories of a Kennedy ghost, and for all I know, he did enough good in this world to be allowed to rest in peace, to truly rest, and that's important because from what little I've heard about the motivations of ghosts, it's that they feel they have some unfinished business or pain that prevents them from getting over to the other side completely.

I stand up, give a nod to the building, and then walk on home in the downpour, but I don't mind, because I feel now I can withstand downpours, people laughing, or any other challenges I may face as I try to find the boy.

14

I can see the apartment just up the street. It looks different now. Quiet. Gone is the sickening sound of sirens dying. Gone are all the people, the squad cars, and the police tape. It's just an old building. I'm now at the exact spot on the sidewalk where I was once mysteriously held back by some invisible power. But there's nothing here today. I walk back and forth through the force field's wall, my hand extended, trying to feel something. But whatever it was, it is now gone.

I'm not sure I should be here. I'm not sure Mrs. Machado will remember me. I'm not sure what I'll say to her. I'm not sure.

Walking toward the building, I see three Hispanic guys watching me from down the street. Our eyes lock, and neither of us turns away. They're really staring me down, and I decide to walk over to them, something I never would have done before in a hundred lifetimes, but I can't be afraid anymore. I can feel a pulsing in my head again, and I'm starting to wonder if there's something new that's wrong with me now, like a brain tumor or some other diagnosis that I have absolutely no time for. As I get closer, their eyes widen. One is wearing a Raiders jersey, another a Metallica T-shirt, and the last man is wearing a white tank-top T-shirt—the kind Jamal refers to as wife-beater shirts. Metallica holds a brown paper bag with the end of a glass bottle protruding. He takes a sip.

"Watup, homie?" the guy with the Raiders jersey asks.

"I need to ask you a few questions," I reply.

"Some questions? What, you the police?"

"No. I'm more like a . . . private investigator."

Raider and the guy in the white wife-beater tank top laugh. Metallica cocks his head sideways, eyeing me hard like he's trying to figure something out.

I clear my throat.

"Were any of you around the other day," I start, "the day the little boy disappeared?"

"Hey, Essé, we answered these questions for the police already." Raider guy does all the talking. "Why should we talk to you?"

"I'm helping out in the investigation. Sometimes, after a while, people remember things they didn't before. Memory is a strange thing. Sometimes, it comes back that way."

I grimace as I place my index finger just to the side of my right eye, where I feel a sharp stab of pain.

"Homie," Raider starts, "you bettah get tuh steppin' . . ."

"Wait, it's *you*." Metallica speaks up, slurring his words. "I talked to the police. I was here. I saw you hanging around the street that day."

Raider and wife-beater stare me down.

"Essé, I'm-a cut you up," Raider says, pulling a switchblade from his back jeans pocket and clicking it open to expose the blade.

I bolt into a hard run down the block. The three start chasing me, yelling in Spanish, but I'm outpacing them, pumping my arms and legs as fast as I can. I'm not turning back to look, but I can hear their voices quickly growing distant, and maybe they're not in as good a shape as I'm in, but I've got to be sure. So, I'm in an all-out sprint, carrying this life-or-death pace farther than I ever have. My heart is pounding. Still, I keep running until several blocks later when I can't hear them at all. I look back and see no sign of them. I know I can't keep this up, but there aren't many places to hide here. It's a pure residential street, and the apartments are all gated. There are no stores to duck into and quickly make a call. But I can't keep running. My legs feel heavy, and one calf feels tight, like it's starting to cramp. If they're close enough to just turn the corner back at the last intersection, they'll see me, even though I've got some distance. I dive into some bushes.

I'm breathing hard, and I'm loud. But I let it out. It's okay. Even if they happen to come down this street, it'll be a while before they get here. So I catch my wind, hard. It will calm me down quicker this way.

I text Ray to come pick me up. *Now*. I tell him that I don't know the street name, but I think I'm just two or three blocks east of Yellow House. Once in the neighborhood, he needs to drive slowly so that I can see him as he cruises by, and then I can make a dash for the car. *Now!*

The wait is forever. But my breathing starts to calm, and I've got a good view from the bushes. No sign of the attackers. *What's happening?* These guys think *I'm* the kidnapper? I don't think they'll go to the police. Not the type. Besides, what are they going to say? They threatened to kill me and chased me all over K-town with switchblades?

I see Ray's ride, a clean blue Hyundai Sonata, and I rush the car, swinging open the rear passenger door, then jumping inside. I slump down low into the tan leather.

"Cole! What's going on? You okay?"

"Yeah, okay now. Thanks. Drive faster."

"What happened?"

"Some gangbangers chased me with knives."

"What? Are you serious? Why?"

A long time passes before I offer up, "I don't know."

"Let me call the cops."

"No! Don't!"

I think I surprise him with my reaction because he goes quiet.

"Why not?" he finally says softly. "They could've killed you."

I beg him to please not call. I tell him I've been running hard and just want to rest. He gives me that, easing up on the questions. Still, I see his eyes from time to time in the rearview mirror, checking up on me.

When we pull in front of my place, he double parks and asks again if I'm alright.

"Yeah, sure. I'll be fine. I owe you, man. Lunch on me, forever."

15

I AM UP EARLY THE NEXT MORNING AND BRUSH ASIDE THE bedsheets, rushing to the closet. I flip on the light switch and see an empty hanger there, separated from the others purposely last night so that I could maybe wear the shirt again the second day. It would have been a complete violation of the ceremony's etiquette, but I really believed I was beyond the strict rules and everything. It would have been totally proper for me to select a shirt I liked by choice. But the shirt is gone now. I can't explain why, but I half expected it. This miraculous gift that came out of nowhere must now return to nowhere. I turn off the light.

I drift over to the sofa and plop down. While not as frazzled by all of it as I was yesterday, I still have a sense of being lost in a forest. Somewhere there is a trail that makes sense, but I have no idea where. But there's also a small voice inside that whispers, "*What if none of it was real? What if I had imagined it all yesterday?*" I wince and rub my temples. I soon realize that while the possibility of having imagined, dreamed, or hallucinated the shirt yesterday would seem astronomically remote, so would any other explanation. If it was real, then how could a shirt like that ever make its way into my closet? The other possibility is that I had indeed bought it, or was given the shirt as a gift, and I simply forgot about it. But that doesn't fly either, because while my memory can be horrible, it is actually a precise instrument when it comes to my shirts. This is the one area I am dedicated to, give all my focus to because I feel these shirts can maybe help me. I have exactly four hundred fifty-three of them, and I know exactly where each one came from. So, while on the surface, to anyone else, this explanation might seem the most likely, I know in my heart that it is, of all the explanations, the only one that is impossible.

Now, I sense something's wrong. I smell smoke, but it's not the burning building kind of smoke or the nice smell of a barbecue grill. It's faint, but it has a tinge of menthol. This has to be from a cigarette. I look around the room, but I don't see any cigarettes, and it's not an old and stale smell like the odor that used to hit me when I was shopping for my used car, and I could tell when the cars belonged to smokers because they just had that cigarette stench permanently locked into the fabric. No, this smell is fresh. But that can't be right because I never light up. I look under the bed and sofa, and then toss the pillows and check the night-stand, where, of course, I find my pack of cigarettes, which are all still in there.

Since it's so faint, I'm thinking maybe someone is smoking in the hall, maybe close to the door. But when I check outside, I don't see any-one. I return inside and consider that it's possible I was just imagining it too. I groan.

I take my meds, only a half dose. It's still early, and I decide to watch the morning news show. It's hard to watch all the horror in the world. The part about the boy comes and goes so quickly, I'd have missed it if I turned away to check the time. *A mid-Wilshire autistic boy remains miss-ing, days after being abducted from his apartment. Police are asking that anyone who has any information regarding the disappearance of ten-year-old Juan Machado call the hotline number below.* And that was it.

What it means is that the police are getting nowhere. There are no new clues, and that's bad because the longer the time goes by that a missing person is not found, the probability increases exponentially that the story will not end well. I've read that again and again in my Internet searches.

The clock says 7:58 a.m., and I decide, well, I may as well go back, back to the ritual that has helped me—*sometimes* helped me—over these past few years. So I return to the closet and walk in. As usual, I allow the tips of my fingers to brush the shoulders of the hanging shirts until one seems to almost stick to my hand. I decide to pull this one out, and flip on the light.

It's a gray shirt with white text bubbles capturing the words: *Everything is easier said than done. Except Talking. That's pretty much the same.*

Today, I don't need to walk for miles through K-town or sit at a café, twirling my scrambled eggs, until some enlightenment hits me about the possible meaning of my shirt's message. I know right away what I have to do. I know what the shirt means.

I drive a few laps around the blocks where the Morning Show's studios are, struggling to find a parking spot. Hollywood is nothing like what most people living outside of Los Angeles imagine it to be. Most television and movie studios are actually not in proper Hollywood, and the few that are reside behind ordinary walls or inside buildings that give off nothing relating to fame and glamour. Hollywood is, in fact, as gray and dirty as most parts of L.A., even comparable to K-town, though I'd say K-town at least has a lot of charm. I kill the ignition and sit there in my car for a few minutes, leaning forward and resting my forehead on the steering wheel. *Is this all crazy, to even attempt this? What will I say to her?*

"Shawna Cleary, please," I tell the peppy receptionist with the big welcoming smile, with red hair and in her early twenties, standing behind the tall counter. I can really tell about her, her spirit. She is the kind that wants to help, and I'm feeling good about this now.

"Yes, of course. And your name?"

"Cole Reeves."

"Mr. Reeves, do you have an appointment with Ms. Cleary?"

"No, actually, but I know she'll want to speak to me."

"And what may I tell her this is regarding?"

"It's private. But I know she'll want to speak to me."

The receptionist's smile melts, and she looks at me sideways as she picks up the receiver of the phone on her desk and presses a button. I hear whispering and a short conversation.

"I'm sorry," she says, "but Ms. Cleary has gone for the day."

I look at my watch.

"But that can't be," I say. "*The Morning Show* should have just wrapped."

"I'm sorry, but if you call back our number and leave a message, she is prompt in returning calls."

"But, but . . ." I stop, hang my head, and turn toward the door.

"If I can say something. . ." the receptionist starts. "Well, if you do come back or call her, you have to state what you want. None of the talent is going to meet with anyone they don't know if they don't know what it's about. They're just too busy, and there are too many crazies out there. You have to state your purpose."

"State my purpose. Okay." I smile, and she smiles back and holds it. I think there's really something there, but I decide I need to focus, and so I step outside and think about calling the studio and what I might say in leaving a message for Shawna Cleary.

As I walk back to my car, the sidewalk hugs a long, tall chain-link fence that protects the cars of the people who work in the studio. I'm checking the cars, the various makes and models, when, from a side door to the building, I see someone come out who looks like Shawna Cleary.

"Ms. Cleary!" I call out.

She turns, smiles, and gives a quick wave, but keeps walking.

"Ms. Cleary, I need to speak to you. It's important."

"Sorry, but I need to run."

"This won't take long."

"They have photos of the news team at the reception desk. Just ask . . ."

"No, no, it's about the boy."

She stops.

"What boy?" she asks.

"The missing boy from Koreatown."

She studies me, narrowing her eyes, and walks slowly over until she's just on the other side of the fence. "You have information about Juan Machado?"

"Yeah. Sure." It's a stretch to say that I have information about him, but since I have her interest, and there is absolutely no doubt I have her interest now, I definitely am not going to walk it back and give her a reason to back out of the conversation. She will be part of this somehow. My shirt basically said so, put me here, and so I need her to come along.

She looks all around, as if she is searching for an answer. She seems confused about what to do. Then she looks at me, hard and penetrating, and I fidget as I've never been assessed in this way—well, except maybe by doctors, but this is different as I can almost read her thoughts. I'm sure she's questioning whether she can trust me or not.

"Go back to the reception desk," she says. "I'll have a security guard meet you there and bring you back."

I hustle back to the lobby area, and when I see the red-headed receptionist, I give her a smile and a big thumbs-up. She does the same. A security guard tells me to empty my pockets and put my belongings into a small tray, then walk through a metal detector just like the ones they have at the airport. We then walk through a maze of hallways, all feeling so un-Hollywood and un-glamorous, with Formica flooring and fluorescent lighting, just like you'd find in any old, boring downtown office building. We finally arrive at a small conference room, where the security guard asks me to take a seat and says Ms. Cleary will be right with me.

I can see him standing just outside a large window, and he glances over now and then, checking on me. Behind him, I see the set of the Morning Show, and the stage lighting is dimmed. The set is empty, except for a couple of technicians who seem to be adjusting a camera. It all looks so much smaller than it does on my television.

She finally enters the room. I rise and shake her hand—her soft, moisturized hand.

"What's your name?" she asks as we both take a seat at the table.

"Cole Reeves."

"So tell me, Cole, were you the one who called my office yesterday and said you had information about the Machado boy?"

Yesterday? I watch her hand tap nervously on the table, as something seems wrong or out of place with that hand.

"I said," she tries again, "did you call my office yesterday . . ."

"Is that a wedding ring?"

"What? Well, yes, of course, but . . ."

"But you never wear that on your show."

"That's right. Most female reporters don't. I'm not sure why; we're just told not to. I think it's about keeping distance and not giving too much away about our private lives."

"Huh. How long have you been married?"

"Five years. But listen, I do have a remote interview I've got to get to later, so I need to get back to the boy."

"I didn't call your office yesterday."

She sits up, surprised. "You didn't? Are you sure?"

"Yeah, I think I would remember if I'd called you. I call television journalists pretty much next to never, so I would remember something like that."

"Huh, well, that's strange. Someone called yesterday while I was on set and left a message that he had information about the boy, but didn't leave a call-back number."

I ponder this.

"Wasn't me," I say.

"Huh, that's just so odd. There have been no calls, no leads, and now, two days in a row, I've got young men coming to me with information."

"How do you know the other guy is young?"

"Well, he sounded young on the message."

She opens a leather portfolio, exposing a pad of paper, then clicks on a ballpoint pen.

"So tell me," she says, "what do you know about the lost boy?" She taps the pen nervously on the notepad.

"Well, it's not so much that I know something. It's just that I'm trying to find him myself, and I think I could use your help."

"How do you mean?"

"Well, I was wondering if your station had videotape of that first day, when the police were at the apartment, going in and out, and people were standing around outside."

"Sure, I'm sure we have footage on that."

"Is it possible for me to take a look at that?"

"Well, that's against station policy."

"It's just that I heard sometimes criminals return to the scene of a crime, and I thought maybe something might stand out."

"Do you know the kidnapper?"

"No, no, not at all."

"Then who would you be looking for in the video?"

"I'm not sure, but maybe someone who's a lot like me." I cringe as soon as I say the words. She stops the pen tapping, a serious look in her eyes as they penetrate mine.

"What do you mean by someone who's a lot like you?" she asks.

My stomach tightens, and I feel the blood leaving my face. There is a checkered flag in my head that flaps wildly, and a crazy car race of speeding thoughts of all colors, shapes, densities, and intensities bursts loose, and I'm trying to contain them, bring them back to the starting line where I can inspect them one at a time, carefully, to determine which ones make sense and which ones are just loud engine-revving noise, but it's too late. They're out and gone, flying away and around in my mind, so I wonder if I can trust her and tell her about the Russian chess player and how he swore I was a child molester, because if I did, then she, being a great journalist, would no doubt track down that chess player, and instead of saying the molester is a guy who looks like me, he would swear it *actually* is me, or the gangbangers at the boy's apartment yesterday, who also were sure they saw me the day of the kidnapping. They were so sure that they pulled knives and chased me down the street, and so if she talks to them, then the next thing I know is that the police will pay me a visit and probably arrest me because things never go well with me and the police, but now I know I've got to say something because she's got this hard look on me and is not going to let me off until I answer her question.

"I just think if I see the video, maybe something will stand out," I say.

"What, you're like some kind of psychic?"

I pause at this question, then quickly realize it's the perfect out.

"Yes, yes, although I wouldn't call myself that exactly. It's just that sometimes things jump out at me, and I notice things others don't, and I get inspired." It really is sounding good. I don't know where I'm getting this from.

"Where do you get your inspiration from?"

"Well, you see . . ." and then I stop myself, because, for just a millisecond before the words come out of my mouth, I am blessed with a sudden revelation that if I tell her my T-shirts are guiding me, she will never understand. "It's hard to explain." I trail off.

"So, Cole, not too many criminals come back to the crime scene. That's TV crime drama stuff. I was a crime beat reporter in Phoenix before getting this job here in L.A. Pyromaniacs sometimes like to watch everything they've set on fire burn down. Maybe first-time criminals, if it's truly some thrill they're getting out of it. You know," she hesitates now, "sometimes it's the ones who want to be heroes who come back and try to fix whatever they started. You know, they commit the crime and then help solve it."

She is staring me down, waiting for an answer.

"I'm just a psychic," I say softly.

She nods.

"Your shirt—it's interesting," she says. "I like it. Where'd you get it?"

"I . . ." and then, I freeze up. Where did I get it? *Where did I get it?* Where? It's not coming to me. This is impossible because I know every shirt and its story, but this one is not coming to me, not right at this moment, and I rub my forehead and beat my fists against my head, and maybe it's just that I'm nervous around her. Yes, that must be it, because there's no way I've forgotten where this shirt came from. It's just *not* possible.

"Hey, hey," she says. "It's okay. No big deal. I was just curious where you got it, that's all."

"Why do you like the shirt?"

"Huh. I don't know. I think it's funny. Also, the whole talking thing appeals to me. I like talking to people. And I've always thought the biggest part of my job was to make it easy for people to talk."

"Yeah. I see."

She smiles; I think she senses the conversation has taken on an intensity she does not want.

"So," she says, "if we're looking for someone who is a lot like you, tell me about you."

I don't know where to start. This is similar to the first question they asked when I interviewed for admission to Columbia, or the job interviews for the cellphone store, or Cup O' Joe's. *So, tell me about yourself,* they said, and then I fumbled through fits and starts. I mean, what an unfair question, because there is so much I can say—*anyone* can say—about myself, and so in the interest of time, I have to sort through what's most important in my life that would be pertinent to this conversation and that I should share in order to give them insight as to why I would be a good student, worker, or partner in solving missing person mysteries. But there's so much I could say that I need to try to calm my thoughts and slow down because it has to be about focus, and my journal entries, and my conversations, and my life must contain more structure and focus now.

"I suppose I should start with my father," I say. Then I tell her about my relationship with him—but not the whole smoking thing because that's just way too personal—my mom, Robbie, Ray, and Jamal. I decide not to mention Julie, though she asks if I have a girlfriend. I just want to give off that unattached vibe in case her whole marriage thing is shaky. *Oh, what the hell am I talking about?* She isn't going to go for a guy like me anyway. But I still decide the whole Julie conversation won't help me look like someone who's got it together and is ready to do anything I can to help find the boy, and even though I can't say what it is—because I don't *know* what it is—I know there must be some special way I can help.

"But why?" she asks. "Don't get me wrong; I think it's great you're wanting to help, but why him?"

"I sometimes ask the same thing, especially since he was pretty mean to me."

"You *know* him?"

"I met him, but just once, so I wouldn't exactly say I know him. It was at a neighborhood restaurant. He laughed at me."

"Why?"

"I don't know. And it really hurt, you know? It wasn't like we were sharing a joke or I made a funny face or did something silly. No. He just pointed his finger straight at me and laughed, and it was a wild, crazy laugh, and he was laughing so hard that his finger was shaking, and even though his mother tried to make him stop, he just wouldn't. I remember crying that night because it hurts to be laughed at, and believe me, it's happened to me before, but it's been a long while, and so I'd forgotten some of that sting, that pain, until it all came back, and I hated him so much. I hated him as much as a person could possibly hate. I hated him! I hated . . ."

She holds down my hand, which is balled up into a fist and slamming down onto the table.

"Sorry," I say, softly.

She's staring at me with a scared look. The security guard peers through the door, asking *Is everything okay?* but Shawna Cleary waves him off.

"You know, I also play Minecraft a lot on my computer," I say, trying to change the subject, but she doesn't seem interested. I also tell her about my obsession with European soccer, and this changes the tone a little because, as it turns out, she played competitively for several years when she was younger and even played for Stanford, one of the best teams in the country. The conversation then starts to loosen up a little, although I feel like her mind is still back there at the Tofu House scene, where I was hating the little boy. Still, she's passionate about soccer, so we have that in common.

It isn't until I finally mention my newfound fascination with Kennedy that her face lights up. She says it's a little unusual that someone as young as me would connect with him, but I explain how my grandfather always admired him, combined with my obsession with the 1960s. She says she minored in Political Science in college, and Robert Kennedy was one of her favorite political figures for taking on unpopular positions in the name of social justice and going on with the fight after his own brother was assassinated. I went on to even quote some of my favorite passages from his speeches for her, and now she's truly impressed. She can't believe I can actually memorize long passages of Kennedy quotes, and I tell her I really can't explain it because my memory isn't very good at all. Then she goes on about some of the highlights of his career, and often I can recite a key part of the speech right off, and I can tell she is truly in awe. She's taking notes of some of the quotes as I'm speaking, though I don't understand why.

I can sense it's all wrapping up here, though I still wish I could see the station's footage of the crime scene. Still, I should feel good. Except for the part about meeting the boy in the restaurant, I've had a good conversation with her—a natural give and take with some depth but also with some humor. It has been as perfect a conversation as I can ever recall having.

We leave the conference room and head back down the maze of hallways, and she says she will give some thought to what we talked about, and if I think of any clues or leads, I should feel free to call her. There is a warmth building inside of me that I'm finding hard to control. She makes conversation so easy. She really cares. It seems like she really believes in me, not taking me as some kind of joke like Jamal, SteFunny, or whatever her name is. Here is a professional journalist who thinks I may be of some help, and she will help me as well. I can feel tears welling up in my eyes. Sometimes, my emotions just escape me, and it's often for something ridiculous—just a hint of sympathy for someone in need, or like now, the disbelief and the infinite gratitude for someone who has treated me fairly and listened and understood, I think—but at least listened—and I want so much to do something for her like buy her dinner, not out of some romantic attraction—although that's still definitely there, even though I'm crushed she is married, but just to do *something*, anything to show I appreciate the recognition that I am capable here, I am a force for good and can, with laser-focus and determination, find this child. And I want to say something, but I'm getting choked up by it all.

We arrive at the lobby, and she extends her hand, thanking me for stopping by.

"I need to do something here now," I say. "You may think this is a bit crazy, but I want to give you something."

She takes a step back.

I lift my shirt up over my head and proceed to take it off. I stand there, holding the shirt in my hand, and then I extend it out to her.

She slowly reaches out to take it, her brow furrowed.

"I thought since you were a soccer player . . ."

She covers her mouth with her hands and laughs. I imagine myself as a champion who has just won the World Cup and, in a sign of camaraderie and respect for his opponent, exchanges shirts at the end of the match.

"Well, thank you," she says. "But I'm not giving you my blouse if that's what you're thinking!"

I laugh at this, then begin to walk shirtless down the streets of Hollywood, back to my car parked several blocks away.

16

I WAS SO WOUND UP YESTERDAY BY THE MEETING I'D HAD WITH Shawna—she said I could just call her Shawna—that I spent the rest of the afternoon just walking around K-town, still shirtless. I guess this would be a small example of me in a manic state, or what Jamal would refer to as me feeling a bit too high—crazy high. Later, I must have stood a block outside Juan's apartment for an hour. But I couldn't move. I don't think I was scared of those thugs returning, and it wasn't as bad as that first day when some unseen wall was keeping me there. I just, I don't know, but maybe I was afraid to face his mother.

Now, looking out the large window of my apartment, I see a soft haze in the early morning sky, soon to burn off, I'm sure, for what will be a clear, sunny day. The Hollywood sign leaks through the haze, fame and fortune so nearby, and I remember Martin Conrad and realize this must have been a daily torture for him—to want so much to break into the Industry and yet have that sign greet him each morning—a tease, as if saying, *I'm right here, just right over here, but you can't touch me.* Every day.

I lean back on my sofa, lift my feet up onto the coffee table, and sympathize with the man Mr. Li said never to have sympathy for. But I come back to what I said to Mr. Li that day, about how cruel it was to have been given that one great—or at least very good—screenplay to coax you into thinking you can really do this, only in the end to realize you really can't. And then there is all that time gone—time you can never get back, and the years that are just a daily reminder that your life wasn't what you thought it was meant to be. And then it's too late. And then a shotgun barrel to your head.

I take my meds, a half dose, then head to the closet and find my shirt for today. It is one with the words, *Back in my day, we had Nine planets*, accompanied by a comic drawing of each of the planets, including Pluto.

There's something to this. *What did she say?* What was it about Pluto? The little girl wanted me to take her there or show her the planet. It was something like that.

I don't know what to make of it, why the girl at MacArthur Park would say what she said, or how any of this relates to me and the missing boy. Maybe it has something to do with something that was once there but is now gone. However, that really doesn't fit because Pluto didn't go anywhere; it's not missing—just reclassified. Robbie once told me that the scientist who discovered that Pluto had an unusual orbit that caused it to no longer be classified as a planet received death threats for years. *Perhaps the boy is dead now?*

Nothing is making sense. I turn on the TV, and this time, there isn't even a mention of Juan Machado on the news. So little is happening that there's nothing new to report. I'm just standing, looking outside my window, and turning over in my mind the wild and random possibilities as to what the shirt might mean.

There is a lone man I see walking down the sidewalk below, maybe on his way to work or to meet a friend for an early coffee, and there's no way he sees me, but I can almost see myself as *being* him, walking a sidewalk alone in the mystery of an overcast morning—just our secret—the beauty and the anticipation of the day to come. Sometimes, I feel like I'm inside of someone else, as if we have connected, our psyches intertwining somehow. *I hope the bus is on time because I can't be late for work again. I can't wait to see Maria this weekend. Why do kids' braces cost so much?* I've heard it all. It's probably my imagination, but I really feel I'm inside somehow.

I look up at the hills, and I'm still struggling. "*Sometimes, the answer is right in front of you,*" my mother used to say. Mothers may love you more than anything in life, but they can be Pollyannaish and say the stupidest things. Staring out right in front of me, I see the same Hollywood Hills I have been looking at all morning.

Wait.

Wait, *wait.* Oh man . . . there it is!

That's it, and it was right there all along, just to the right of the Hollywood sign. The answer. The Griffith Park Observatory.

I call both Ray and Jamal to see if either wants to go to the observatory, but I only get their voicemails. I decide not to leave messages since I want to leave right away. I know they're busy. Ray's business is keeping him going round the clock, and Jamal's hooked up with a new girlfriend and also got commissioned to paint a new mural on the side of a government building up in the Valley. I don't really *need* them for this, but I think it might have been good to have someone with me—someone who might help piece this together with me. I wouldn't even need to tell them what I'm up to, especially Jamal, since he's already laughed at the idea. We could just check out the observatory and learn about stars and black holes—especially black holes, since I've read and re-read about them countless times and still don't understand them. Then, as we talk and observe, I could have them play off my questions and clues without them even knowing, and maybe, with a little luck, have this start to come together.

But I guess I'm on my own.

The Griffith Park Observatory is a landmark in Los Angeles, and yet, aside from a field trip in the fourth grade, which I can't even remember, I have never been there. As I arrive, the building looks familiar, with its large block structure capped by three domes, the largest being in the center at the main entrance. However, off to the right, I see the Hollywood sign clear and big, a much closer view than I get from my large apartment window, and so I decide to walk over and get a better look. Children run and play on a large grass field, and as I'm walking, I notice a bust with a sculpted head sitting atop a tall white block pedestal. The name on the pedestal reads *James Dean.*

"You have the same hair," a boy says to me as I step up next to him, looking up at his bust.

"Ha! You're right!" I exclaim, studying the way the hair pulls up and back, and the locks look just like mine after I've raked them through out of anxiety, which haunts me pretty much all the time.

"I saw a lot of statues at the museum yesterday too," the boy says.

"The County Museum over on Wilshire?"

"Yeah. A lot of cute girls there too," he smirks.

"How old are you?"

"Thirteen. Hey, who knows, maybe even you might find yourself a cute girl."

I turn and head back to the Observatory, deciding I don't need the pity of anyone not old enough to shave. And why are kids coming up and talking to me all of a sudden anyway?

Walking into the main building, I see there are children everywhere—bright supernova bursts of excitement with every laugh, push, and dash to the restroom or gift shop. I look up at the brightly colored mural on the ceiling and try to make out who all the people are up there. I sense they are the Roman or Greek gods, the likes of Zeus, Poseidon, Cupid, and so on. They're looking down on us—the tourists—who are waiting to buy tickets.

I feel the first twinge of another headache just starting up. I pull out my cellphone and start to make a note to research my symptoms on the web later and stop by the store for some aspirin, but I'm interrupted.

"You don't have to pay again," the lady with the white hair, Clark Kent glasses, and deep stoop tells me as I arrive at the ticket counter.

"What?" I say, turning to look behind me on the chance she may have been talking to someone else.

"You don't have to pay again," she says, directing the statement to me. "Weren't you here before?"

"No. I just got here."

"Oh, I'm sorry, you look so much like someone who was just here."

I pay for my ticket, but a wild vertigo hits me hard, and I clutch the counter with both hands.

"I'm sorry," I say, "but I really need your help. Take a good look at me." I open my eyes and hold myself steady. I give her a moment.

"I need you," I tell her. "I *really* need you to let me know now if it was *me* you saw earlier."

"I'm pretty sure . . ."

"No!" I shout, slamming my hand down on the counter. I can sense the eyes of her coworkers, tourists, and kids all falling on me. "I don't want *pretty sure*. Was it *me*?!?!"

"Sir, is there a problem?" says a burly, bearded coworker, with authority in his voice.

"No, no," I say meekly. "I'm sorry."

"Oh, and no smoking here, sir," he says, and I yank the cigarette from my lips and walk away.

I veer off and wander through the large hall, my head still spinning. This is crazy. I watch the people—their faces—for anyone who looks like me. I place my palms on my forehead and try to steady my head. I realize I've wandered off into an exhibit that's dark and has benches for what appears to be a film that's about to start, and I sit down because I'm starting to feel overwhelmed by the incessant chatter of the children, like bees working a hive.

"Do you like black holes?" says a little girl sitting next to me, a big grin of anticipation on her maybe ten-year-old face.

"What?"

"The movie. It's about black holes. We just learned about them in school."

"Really?" and I am sincere in my fascination. "You know, I've always had an interest, but I've never really understood them."

"Didn't they teach you about them in school?"

"Sure, but it never made sense. And then, I've read articles over the years, but I just couldn't get my head around them. I mean, something that swallows up everything that comes near it, including light?"

"Did you go to college?"

"Yeah, one of the best. Columbia. That's in New York City."

"Wow, you must be smart."

"I don't know . . ." my voice trails off. "I got perfect scores on every entrance exam, but I think when I took the tests, I just happened to be feeling . . . good."

The lights dim a bit more, the film starts, and the narrator states that we are about to journey through the darkest parts of our universe as we study the mysteries of black holes. He says something about them not being actual holes at all, and I sit up in my seat because that's exactly what I'd always thought they were. But he's saying they are actual masses so dense that they have an unbelievable gravity pull, and this is what sucks everything into them, even—and I still can't imagine it—*light*. This is why they're called black holes, because even light can't escape them.

I scan the audience, still looking for whoever this person is who looks like me. The girl I spoke to looks as if she is in a trance, in awe of the mighty force of such powerful galactic beasts. Among the other faces, no one stands out. I look at the closed door just behind me and consider stepping out because I'm wasting my time here. Nothing's coming to me—not anything related to the boy and not even anything about black holes.

The narrator continues, saying there is a boundary—something called an event horizon—that is a point of no return, and if anything crosses this line, then it cannot escape the pull of the black hole, and it's finished.

I nudge the little girl and tell her I really need to get going. She just nods, not really caring, I think, and waves goodbye to me.

I rise, just as the narrator says something now about newer theories relating to black holes: that maybe not all matter is incinerated when it hits the event horizon and that there are twin particles to everything and that one particle gets sucked into the darkness but the other escapes. I rest my hand on the door, ready to push out and get on my way, but this intrigues me. The narrator mentions the word *Entanglement*, a theory stating that two twin particles can be separated over an infinite distance and yet still be connected. They actually continue to act and react to each other as if they are still one. I shake my head and can't really fathom any of this. Another concept even more astounding than black holes is that twins separated over billions of light years are still essentially one. I decide as soon as I get out of the theater that I will make a note to myself to look up *Entanglement* and try to better understand it, but for now, this actually makes me feel a little better—almost relieved. What may have brought me down so much before about black holes was the inevitability, the certain doom for anything that crosses a line and is drawn into the infinite blackness. But now, just maybe, half of that doomed thing may escape the death pull and find a way to stay in the light.

17

It's still early in the afternoon, and I'm not sure I got anything out of the observatory or my Planets shirt, but I decide I can't wait until tomorrow morning, so I head back to my apartment. I'm going to pick another shirt. It goes against all the rules, but I have to do *something.* I have to do something now. I'm feeling depressed and like time is running out for Juan, and I'm just not helping. I'm trying as hard as I can to push these experiences out of my mind, where people keep thinking they've seen me before, but it's getting hard. I can't figure any of it out.

This time, it's a white T-shirt with an etching of the face of Leonardo Da Vinci. Da Vinci is saying, *Je suis un genie*, which translates to *I am a genius.* It's a shirt from my trip to France. I stare out of my window, again at the hills, and search for what meaning this could possibly have. After a while, I start to get really down, and I'm drowning in doubt about whether any of this is going to work, if I'm really meant to help in any way here, or if maybe I'm going about it all wrong. Maybe, I should go to the police. But I've got no real information, and there's no way the police will ever take me seriously. I've never had any luck with them, and I'm sure they have a file on me and will immediately discount anything I say. The Shawna Cleary meeting was good, or at least it felt good, but I'm not sure where that's going to take me. A meeting that closes with, essentially, L*et's just keep in touch*, means neither person could come up with any sort of definitive action plan. There was no next step; no *this is what we're going to do and how we're going to get it done!* Nothing, except an unspoken admission that no one knows where to take it, so I guess we'll just think about it, and if something, by chance, pops into our heads, then we'll keep in touch. I sour.

I call her, but I get her voicemail.

"Hey, Shawna. This is Cole. Listen, can we talk? I'm really feeling like it would help me a lot to see that footage you have from outside Juan Machado's apartment. It, um, might help my psychoability, and images may start coming to me."

I hang up.

Psychoability? What the hell am I even talking about? At least I should use real English words if I'm speaking to a journalist.

I tap my Notes app, and I'm about to enter some thoughts on how to best approach Shawna again when I'm greeted by strange words. They read *Liberar a Juan*. I don't recall making this entry. Clearly, I must have wanted to save some thoughts about Juan or my search, and I'm guessing the app's autocorrect feature butchered whatever I had started to write. For just a moment, I try to bring back what I might have wanted to say, something likely beginning with the letter L, but then give up and delete the entry when my phone rings. I see, it's Ray, finally returning my call from the morning.

"Hey, not too late for Mexican!" he says. "I've been killing myself. Need a break."

Because I want so much to talk to him, anyone really, and perhaps in an indirect way, get his take on some of this, I agree to meet him.

"S'up?" he smiles, toasting me with a shot glass as I enter.

"Hey," I say, pulling up a chair. "Done with work?"

"Yup. Going to the range right after lunch. Hey, come with me."

I consider this for a moment, as I do enjoy going to the driving range with Ray. There's something about golf that makes him philosophical and yet still very funny. We typically go to the big place just off Wilshire, a monstrosity of a facility smack in the middle of K-town. Because you can't just crush golf balls out into the city with all the cars and glass buildings around, the place is encased in massive green netting.

It's a four-level facility, and we like to go to the top floor, which gives us the feeling of playing golf, yet it's more like just crushing golf balls off the top of a mountain into a bottomless ravine.

"Man, I really want to, but I can't," I finally answer.

"Why not?"

"Just . . . busy."

"C'mon, you're never busy. Let's go crush a few."

I think about the time I've wasted and how the puzzle pieces aren't fitting. I really need to focus here.

"I think you need focus," Ray says, and I pull back in my chair, stunned that he would say that just when I was thinking the same thing.

"Golf will help with that," he says. "They say this game is played between your ears—get it? It's mostly in your mind. But most people's minds are messed up. That's why hitting a little white ball that's just lying there—it isn't *even* moving—is the hardest thing in the world to do. At least, it's the hardest thing in the world to do *well*."

I nod in agreement but still say, "I'll pass."

We order, and I quietly play with my silverware, occasionally looking around the restaurant to see if the waitress from last time is here, but I can't find her. The one today is neither attractive nor friendly.

"I ate Mexican just yesterday, so I may go light," I say.

"What you did yesterday has nothing to do with today."

I nod.

"So are you still looking for this kid?" Ray asks.

"Sure. Jamal told you?"

Ray nods. "So . . ." he starts, fighting to find the right words, "this kid, he made fun of you, or something like that?"

"That's right."

"Laughed in your face?"

"Yes."

"So, why are you looking for him? I mean, no one, in general, wants to see a kid hurt. But why do *you* feel you have to do it? What's it to you?"

"I don't think I'm 'in general' anyway. I'm me. I sometimes wish I could be a part of 'in general.' Hell, Ray, it seems like every day, all I want, more than anything else, is to be 'in general.'"

"Okay, I feel ya. But why you and this kid?"

I shake my head and shrug.

Our food arrives, and Ray moves his plate of chapulines over to me with a questioning look in his eye. I laugh and look at the plate for a moment, really considering what it might taste like, then wave it away.

"Hey, are you okay?" he says.

"I think so."

"What's up?"

I often feel like there's a never-ending war going on in my head—the decisions surrounding what information to share. I am so afraid that if I speak up and say the truth—the straight, pure truth—that someone might laugh, suggest I see a doctor to prescribe me different meds, or call me a freak. This war goes on during almost every waking moment, and I feel what it must be like for that zebra or antelope grazing or doing whatever they need to do during the day while always keeping one nervous eye out for the lion. I, too, live in constant dread of the lion.

"There's just been some things happening to me that are a bit hard to explain." And here I stop, reminding myself, actually talking to myself in my head, *Do not say I am chasing someone exactly like me; do not say this person seems to be in places right before I arrive; do not say, do not say —*

"Explain," he commands.

"Just some strange . . . coincidences."

Ray takes an especially large handful of *chapulines* into his mouth, chews loudly—no effort is made to suppress the unnerving, crunching noise—and stares at me blankly.

"Coincidence does not exist," he says.

"What?"

"CO-IN-CI-DENCE does NOT exist!"

"Where'd you get that from?"

"My sister says that. She says everything means something. Every little thing."

"This is your Zen Buddhist sister?"

"You know it."

If *she* said it, then I really need to give this some serious consideration, but I'm quickly dazed by all the little things that have been happening to me, and if every little one of them means something.

I feel dizzy again, and I'm struggling through my taco salad. I'm drinking more water than usual, but I feel thirsty and a bit lost and disoriented. I look at my shirt, and I think about all my shirts and what if Ray's sister is wrong. What if they don't mean anything, and none of this has meant anything, not the angels mural or the observatory? But the *I Am A Man* shirt—how to explain that one? How do you explain a shirt that did not exist and shows up just for me? And what about the Internet and Pi shirt? Every other shirt has had some meaning and some direction. But it's nagged me for all these days that I can't figure what that one was about. And yet, I want so much to believe what Ray's sister says, and this shirt must mean something too.

"Here you go," Ray says.

"What?"

"The bill."

"Oh yeah, right."

"You okay?"

"Yeah, yeah."

"Hey, lighten up. Don't take things too seriously, you know?"

I nod. "Ray, maybe I'll head to the range with you after all."

"Cool."

We rise from the table. Ray waves to the waitress, who just barely tips her head in acknowledgement. As we walk out, Ray slaps my arm.

"So hey, you wanna tell me what 'Jeh swiss uhn genie' means?" he says.

"It's '*Je suis un genie*,'" I respond with the correct French pronunciation. "It means 'I am a genius.'"

"You are, huh?"

"Well, no, it's actually Leonardo Da Vinci. See, that's him on the shirt."

"Huh, that's strange. Just before coming here, a hot young thing had me give her a ride to the museum."

"The big museum over on Wilshire?"

"Yeah, she said she really wanted to see some Da Vinci and asked if they had any. I said I didn't know, but I saw that bad movie about him years ago, and she said that was nonsense. She was really nice to talk to and really easy. What do you think? What are the chances? You wear some foreign language shirt about some painter who's been dead hundreds of years, and I've never given any thought to, and just this morning, I drive some cute Asian girl to the museum to see this same painter. I'm telling you, that was one nice fare, Jack. Thank you, Da Vinci!"

18

Ray drops me off in front of the L.A. County Museum of Art, and I apologize again, saying there's just something I need to do and we could golf some other time. He had been trying to talk me out of coming here and joining him at the range instead, but I caught a break when Robbie called me, completely unexpectedly, and said he'd be in town in two days and wanted to get together. Of course, I said *Yes*. Robbie's cool and always fun, and I tried to keep him on the phone longer so as not to have to argue with Ray, but Robbie said he had to go, promising he had the greatest story to tell me, and though I insisted he tell me *now*, he said he had to go but that it had to do with *Torture*.

The museum entry building is massive, resting right on the busy boulevard, just a little west of K-town. I haven't been here in many months and had forgotten, or perhaps not closely noticed, how much the big stone, blocky architecture reminds me of the buildings in Minecraft, which is a video game that's ridiculously popular, even though the graphics look like a five-year-old had developed them—crude and blocky.

This must be a special day for field trips because schoolchildren are everywhere. They bustle with energy, running and laughing as school escorts try to reign them in. I'm guessing they *had* to behave, be still, and be quiet inside the museum, and now that they're finished with it, their true selves explode outside, and they want to be kids again. I feel a hint of nausea as I watch them, and a soft sadness, which I can't explain, falls upon me. Their sheer joy and energy—I can't take it, feeling overwhelmed by the throng of people, children, and noise, and nothing here feels like the Da Vinci Museum, which is more like a large house, outside the

Amboise Castle in the Loire Valley of France. It all feels wrong. I don't know why I'm here or what I'm looking for. I feel repelled by the museum itself, as if I am the polar opposite of its magnet.

The nausea gets heavier, and another headache starts, so I step out of line and find a place on a bench, squeezing between two elderly ladies who I'm sure are wondering why a young man in his twenties desperately needs to take a seat. I rest my head in my hands and sit here for a long time. I close my eyes but cannot escape the noise all around me, which is no longer just around me. It is seeping inside of me as if someone has made a deep cut and poured the laughter, footsteps, chatter, and scolding into my open wound. As soon as I can muster a little strength, I will leave, I decide, but I am afraid it's too long a walk. So I'll need to call Ray or get a real cab or something because I'm feeling short of breath now, like the simple decision of how to get home is smothering me, and I gasp for air while I say to myself, "*Slow down*," and then again, "*Slow down*."

In the throng of faces, I see one that looks familiar. Only the head sticks up above the crowd—the hair, the profile of his face with the defined jaw, the way he's squinting as he looks into the distance. I blink hard several times, the vision just a click out of focus. I shut my eyes tight to try to adjust and get my eyesight clear, but when I open them again, he's gone. It was *me*.

Staggering, I rise but need a moment to get my balance, then rush off to chase down whoever it was. It's like driving bumper cars as I struggle to get through the crowd, and I can sense I'm getting dirty looks, but no one says anything. Maybe because of the way I'm walking, they must think I'm drunk or something. But I can't find him.

I keep on fighting through the people, occasionally tripping over a kid, and then excusing myself, but I don't see him anywhere. Think. *Think!* What's going on here? But the more I strain to make some sense of all of this, the worse my head feels. When I finally tire, I see the crowd has thinned and dusk is falling. I begin to wander the grounds but soon decide to walk back out to the street and head west on Wilshire. I take it slowly, breathing deeply, and then begin to find my balance.

A chorus of lights switch on just ahead of me, all sitting atop what appear to be a hundred lampposts, clustered together in organized rows. The configuration makes no sense, but it becomes obvious that this must be part of the museum, an exhibit of some sort that is instead situated outside, in the museum plaza. Walking closer, my impression is confirmed, and they are, in fact, tall, gray lampposts of varying heights and styles with their ornamental bulbs at the top burning brightly.

Leaning against one of the poles, a girl whose face glows with unblemished alabaster skin looks off to the west down the busy street. Her complexion is perfect—smooth and glowing white—while her lips hold a half smile, or maybe it is no smile at all. *It's Julie.* She is different, wearing a loose chartreuse blouse and a long, tan skirt. She has a pearl necklace, and you would think she's a junior lawyer at some Century City law firm or a model for some stylish but conservative high-end designer, like Brooks Brothers or Ralph Lauren. There is something different about her hair too—the way the curls softly flow down to her shoulders. It just seems, I don't know, wilder when she's at Q Bar. And there is no Lolita-echoing schoolgirl outfit on her like I see each night I visit the bar.

I pull my phone from my back pocket, wanting to capture a picture of her right now, at this moment, with the sunlight and lamplights hitting her perfect white skin, but then, as if sensing someone is watching her, she turns to look straight at me.

"Oh, hey!" she says and gives an energetic wave.

"Hey!" I say, slowly lowering my phone so that I'm pretty certain she doesn't suspect I had been trying to get a shot of her and was maybe just taking a picture of the lamppost exhibit. I wave back.

"Well, come on over," she says with a wave of her hand.

I take a step, then another, and can feel an energy welling up inside me—an energy I don't like because I recognize it as the one I can't control, and I try not to think about how I'm walking over to see the girl I've longed for ever since I've moved here, or that I'm now going to see her outside of her workplace, where the rules that we must stay on opposite sides of the bar do not apply, or the worry that goes hand-in-hand with these situations that the energy will overpower me, and I will say too much or the wrong thing because that energy has a way of bursting through any filters I might have in my mind, like tsunami waters pounding through a village. So I try to think of the lampposts and museums and not the girl, but, of course, the more I think, *Do not think about the girl,* the more I'm actually thinking about the girl.

"Hey, did you change your shirt?" she asks.

"What?"

"Didn't you have a different shirt on earlier? I thought I saw you a while ago. I was going to say hi, but there was a small crowd between us, and I didn't want to just yell over. I was waiting in line and didn't want to lose my place."

"No. I had a different shirt on this morning, but not since I've been here."

"Hmm. There were a lot of people in the way, coming and going, but I think it was *you*. It's strange, but at first I was sure it was you, and then you seemed different. Like it was someone else. And then it looked like you again. You seemed to be looking around and didn't turn my way, so we couldn't make eye contact. Anyway, I thought it was a cool shirt."

"What did it look like?"

"It was white, with long sleeves, with three blue stripes sitting on top of each of the shoulders."

"Really?"

"Yes. And on the front, it had the word *Emirates*. There were smaller words just below that, but you turned quickly, and I couldn't make them out."

"Was it *Fly Better*?"

"Yes, I think that's it! *Emirates Fly Better*."

"I would never, ever, ever, *ever* wear that shirt!"

"Huh?"

"That's the shirt for Real Madrid. I am Atlético!"

"You're what?"

"I am a fan of Atlético Madrid, not Real Madrid. That couldn't possibly be me. There's just no way!"

"Sure. Whatever."

Please, Cole, just shut up. Shut up now. Figure it out later. Figure out how there is some shadow of myself hovering through my life just a half-step ahead of me. Figure out how the shadow likes Real when I like Atlético. What does that mean? And then a coldness fills me as I realize I am the one who is always just a little bit behind. What if it's not a shadow, but it's real—a more real side of myself—and I, or at least the *I* that is here now speaking to Julie, is actually the shadow? I rake my hair back, as I need to really understand this. *But figure it out later. Just shut up now. No, wait. First apologize; otherwise, she will just be left thinking I go nuts over little things like soccer teams.*

"Hey, Julie, I'm sorry. I'm just a little too passionate about my soccer."

Her look of dismay builds up to a smile.

"That's okay," she says, "I like passionate."

I pause and am about to make some comment about how she doesn't have to do that bar-talk here, now, with me, and how, in fact, I'd prefer she didn't because I'm falling in love with the image of this pearly-skinned, smartly dressed girl by the lamppost, but she jumps in first.

"Is that Da Vinci?!?!" she asks, pointing at my shirt.

"This? Uh, yeah."

"Unbelievable! I came here today specifically looking to see if they had any Da Vinci pieces here at the museum. Of course, they didn't. I guess I should have checked it out first online or called. It was just a whim."

"Why are you interested in Da Vinci?"

"I just finished a paper on him for my Renaissance History class at City. It's pretty much ready, and I'm turning it in Thursday, but it's all researched from books, you know. I thought it would add a lot if I could somehow experience it myself, maybe really feel something from the art directly, and maybe that could inspire me somehow."

"Well, it inspired *me*, that's for sure."

"You've seen his work?"

"Sure, at *The Louvre* in Paris, but more at the museum that exists at his former home in France. It's in a region called the Loire Valley, and I really think it must be one of the most beautiful places on earth. There were fields where you could see tall sunflowers that stretched to the horizon. And they have beautiful castles there, which the French call *chateaux*, and outside one of the castles called Amboise is the home where Da Vinci lived and wound up dying. That's now a museum with some of his work."

"Oh my. . ." she says softly.

I freeze. She looks up at me with a look of—I don't know—*awe*. I want to stop here. Or maybe not stop, but just ask her out. Or, better still, just kiss her. But wait, no, I can't do that.

"So," she starts, "how did it inspire *you*?"

"Well, let me first tell you that I don't know anything about art. I like some paintings and some sculptures, and I don't like others, but I can't tell you why. I do, however, love the feeling of museums, the wandering around, and the discovery. But it was at the museum in the Loire Valley—it's called *Clos Lucé*, by the way—that some girl, another tourist like me, said something about how we humans only use about ten percent of our brains. That's it. Just ten percent. But then, I saw everything Da Vinci had done—the paintings, sculptures, architectural designs, notebooks, and plans and ideas—even mirror-writing, which means the words and sentences are all written backward, so they can only be read in a mirror, and do you know how unbelievably hard that is? Anyway, it gave me hope that we could do more. *I* could do more. It's at least possible. Maybe it's super hard, but it's possible. And so, that's what I want. I want to do more."

She looks at me in such a way that I'm sure she's not just reading my face or checking my shirt. Her eyes are penetrating. She is inside of me. I can feel it somehow. There is a warmth, or maybe I am imagining it because her soft smile is something I have wanted to see for a long time. A sincere, *accepting* smile.

"I'm getting hungry," she says. "There's a restaurant I know just down the block, if you're up for it."

We walk east down Wilshire and cut back through the museum grounds, where there is a park and a plaza. We walk close together, and as we do, our hands brush against one another until I decide to gently hold hers. She does not resist. Then our arms begin to swing gently to the rhythm of our steps. I whisper a prayer—and I never pray—but I say, *Please God, let me be real and not the shadow—let this be the real me right now.*

And then, I can feel the energy stirring again, and I think, *No, no, not now.* I begin to swing our arms higher and more wildly, as if doing so will make this more true, the bond more firm and permanent, the acknowledgment that this is really happening and can never stop. I don't want it to stop, but now it's getting ridiculous as we look like a couple of second-graders playing some game, and I know I must break this spell, the exaggerated movements of a reality I am getting a taste of that I want to make permanent.

She breaks my hold, though we continue to walk. I close my eyes—though I don't think she notices—as I'm thinking I have surely just blown it, and when we get closer to the restaurant, maybe I should just apologize and tell her I'm not feeling well and keep walking, then disappear from the bar for a few weeks, hoping she'll forget until I return one night when I've taken my full meds to make sure I'm under control and . . .

Julie then wraps her arm around mine, high up at the bicep, and we continue to walk on.

It turns out, I have been to this restaurant before, though it's been months. So it must have been right after I saw the Japanese exhibit with the tea ceremony. I order the cornbread with the sweet honey butter to start, and it hits me how this is perhaps my favorite food of all time, even though I haven't had it in what seems like a lifetime. I'm dumbstruck by how I could have forgotten this place when it would be so easy for me to get over here on just about any day of the week and gorge on cornbread and honey butter.

We chit-chat through dinner, and I come to the glorious discovery that if I'm in a restaurant, I can control my tsunami energy by merely stuffing food in my mouth. It's the perfect antidote, because if I just leave it to my mind to try to control my mind, then it's like trying to change the current of flood waters by splashing water at it from the opposite direction—but if you place something physical there, say, a mountain, then the water has to stop. I don't usually go for metaphors in my journal because they are very difficult and usually bad, so I'll just say the best way to keep my mouth from spewing endless meandering talk is to physically stick some food in there.

Turns out, Julie goes to school during the day, getting General Ed out of the way and hoping to transfer to a UC school later, maybe UCLA if she can make the money thing work out, but she hasn't settled yet on what she wants to major in. She tells me she is actually half Korean and half Japanese, which comes from her mother's side, and her mother makes certain she keeps with Japanese traditions and so she actually knows how to perform the tea ceremony. When I tell her that I had actually participated in one long ago and that I'm very interested, she says she can perform one for me if I'd like.

When the conversation turns to me, I always get a little nervous because, sometimes, people can't relate to a guy who's still struggling and not heading in any particular direction—not yet—but I think it's going well with Julie, either because I am timing my bites of cornbread just right or because it all doesn't sound so bad to someone who, herself, is an undeclared major. But, of course, there is more, and I hesitate before crossing the line, giving her a similar penetrating look to the one she gave me earlier, in an effort to go deeper beyond just the façade of her body language or even the words she speaks, because they could be deceiving. What I'm looking for as I search her is that judgmental gene, the strand in her DNA that laughs—or doesn't laugh—at others' dreams. I decide it's safe to tell her about my hunt for the boy—not about the shirts, but just my desire to help and that I will figure it out somehow. She smiles in approval.

Over dessert of custard cream pie, which is so filling that we decide to split it, she begins fumbling for words.

"So, uh, I want to ask you something," she says. "Is there a reason you don't ask me out?"

With that, my mind goes into overdrive, as if it's a computer running its search-engine algorithms through all the data housed in its memory in search of the right answer based on the delicate question.

"Well . . . uh," I stammer, buying time. "I'm not sure how to say it," buying more time. "I usually . . ." and then stall. I mean, I couldn't tell her the truth: I hesitate to ask beautiful girls out because I'm tired of hearing *No,* and even if they say *Yes*, the whole thing usually falls apart after the first date because they see how I really am, and that will be the end of it. No, I don't want to say that at all.

"I usually . . .," I start again, "don't ask girls like you out—girls who work in a bar—because I know it's part of the job to flirt with the customers and make sure everyone has a good time. I get that, but what I'm really looking for is someone who is sincere. And so, I actually would really like to ask you out, but first I really need to know if you're sincere."

I stop talking, shoving a piece of custard cream pie into my mouth as fast as possible. She looks straight at me, her big Manga-girl eyes wider than ever but softer and more vulnerable. Her bottom lip quivers.

"Yes," she whispers.

I need to put another, bigger piece of custard pie in my mouth to keep from screaming out. I refuse to speak or even move since I'm afraid she will pick up on my excitement.

Maybe out of awkwardness, nerves, or whatever, she decides to change the topic and tells me how much she likes bookstores, maybe even more than museums. I think I say something about how my grandmother loved them as well and how books represent infinite possibilities and how she influenced me with books, but I must really be out of it, talking nonsense, because Julie is giggling. She asks if I'm okay, and I tell her *yes, yes,* but I'm not sure she believes me. I think she says that we need to someday go to a bookstore together and see if we like any titles in common, or something like that. I tell myself I have to remember this; I *cannot* forget. *Bookstores.*

Outside, we stand on the sidewalk, waiting for the K-town cab she has called. I slip a cigarette between my lips, savoring the silence this too provides me.

"So, what's that about?" she asks. "The unlit cigarette."

I narrow my eyes, trying to focus, but feeling much more confident than just a moment earlier when dealing with the *why don't you ask me out?* question, or earlier still when holding her hand, or any other time when I've stepped out on that high diving board and been asked to plunge down into a deep pool of vulnerability, infested of course with piranhas of criticism. But I am not feeling any of that. Looking down Wilshire, the white and red car lights shining and flickering, the coming and going, I inhale, and I feel as if my Da Vinci shirt has magically transformed into *I Am A Man*. And so I tell her.

"In high school, I tried really hard to take up smoking," I say. "Yeah, I know—stupid. But my friends had started smoking, and it was hard enough back then to find and really connect with a circle of friends, and I didn't want to lose that, so I really wanted to smoke. The only problem was that I couldn't do it."

"That's good."

"Yeah, well. I kept trying, but I also kept gagging, and I hated the taste. So finally, one time, as I was choking on a cigarette in our garage in the Valley where I grew up, I decide I've had enough. It wasn't worth it. I hated it. So I was going to quit, right there. And sure enough, just as I reached up to yank that last cigarette out of my mouth, my father walked in. I'd seen him angry a hundred times before, but this was beyond that. His eyes bugged out and reddened right before me. He didn't even say anything; he just swung as hard as he could and cracked my jaw."

I check her reaction before I go on, her lips parting as if wanting to say something, but there is nothing.

"And so . . ." I continue, but she interrupts.

"I understand," she says.

But I haven't finished the story, and so I don't think she can really understand—I mean, how could she?—but then little sparks of thought shoot through my mind, and I think maybe she's like Jamal, assuming this is now some act of defiance, and that I won't actually light up the cigarette because I don't enjoy smoking, but that I definitely place it there as some sign that *I* decide—and no one will tell me not to. But that's not it at all.

"Julie. . ."

She reaches out and holds my cheeks in the palms of her hands, pulls me close, and kisses me deep. She holds it there for a long, delicious time.

Please, God, do not let me be the shadow.

19

It's night, and it's very late. I took some Jack Daniel's a couple of hours ago, even though I don't like whiskey. But I needed to calm down, to finally come back down to earth, having relived the evening over and over again in my head—the fantastic night that left me on a high that I could not climb down from. The Jack was the only way to get to sleep.

I never remember dreams and can count on one hand the dreams I've had that I can actually describe in any detail, but now I am dreaming a dream so lucid that it feels as though I'm actually there. It is a memory dream, and I'm back inside the Woodland Hills office of the admissions interviewer from Columbia who lives in the Valley. He is a friendly alumnus who owns a big commercial real estate firm, and yet, I am more nervous than I've ever been. They say these interviews don't mean a whole lot. But I really think I need them to have a chance because, although my test scores were through the roof, I didn't have a whole lot else on my resume in terms of other activities or really doing something with my life other than just being smart. Similar interviews with Brown and Dartmouth did not go well. This was my last chance. I suppose there could have been some non-Ivy League alternatives I could have squeezed into if needed, but with my test scores so high, the expectations were great. No one said anything about expectations directly to me, but sometimes the unsaid pressure is even more powerful. Here, in the interview, that pressure seems to always break. Most of the time, I stick to just answering the questions without elaborating, much like a defendant being questioned on the witness stand, but that leaves an entirely lackluster impression of a kid who hasn't really done much, especially in extracurricular activities, sports, community service, or any other facet of life these interviews are supposed to glean—something beyond the scores on the exams, which, at this stage in the process, were high for everyone.

The interviewer has a gray, mock turtleneck sweater that is thin and tight enough that I can tell he works out, but what's more is that he has the slim, low-body-fat physique of a swimmer or distance runner. As he talks, he occasionally wipes his hand across the top of his cherry-wood desk as if to gently wipe away some subtle dust that may have built up. The wood is polished to such a high sheen that it serves almost as a mirror, and I can see his ghost there reflected on the desktop. He speaks slowly and deliberately, but there is fire in his eyes and a warm, welcoming smile. The window behind him is wide open, and the brilliant sun fills the room with an energy I can't explain.

I am filled with the sweet honey residue of this light, and it makes me strong. There is a desire in my heart like I can't ever remember experiencing before, and it's so powerful that I don't hear any of the questions or the answers, but our mouths are moving, and I can tell every response is perfection. I am in a zone beyond mere words, and though I'm sure I'm saying them, they are, in the end, not important, because it is the desire that has taken over and my will to make this happen—for it all to go well here, now, on my last chance—that I have lost the fear and remembrance that my father is waiting for me just outside and perhaps willing more than I am that this will all go well.

Though I don't even hear the words—not in my dream anyway, and not at that moment, years ago, when all of this happened—I do somehow know the counselor seems impressed that I am a swimmer, and I explain how I was always in the water since I was very young and how it terrified me at first. I'm very precise here about the word *terror*, and the reason for this is hard to explain, but it was probably the sensory deprivation of not quite being able to hear or see well underwater. This quality of my existence being altered was not something I could withstand for very long, and I wanted to quit every day because of it. But I never did, and though it took a long time, I eventually came to terms with it, and the water ultimately altered my existence in a positive way. The interviewer seems impressed by this, and so I tell him the pool was probably one of the best things to ever happen to me, but with all that sun exposure, I'm sure I'll be needing some anti-aging products soon. This, or maybe something else I say, makes him toss his head back and chuckle. When his body swings forward again, it smoothly lifts up from the chair, and he extends his hand in one smooth, graceful motion. Then he says the only words I actually hear—the words that made me happier than any other pinpoint of time in my life.

"I believe there's hope for you here," he says, and we shake hands. By 'here,' I presume he means Columbia.

When I walk out into the hallway, my father is there, sitting with a sour, questioning look, but it softens slowly as he sees my confident glow and my thin, parted smile of satisfaction.

"He said, 'I believe there's hope for you here.'" And with that, I flip my wrist in a cool *We'll see* motion. He puts his arm around my shoulder and taps lightly, and we walk out together.

In my dream, we are now in the living room of our house, months later, with the open letter announcing my acceptance to Columbia still in my hand and my father holding me in a full embrace. I don't remember him ever doing this, and so I am crying openly into his shoulder, and though I try to control it, I can't stop the words repeating in my head, the most glorious words in the English language: *I believe there's hope for you here.*

The dream continues but is starting to fade, my dad still hugging me. When we finally break our hold and I take a step back, he reaches into his pocket, pulls out a pack of cigarettes, and extends them to me. I take them hesitantly from his hand.

"Anytime, anywhere you want," he says. "I love you, son."

20

Though I didn't sleep well last night, the positive energy from yesterday afternoon's time spent with Julie gives me a conquer-the-world spirit. Still, I'm anxious to see if today's shirt gets me any closer, in some real way this time, to finding Juan. When I lift the shirt I've selected, I scratch my head, not knowing what to make of this one. It's a basic green shirt with the words *Let's eat Grandma / Let's eat, Grandma / Commas save lives.*

Generally, when I pull a shirt having to do with writing or literature in some way, it gives me a little hope that my journaling is somehow taking me in the right direction. Maybe someone will even read all of this one day and find it mildly amusing. Other shirts that have given me a boost include *Similes are Like Metaphors*, which made me think a lot about how things I see and experience may, in fact, be symbolic of something else: *Every time you make a typo, the Errorists win*, which reminds me to pay attention to detail and inspires me with the idea of using words that don't really exist. *Misuse of Literally makes me Figuratively insane*, which really influenced me to try to be more precise in my words, because I was one of those people who casually threw around words and terms in a haphazard way, and though I'd remind myself a million times, I would keep doing it, until this shirt provided that spark and an understanding that's helped me change my ways; and, actually, my *I told you a Million times, Stop Exaggerating* shirt probably deserves some mention here too.

I watch the news, and there is no mention of Juan. I go to breakfast at the diner down the street, but the waitress, whose life is over, isn't there.

While eating my eggs, bacon, and toast, I think hard about my shirt, but it's no good, and I'm not making any link to a clue.

I decide I need to get some grocery shopping done, and so I ride my bike to the H Mart over on Western to pick up some fresh food, which I really need to eat more of. On the ride, I'm checking people and storefronts, especially people who might resemble my grandmother. But there's no one even close.

I don't always go to H Mart because I don't understand all the Asian cuisine, and so I feel a little out of place there, though that doesn't bother me a whole lot because if it did, I certainly wouldn't live in a place like Koreatown. But I do like the overall vibe of the multilevel shopping center. It is modern and clean, at the bottom level of which rests H Mart—a foundation for the rest of the center. They also have some great pastry shops and a bookstore that sells books in both Korean and English that is well lit with excessive windows that give it a more welcoming feeling than a library or the small, independent bookstores that are often windowless, which, to some people, gives these stores "charm." But I find that actual light makes this particular store feel open—open to thought, open to the world. *Infinite possibilities.*

At the top level is a cinema, where half the films they show are in Korean. I have watched a few films there—typically when I had a slight hangover and English subtitles were just a distraction—back when I first moved here, in some strange attempt at immersion in the Korean language, which they say is the best way to learn a language. Though I picked up virtually no words in Korean, I discovered something strange. Even though I couldn't understand a word, I would fairly easily get the general plot and understand the emotions and motivations of the characters. I even checked this with Ray on a couple of films he was familiar with, and he was amazed at how much I understood of the films. It made me realize the huge importance of body language as well as context—the setting in which something is happening—because if you are good at understanding these things, then you can probably understand—maybe even on some deeper level—what is truly going on. I prefer to read people—the body language, the expressions, and especially the silences—as much as I can.

Having finished my grocery shopping, I decide to stop in at the pastry shop on the second level. I take a seat, and a waiter kid comes to the table quickly, bobbing and weaving like a fighter with a big smile on his face. He's Korean and can't be more than eighteen, and he's definitely got all the jumpy energy of a guy who's brand new on the job.

"I'm sorry; we don't serve Grandmas here," he says, pushing his black glasses higher up on the bridge of his nose and laughing.

"Ha." I give a short, courtesy laugh.

"Just kidding. We're equal opportunity. But Grandmas are definitely not on the menu. Out of season." He laughs harder, his whole body really bouncing now in sync with his laughter.

"Good one," I say, and I actually sort of mean it. I mean, it's a little funny. But I'm not really into jokey people like this; I never have been, and I'm not sure why, even though I'll admit to sometimes laughing at my own jokes, sometimes out loud, just like him. I suppose if you really had to do a slam-me-down-on-the-couch in-depth psychoanalysis, you would probably find a well of jealousy there because jokey people are, ultimately, happy.

I order a couple of the cream puffs, which turn out to be larger than I expect, and I begin to worry about the sugar high and the subsequent collapse that always seems to hit me hard, and aside from not wanting any of that due to my fight to find a certain balance in my body, I also can't afford to deal with that now because there has been a nagging worry for some time now—just there beneath my consciousness but now rearing its head in an ugly way—that I am running out of time. The boy has been gone too long, and so I can't really nap off a sugar crash like I usually do. I push away the plate.

I have a strong desire to see the boy's mother and have had this from almost the beginning, just to let her know I'm on this and doing everything I can. I don't know. Maybe that will help her feel better, especially if the police aren't coming up with anything. I just want to get to know her, as she seemed so nice that day in the restaurant when she was trying to quiet Juan and stop him from laughing loudly at me. I can't imagine what she's going through now—the emptiness. Still, I'm scared. What if there's something I did or said that I'm not remembering, but she recognizes me and says, *You! You are the one,* and the next thing I know, she's calling the police. And then I would have no chance of ever finding her son.

I ask the jokey waiter for more water and ask if it's okay to hang out a bit even though I'm finished.

"Sure. Here's the check, but no hurry."

"Thanks."

"Hey, did you get the shirt at the bookstore down the way? It looks like something they might sell."

"No, I can't remember where I got it," I lie, because I don't really want to continue the conversation with him. I actually bought it at a bookstore in the Valley that has since gone out of business. This was just after my grandma died, and while that may sound morbid, it was actually an homage to her because she had introduced me to reading quality literature when I was young, thinking that would help me with all my issues—and many times, it has, especially Hemingway. His prose was simple in structure but deep emotionally. American Zen. Whenever I read his books, I sometimes start from the beginning, but other times, when I need to just relax and get lost in the words, I'll flip to a favorite dog-eared passage—proven for its calming, transformative effect. And that's what it's really about. Calming down. My grandmother first introduced me to Hemingway and other writers of classics because she thought the reading would help me to be still. She was the one who gave me the edition of *The Sun Also Rises* that I read to this day, and so I'll always owe her for that.

That's it!

I then quickly put a twenty on the bill plate, leaving a big tip because I don't want to wait around for the change. I bolt through the door, hearing the distant voice of the jokey waiter yelling, *Hey, thanks!*

In the bookstore, I stop just inside the door, and my heart is racing, but I try to calm down and survey the store—the layout, the people, anything that stands out. Though it's cloudy outside, it's still bright in here because the storefront is all glass. I don't see anyone here, and I slowly enter, surveying the shelves, the sections, and the signs on the wall written in Korean, likely promoting a new bestseller. A young lady then pops up from behind the counter.

"Let me know if you need anything. Oh hey, you're back!" she says.

I walk over to her, really studying her. A dull headache is starting up.

"Sorry," I say, "but I just have to ask. Did you help me here earlier?"

"No, not me. It was Jin, my coworker. I think it was you. Was it?"

"Is she here now?"

"She's at lunch now. But if she were here, she would tell you she made a big mistake and shouldn't have taken that journal back that you returned. It's all written in! We can't resell it."

I stare at her, confused.

"But listen," she continues, "I won't say anything. It doesn't matter to me. I'm just part-time here."

"Um, can I take a look?" I ask.

"Okay. It should be easy to find. You just returned it. Yep, right here on top," and she hands me an all-black leather-bound book with no title on it.

As I hold it in my hands, one placed underneath and the other on top, ready to open the cover, I stop.

"Hey, did I have a receipt with this return? Was it charged?"

"Hmm, looks like it was cash," she says, showing a crumpled receipt.

I open the book and find it gibberish. But it's a little familiar. The words, they just run on. It reads *Liberar a Juan Liberar a Juan Liberar a Juan Liberar a Juan Liberar a Juan Liberar a Juan Liberar a Juan Liberar a Juan Liberar a Juan Liberar a Juan Liberar a Juan Liberar a Juan Liberar a Juan Liberar a Juan Liberar a Juan Liberar a Juan,* and it continues—on every single page—from the very first page to the inside back cover.

I set the book on the counter.

"Hey, I don't really care," the girl says. "But what does it mean?"

I turn away, dazed. The eyes are smarting badly now. My feet drag as I drift slowly through the aisles of clean, white shelves, and I'm losing energy. I see the titles, mostly in Korean, and they mean nothing to me. There is an English section, but there is nothing remarkable. There are the bestsellers you would find at any common bookstore. Of course, there are the classics, cookbooks, and computer books for those who want to program in Java. I lean against a shelf, feeling tired and light-headed, the shooting stars of thoughts in my head still firing but in slow motion now. *Was I really here today?*

I take out my cell phone and punch a translation app icon. I type in *Liberar a Juan*. It detects it as Spanish. The English reads *Free Juan.*

There is a whirling in my head, and I hold onto a shelf as I feel I'm losing my balance. I take a lot of deep breaths, really focusing on the air I let out. After a few minutes, there is an easing, like something is releasing out of me.

"You okay?" a soft female voice, different from the store clerk's, says to me.

I look up slowly and see a beautiful girl. She looks familiar, but I can't place her. She's beautiful.

"Oh my gosh, it's you!" she covers her mouth with her hands.

I open my eyes as wide as I can in hopes that this will help my brain to focus and recall where I've seen this girl before. And then the answer arrives. It's SteFunny.

"Oh, hey," I stammer. "Yeah, I'm okay. Just felt a little dizzy. Thanks."

"I can't believe it's you! This is so weird. I've been wanting to talk to you again but didn't know how to find you."

"Wha—?"

"Yeah, I just wanted to say I'm sorry about that night. My friends were really down on me about how I acted because they really liked you."

"Your friends liked me?"

"Yeah, totally. They said you're cute, and you were probably talking strange because you were drunk, and yeah, I was a little drunk too, and it's really a great thing to be on a new path because, you know, how many losers are out there hitting on me without any path what-so-ever? So whatever you're trying to do, whatever it is that made you so happy that night, I'm sure it's a good thing, and my friends said maybe the alcohol just made you a little excited and besides, you're cute."

"Wha—?"

"I'm sorry. I'm just a little nervous."

"Do you always talk so fast?"

"I'm sorry."

"No, no, it's okay. People who talk fast are great. Really. And I mean, *Really*. I just have a little headache, and it's hard to keep up."

"I think . . . I think your shirt is funny."

On reflex, I look down at my shirt, even though, of course, I know what it says.

"You must have a thing for shirts," she says. "I know, because you had a great one on the night we met. Remember? *I'm only here to establish an alibi.*"

"Uh, yeah."

"Anyway, you have great taste. They're so clever."

I grunt.

"Okay. Listen. Can I give you my number?" she asks. "Maybe we can talk once you feel better."

I rub my temples, and if I was losing touch with this world before, I am well into another dimension now. Why is any of this happening? Now SteFunny, out of the blue, finds me and flirts with me, and the funny thing is that she's beautiful and her friends actually like me. So maybe this is something new, a desperately needed turning point for me, but it doesn't feel right. Everything around me feels loose, like I'm on a sailboat in a hurricane and all of the sails have come loose from their moorings, and I'm trying to tie them all down in the middle of hundred-mile-an-hour winds, and that is exactly me and my life right now. *So, I focus*—right now—and I find the eye in my mind picturing only Julie. I don't want to mess it up again like that evening at Q Bar, where I'm pretty sure she wasn't happy with me talking to SteFunny, and though the girl in front of me seems nice, I just don't need another sail to tie down right now, and I really need to get it all under control and gain structure—just like I wanted to with my writing, my journal, but I'm not sure any of that is working—to be happy, to find true and direct, declarative focus in my life. Structure. That's all I need. To be happy. To write like Hemingway.

"So, I guess you don't want my number."

"No, hey, sorry," I say. I look up to eye her straight on. It hits me that I should at least be nice here, like Julie putting up with me or any other bore at the bar, and at least play along for the moment. I can back out later, somehow.

"I'm just really not feeling good right now," I say. "But sure, give me your number. We'll talk."

I take out my phone, type in her name, making sure to spell it with the F, and as she calls out each digit, I enter it into my contacts.

"Now, call me," she says.

"Huh?"

"Just hit the number now."

I press the number, and her phone starts to ring. She quickly declines the call and shuts it off.

"Perfect," she says. "Now I have your number."

"Perfect," I say.

She brushes her hand along my shoulder and tells me to take care of myself, then leaves.

I linger a while longer, focusing on deep breathing, just like I do during my morning ritual, and soon feel better, just enough to get my bearings. I start to head home.

I am, in fact, not feeling as well as I thought. It's a few blocks from Western to Normandie, and that's typically nothing for a roamer like me, but right now, it feels like a marathon. The sun feels hotter than before, and I can tell I'm walking at a much slower pace. Across the street at the Wiltern, there's a long line of people waiting to get tickets, so there must be a big act coming soon. I pass a few homeless panhandling in the alcoves of some businesses that appear to be shut down, or at least closed for the moment. When I finally reach St. Basil's, a Catholic church, just a short distance from my apartment, I rest. I don't go inside. I've never been inside. I just place my palm against the large stone block that bears the church's name just outside the entrance, holding myself up, and rest. I breathe slowly again, and this time, I feel like there is fresh air breathing back into me. After a few minutes, I feel fine and continue on.

At my apartment building, when the elevator doors open and I'm about to step out onto my floor, SteFunny is there waiting.

"What do you think you're doing?!?!" she demands.

"What? Why are you here?"

"No, Cole. The question is, 'Why are *you* here?' I try to be nice to you because my stupid friends think you're a great guy, and it turns out you're a stalker. I should have known. I should have known something was wrong with you—you and your whole weird Path thing—but you're just a . . ."

"Hey!" I shout. "I *live* here!"

"You what?"

"I live here. Right there, actually," and I point to my apartment door.

"You live . . . there? In Mr. Conrad's old apartment?"

"Yeah. And I'm pretty messed up right now in so many ways I can't possibly even explain, so I just want to go in there and lie down. So can you *please* step out of the way?"

"I'm . . . I'm so sorry," she says softly. "I live right over there." She points to an apartment at the far end of the hall.

My mental gears still grind slowly, but I soon figure that she must be the beautiful girl Mr. Li was talking about. Just down the hall. We look at each other, bewildered.

"Life . . ." she says, "it's so strange. Isn't it?"

21

Though I went to bed early last night and stayed there for nearly twelve hours, I didn't really rest. No clubbing, no flashback dreams, yet still a rocky, turbulent night where my mind just could not shut down. Still, I rise in time for the selection of a new shirt, about which I'm feeling a little *scared*—yes, I suppose that would be it. I feel as if I'm failing, and I don't mean just falling behind or hitting a bit of a stumbling block, a speed bump that's only meant to shake me up and maybe test my resolve, or some other minor nuisance on my overall journey. No, I mean failing in a grand and spectacular rocket-ship-exploding-on-the-launch-pad sort of way. The way a soccer team gets smoked seven-nothing or a champion fighter gets clocked in the first round and is done. My shirts have taken me to the observatory, museum, and bookstore, and I've really gotten nowhere, and my fear is that either I'm misreading the clues of the shirts, or maybe—and it's hard to even think this—maybe the shirts have nothing to do with this at all.

"Stop!" I yell at myself. "Stop thinking like that! This is the way. This is the path. It *has* to be."

I sniff, uncertain at first, but then I repeat with a deeper inhale, and I notice the same cigarette smell again.

"It has to be me. I'm lighting up, but I'm just not remembering. That's got to be it."

For the briefest, most infinitesimally smallest speck of time, I am satisfied with this conclusion, though obviously I'm discouraged as I can't even recall doing this. And then I realize I don't even own a lighter or matches.

I calm myself, focusing on my breathing and trying with difficulty to expel the negative thoughts from my mind. I've just got to keep going.

At the closet, I bow before entering, step onto the tatami mat, and begin, in the dark, to gently feel across the shoulders of the hanging T-shirts. For some reason, it is taking some time—a long time—and nothing is coming. Nothing. I stop and breathe deeply in and out, trying to calm myself, but I'm feeling agitated. This is strange. It's never taken so long. I try again.

Still, the soft brushing only produces some very slight pulses and makes me question whether there truly was a signal there or not, because the energy from the shirts has always been stronger. I feel my breathing quicken, and I mouth the word *please* over and over again as my hand now passes quickly over the shirts, which I know is all wrong, but nothing is coming. Nothing.

Then a quick spark of static shocks me. I stop because I've never experienced static during the morning selection of a shirt. I try to recall what causes static, the scientific phenomenon that produces energy out of nothing, but I can't remember. I know I'm not wearing socks or standing on a carpet because I'm barefoot and only have wood flooring, except for the tatami mat in the closet, which I don't think can produce electricity.

I decide to touch some shirts at random and feel nothing, but when I get to this particular shirt, the static strikes me again, and I pull the shirt up from the hanger. Turning on the light, I'm immediately confused. It's another shirt that's not mine, another shirt I've never seen before.

I pull it from the closet and step out into the morning light blanketing the room. I flip the shirt over to take a look at the back, but it is the same as the front. A solid black T-shirt. No lettering, images, or symbols. Just black, front and back.

Falling back onto the sofa, I feel numb, completely without feeling, a deep and true numbness all over, and I haven't even taken any medication yet. As lost as I felt just a little while ago, doubting the meanings of my previous shirt selections, I am more lost than I've ever been.

There is a heavy knock at the door. I jerk upright because, honestly, no one ever visits me here except my mother, and that's not her knock. I think about SteFunny and wonder if she might be reaching out, maybe to apologize for calling me a stalker yesterday. But this knock sounds hard and cold, not like one that would come from an attractive, apologetic female just wanting to—

"Mr. Reeves?" a booming male voice says, accompanying heavier knocking. "This is Detective Harrison. LAPD. If you're there, can you open the door, please?"

"Yes, I'm here," I say quickly, and I jump from the sofa and start to rush to the door, but then slow down as all memory of my past interactions with the police and campus cops starts to catch up to me. I look around the apartment as I battle doubts about my innocence. I have no unpaid traffic tickets, and when Ray or Jamal were taking Molly—ecstasy, whatever—I didn't participate. So what could they want?

"Mr. Reeves?" the voice asks again.

"Coming!"

I open the door, and there are three policemen standing there, two in plain clothes and the other in uniform. One of the plain-clothes officers does the talking, says he's Detective Harrison, and introduces Officers Kincaid and Smith. Harrison is black, tall, and dressed in a perfect-fitting gray suit. He talks slowly and calmly, pretty much exactly the opposite of Jamal. Smith is white, in uniform, and doesn't smile; his jaw is set firm as if to say, *I'm watching you, so don't try anything*. But it's Kincaid who fascinates me. I think maybe I've seen him somewhere before.

"May we come in?" Harrison asks.

"Are you here to arrest me?" I reply.

"Is there something we should be arresting you for?"

I go back to thinking about my whole disassembled jigsaw puzzle of a life and realize I must be looking really guilty right now in my extended silence.

"No," I say sheepishly.

"We want to ask you about the missing child, Juan Machado."

I lead them in, and we settle on the dinette set I have in the kitchen area. This being a studio apartment, there are not many choices.

He asks some basic questions, confirming who I am, and that this is my apartment. He even confirms that I am the only son of the late actor, Henry Reeves, and when I concur, he nicely states he was a fan and was saddened when he heard of his death. Even though he speaks in a calm, reassuring voice, I am blue-knuckled, stiff-necked, and tense, sensing these could be trick questions because they're just too easy. I know about the police; I've dealt with them before, and they're all about tricks and getting you to say things, but I'm ready. *I'm ready.*

"We understand you know this missing person?" Kincaid asks. And then it hits me.

"You're Roger . . ." I say, "from the search party that day."

He only nods, then repeats the question.

"I don't know him," I say. "I only met him once."

"Where was that?" Harrison asks.

"At the Tofu House, maybe three months ago. He laughed at me."

"He laughed at you? Why?"

"I don't know."

"No idea at all?"

"No. I said, I don't know."

"Have you seen him since?"

"No," and I say this affirmatively, with conviction. And now, I resolve that the way I will handle these police will be different from the

Columbia campus police and the cops who interrogated me at Cup O' Joe's. I will be strong, focused, and determined and not cower to authority thinking it might score me some points with the subservient *Yes sir* or *No sir* because that never got me anywhere in the past.

"Did you have a meeting last week with reporter Shawna Cleary?" Harrison continues.

"I would call her more of an anchor, not a reporter. But yes, I met with her."

"And did you say to her," and he pauses to check some notes he has in his pad, "did you say to her 'Perhaps this world is a world in which children suffer'?"

"What? No. I mean, yes. I mean, that wasn't me. I mean, yes, I said the words, but I was quoting Robert Kennedy. And he was quoting Camus, I think, and I was just. . ."

"What were you doing at the Observatory recently?"

"I—I don't know. I think I was learning about black holes."

"Is that why you went there?"

"Um. What's this about?"

"Why did you go there?"

"Just to do something, you know. Get out of the apartment."

"You usually go alone?"

I knew the answer was *Yes,* but there was something in my gut that told me that would sound bad, for some inexplicable reason.

"Sometimes," I finally state. I feel myself clenching my fists and fidgeting in my chair, and then I realize I haven't taken my meds this morning, not yet, because these cops interfered with my morning and I didn't get to it. I'm not sure what to do because if I tell them that I need to take them, maybe that will lead to all sorts of questions about my numerous diagnoses and make me look weak, like I am less than them, less than a man, when the truth is *I Am A Man* because, after all, my shirt said so, and I believe in my shirts more than anything, and so I decide to ride this out. Yes, I can do it, even though I feel the propulsion of inner energy beginning to rev, like an Indy racing engine gunning it at the starting line.

"And you like the museum too?" Harrison follows up.

"Sure, I like the museum."

"And yet, the last time you went, you didn't go inside. Why?"

"Were you following me?"

"You went to the museum, but you didn't go inside. Why?"

"I don't know. I wasn't feeling well."

"There were a lot of children at the museum that day. Just like the observatory," he states. It is not a question.

I say nothing but stare at him coldly. *Where is he going with this?*

"Do you have any issues with, say, managing your anger?" he asks.

"No. I mean, I don't think I'm different than anyone else," I say, and think that's the best answer because I can't really tell him that sometimes I am overwhelmed with internal volcanic anger bubbling beneath the surface whenever I hear of the horrors told in newscasts, or I ask God why I am this way and receive no answer, or someone, anyone, laughs at me. No, I can't say that.

Officer Smith sits in his chair quietly, never taking any notes or taking his eyes off me. He doesn't even seem to blink. Kincaid almost looks bored. Now, Harrison has his head down, studying papers as he pulls them from his pad.

"It says here," he starts, still not looking up, "you were formerly employed at Cup O' Joe's on La Cienega Boulevard?"

"That's right," I whisper.

"What was that?"

"I said, 'That's right.'"

"Tell me about your last day there," Harrison demands, his eyes buried in his papers.

"I have . . ." I begin, "an issue with my memory. I can't remember things sometimes. I mean, really big things sometimes."

"Just try," he says, and his whole no-eye-contact shtick is really bothering me now, and I don't know what that's about. I wonder if, perhaps, it's because he's going to arrest me or feels bad for me in some way, like maybe the way a jury hesitates to look into the eyes of a man they've just convicted, but even if it's all a pity thing, it is *really* bothering me.

"Even though I was there," I say, "I admit, I can't remember most of it and . . ."

"Just try," he repeats.

"It was my third day, and I didn't feel good about how the first two days had gone. I felt slow—slow in my movement, slow on the uptake, and so I wasn't getting the instructions right on how to do things properly. I had no experience working in a place like that, but my mother knew Joe, the owner—it's called Cup O' Joe's—and they gave me a break. So, I cut back on my meds, taking only a super small dose. It was the first time I had tried that—and had some coffee that morning, and if you've never had Cup O' Joe's coffee, you're really missing out, and though I know I wasn't supposed to mix caffeine with my medication, I just wanted to be more present, really do well, and have a little more energy. But then, I had another cup and another, and honestly, it was a great iced mocha mixed with salted caramel. I would always like my coffee iced. But all of this wasn't smart, even though it started out as a good day and the added energy and focus seemed to be working. Later, it began giving me a headache, and I was jittery, and that made me feel scared. The manager on duty that day must have sensed something was wrong because she had me go out and clean the tables, getting me away from the coffee makers and the customers in line. I thanked her.

"When I was out wiping down the tables, I saw a man sitting at one who I had served at the counter the day before. He had complained about how his coffee was taking too long to make, but that was only my second day, and I was just learning, and even though I had help, it was during the morning rush, and my coworker had to remake some drinks I had messed up, all the while being kind about it all. But this customer wasn't kind.

"So now, I'm just wiping down a table, and he's seated at a table next to me, and even though I recognize him, I try to avoid eye contact and wipe furiously with jittery, fast strokes. He notices me and says, 'Hah, they finally found a job you'd be good at.'

"I ignore him at first, although I'm beginning to boil on the inside, but then he says, 'Hey, I'm talking to you.'

"So I turn, and we look at each other for the longest time. Well, actually, it was probably for just a few seconds, but you know how sometimes a very short period of time can seem like forever? Well, that's what happened here, and in those forever-seconds, I am shaking, and part of it is the caffeine, part is my meds, and the other part is the anger at this guy for talking down to me, and yet all of this seems to bring him *joy.* I think that's the best word because he has a big smile on his face and as he's smiling, never losing eye contact with me, his fingers are slowly pushing his coffee cup closer to the edge. And then it drops, falling to the floor and spilling all over. I think the cup was only half-full, but still, it made a mess, and it was deliberate, calculated, and done with the full knowledge I would have to clean it up and that my cleaning up would bring some satisfaction to this monster.

"The storm inside of me is raging and my fists clench and I'm shaking hard now, and seeing this, he leans in to me, almost as if to tell me a secret, and so I lean in too.

"'Life's a bitch,' he says, and he's got this arrogant look. A sneer.

"I raise myself back up, closing my eyes, taking in his words, feeling—actually *feeling*—the blood pump through my arteries like a flash flood. I'll be honest. I wanted to kill him. *Really*. But I didn't kill him. Instead, I speak to him with the blinding speed of a man who, let's say, is possessed with the knowledge that the world will end in three minutes and has to express everything in his heart and fully capture the essence of his soul and he only has three minutes to do it.

"'No,' I say. 'Life's not a bitch at all; it's only if you *choose* to look at it that way, because you know what? Life's a *Beach!* That's right, I said life's a *beach*—and you know how I know that? Because I have a T-shirt that says so, and even though I haven't pulled it from my closet in a long, long time, I know in my heart it's true, and believe it or not, I can actually empathize with cretins like you who breed this negativity because there is so much evidence out there that might lead you to think this way, and that's why it's important to never watch the news because there, on the news, small innocent children battle cancer like the little girl who just died of leukemia at City of Hope, although actually it wasn't the leukemia that killed her because, after fighting through two years of chemo and actually beating the leukemia, her immune system failed, and she developed pneumonia and that's what took her away; or the young woman who was gunned down and killed in Hollywood near Sunset Boulevard on a Sunday night while she was just walking with her boyfriend until someone comes out of nowhere and without a word, blows her head off from behind with a shotgun—no robbery or motive. She was completely innocent, and the killer was never found. Either he shot her by mistake, thinking it was someone else, or he killed someone he didn't even know for absolutely no reason, and they haven't caught him because the police have nothing; and don't get me started on the Middle East. But hey, in spite of all of that, we need to focus on really changing, and I mean the word *really*, because if you look at me—a guy just struggling to get by every day—and I choose to see life as a *beach,* even though I feel so low on so many days, when all I want is to be happy and write like Hemingway, even though my journals are more like Faulkner who, if you don't know, could write really long sentences that would twist, curl back, and choke on themselves. At least that's how it feels to me—a gripping, choking Boa Constrictor—and it's not just about words on a page, but about the thoughts in my head. So I am like Faulkner, even though I don't want to be and something else he would do is make up new words, that is, words that you might think would be actual words but are *not,* and I actually like that, the boldness of it, because it's a lot like what I do whenever I play Minecraft and create endless beautiful worlds, and so I decided to create a special word that would capture the greatest feeling imaginable, an elation, a happiness, one so powerful it's almost spiritual, and yet, not so spiritual it loses its rush, you know? – essentially the greatest sensation a person can possibly ever feel on this earth, and so I come up with the word Zenisenz, where I start with the letter Z because of its finality, the last letter, the ultimate—it's as far as you can go—and then, I type in my phone's Notes app with crazy, wild abandon and close my eyes as my fingers continue to work and I decide the word should have *zenith* as its root, since I'm trying to arrive at the highest form of a sensation, and I quickly decide while in this effortless no-thought zone of pure will that I should add *sense* to it and then combine the two, but this bothers me, the way it looks on the screen, the useless 'e' at the end – and aren't ending 'e's always useless? – but leaving the word hanging with an 's' looks weak, and then it comes to me to end the word with another 'z' as well, the perfect bookend, again the finality, where it takes you to the edge – the most you can experience in this world, the poetic Zenisenz, and I promise you that would be the feeling in my ideal world, a world where four-year-olds would not die of pneumonia and people would not be senselessly gunned down and life would be a glorious sensation, but in order to do this we have to do *more*, just like Da Vinci, who was brilliant in so many ways while the rest of us are only giving ten percent or less of our minds or abilities or efforts, but we all need to do it, everyone, so that we're all a little better because it's not enough for just *me* to do it – so if we all send out waves of enlightened positivity or, or better still, positive *actions*, then maybe things can change, but the problem is there must always be some good and some bad, the yin and yang of a truly neutral universe, and yet we're connected, all of us, and I mean really physically connected, and every particle has a twin particle that you can separate even a billion light years apart and still have connected and it's called Entanglement and even Einstein didn't believe it at first but it's true so maybe there is someone, my other particle, out there who is just like me and he is evil – a life's a bitch kind of guy – but we'll always be connected, or maybe it's just evil parts of *me*, within me, and so I'm both good and evil and though this terrifies me knowing there may be another side of me so dark I may not even be able to see it, I want to believe maybe this is actually better because it means I – we – can change – with focused and purposeful intention – and have that good side *kill* the bad side, and maybe you should think about that because if we can accomplish this – really, truly *get* there or, or at least get much closer or, or even just a *little* closer – then we can all realize life is not a bitch – LIFE IS A BEACH!'"

I find I am standing there next to my dinette set, but I am winded and bent over, hand resting on the table to steady myself, gasping for air. Officer Smith has, at some point, moved away from the table and is now standing closer to the door, eyes bugged out, his hand resting on his side-holstered handgun. Kincaid's jaw is dropped. Detective Harrison is still staring down at the notes in his file, except now he has a curious look on his face.

I cough.

"Curious . . ." Harrison says.

It takes me a few seconds more before I finally have the air to speak.

"What's curious?" I'm barely able to get the words out.

"Mr. Reeves, you say you don't remember and have issues with your memory, but you just repeated, word-for-word, exactly what you said that morning at the coffee house."

"Wha—?"

"It's all here in the official report. It was all transcribed directly from a cell phone video some customer took that day in the restaurant. He started recording as soon as he sensed some tension in your exchange, right after Mr. Sellars deliberately spilled the coffee."

"I was recorded?"

"Yes, and a good thing for you. That's what got you off. Despite the beating you gave Mr. Sellars, the video showed he swung at you first. That's why the D.A. didn't press charges. It didn't help him that, in his original statement to the police, he swore you attacked him first—physically assaulted him without cause. When he was caught in the lie, everything went away pretty quick."

"Huh."

"So the cell phone saved you."

Detective Harrison then tells Officer Smith to get a glass of water for me and tells me to have a seat so we can talk some more.

"So," he says to me, watching me slowly sip my glass of water, "I need to get back to this memory thing. You want to tell me how, after insisting you don't remember any of the details of that day, you go on to repeat some wild rant, and you repeat each and every word, verbatim? You want to tell me how that works?"

" I don't know. It just came to me right now. But I swear, I really didn't remember any of this just before."

"So you block things out?"

"I don't know. Not deliberately, but I guess . . ."

"Where is the boy, Mr. Reeves?"

"What? I don't know where he is! I'm trying to look for him. Didn't Shawna Cleary tell you that? Didn't she? Since she told you about my quoting Kennedy, I'm sure she mentioned that. I'm trying to find him. I'm really trying, and I'm doing everything I can, but it's not making sense."

"She said you're looking for someone a lot like you. What does that mean?"

I rub my temples hard now, struggling with how to respond given the fact I can't tell him what I experienced in the park with the Russian chess players or the gangbangers outside Juan's apartment because he would just go interview them, and they would swear I was some molester they had seen in the area just before.

"What does it mean when you say you're looking for someone a lot like you?"

"I just . . . I just have this sense."

"And where does this sense come from?"

"I don't know. I can't explain it."

"Where is the boy, Mr. Reeves?"

"I don't know."

"Ms. Cleary states you said you were some sort of psychic."

"What? Oh, that. I mean, that's just part of all of this that I can't ex—"

"What, do you have visions? What are you seeing?"

"No, it's not like that."

"Where is the boy, Mr. Reeves?"

"I told you. I'm trying to find him."

"Where were you Tuesday night?" Kincaid asks, leaning forward, totally accusatory. "At around eight o'clock."

I squeeze my eyes shut and can feel myself scrunching up my face because I know I need to remember this. Right now. I can forget a lot of things, but given the way he asked, I just have to pull this out. *Remember.*

"I know," I say, smiling. "Yeah, I was at the Q Bar. That's right. I'm certain. Why?"

"There was an attempted abduction of another child, not far from here. The Q Bar? Is that your alibi?"

"You can check it out. I know a waitress there named Julie. And I met a girl there named Stefunny."

He's writing everything down fast.

"That's my alibi," I say softly to myself.

"You know," Kincaid glares, "there are people who have lives that are lacking in meaning and purpose, and they sometimes commit crimes that they then help to solve, and it's all some sort of hero complex."

"I don't know what you're talking about! I'm trying to find the kid!"

Harrison's cell phone rings, and he raises his eyebrows when he sees the phone number that's calling him. He stands, then turns his back, and walks away from the table to answer the call.

"Harrison here" is all I can really make out clearly, yet walking to the other side of a studio apartment only gets you so much privacy, so I also pick up the occasional word or words like *Did you double-check?* and *Are you sure?* but I can't piece them together to get the overall context of the conversation, and it is much easier to watch a film in a foreign language than hear only one side of a muffled conversation. He presses down on the phone's screen, ending the call.

"We have to leave, Mr. Reeves. I would advise you to let go of this case. We will handle it."

I narrow my eyes and jut out my jaw, clenching my teeth to keep from saying anything because I'm feeling a high-voltage attack of ODD right now.

"I said, 'Let it go,' Mr. Reeves. Let it go."

22

I HAVE TO GET OUT.

I have to walk, get out of the apartment, and the blizzard of thoughts blowing through my mind is so intense that I cannot focus on any one of them, and convulsions of memory and dialogue bombard me until it all blurs into a seamless white flash of *HappyFaceEDMteaceremonyJulie'sEyes51/50DavinciPilatesCreampuffsSoccerGrasshoppersTequilaHyenasWeddingringObservatoryDeerAntlerVelvetHMartShotgunCigarettesHemingwayMedsChessColumbiaKennedyShamanHappyFace* NOISE.

It is all noise.

I have to focus—focus on something—on anything.

On the sidewalk, I am almost running, yanking my cellphone from my pocket, nearly dropping it, and dialing Shawna Cleary, but I get her damn voicemail again. I yell, *How could you sell me out?* and I'm so amped up I can't even talk, so I just press the *End* button again and again.

I hear a car horn blare just up the street, then it goes off again. This time, the driver is leaning on the horn and not letting up, and I can't even tell what he's angry about, so maybe whatever it is already happened, but he won't let it go, and the noise and the horn are incessant, and they cut through everything in the hot morning air, and then other drivers start honking their horns until it seems everyone is honking and the sun feels like it's beating down on me. The noise is like a thick liquid filled with shards of glass being poured into my ears, and this thought makes me clasp my hands over my ears and turn and run in the opposite direction.

I stop several blocks down, sweating, and I can tell the honking has stopped back there, but I don't want to turn back. The homeless seem to be everywhere as I pass an old lady pushing a shopping cart holding all of her possessions in the world, and then a man with a gray shirt and pants, or maybe they're just dirty, and even his wool beanie is gray, though a shade darker. He sifts through a trash can looking for—I don't know, anything, I suppose—and there are more, and then more of them—and each of them is muttering to himself, sometimes loudly, sometimes yelling, and all I can think is, *At least I'm not there. At least I'm not there.* Not yet, anyway.

The energy doesn't subside, and yet I have to control it somehow. I decide to slow my walk and force myself to sit. If I physically shut down the mechanics of my body—the movement—that will somehow help to slow my mind. I realize I still haven't taken my meds, and I know with the panic injected into me by the police and everything else, this is why I'm losing it now, so I have to find a place to sit.

I grab my shirt and pull it out in front of me to see it up close, and I want it to talk to me in some way, any way at all, even if it's some subtle metaphorical symbolic way, because all that I've come up with so far for an absolute black T-shirt is that it means nothing or that it means death. The other shirts seem to have led me to some particular place—driving me to a location that maybe means something, though those clues have not been clear except for the fact that I seem to be close to someone everyone keeps confusing for me. Or maybe it *is* me. So maybe this shirt is different. Maybe it means absolutely nothing because it is empty. Is it trying to tell me that none of this means anything? That I'm going about finding the boy the wrong way? Or is it referring to the infinite blackness of that night that does not end? Nothing or death. That is what my mind is saying. Nothing or death. And yet, there is some other voice, coming from somewhere deep that has nothing to do with the mind, telling me those are not the only options and that there is a third option too. I'm just not seeing it.

I see The Line hotel up ahead, and I decide to try and rest there, but when I enter the lounge in the lobby area, it's full with people everywhere. I can't figure out what's going on, but then I remember there is a pool area and a great bar and restaurant on the second floor. When I step out of the elevator and enter the patio and pool area, there is a large crowd here too. I stop and begin to breathe hard with deep gasps, and it feels like a panic attack, which I recognize, though it's been a long, long time since I've had one. So with all the people, I figure it must be a Saturday, although I'm not sure, and something flashes into my mind about not knowing what day it is, and my mother saying that is a sign of not being accountable for anything, and that is bad.

"Hey buddy, are you okay?" asks a waiter.

"People . . ." I say, "everywhere."

He guides me by the forearm and shoulder, and we veer off to the right to an outdoor table. I say, "Thanks." I turn my chair away from the people and face the wall.

"I'll get you some water," the waiter says. "You're sweating, man. Just try to relax."

"I'll be fine," I reply, but these are just words. That's all. Words that are meant to convey *Hey, don't make a fuss over me*, but they are contradictory to my goal of being more accurate and precise because I don't, at this moment, know that I'll be fine at all.

"Here, drink up," he says upon returning.

I gulp it down, and it does feel good. I exhale and feel my pulse starting to slow just a bit.

"What's wrong?" he asks.

"Oh, I have . . . multiple disorders."

"Should I call someone?"

"No. Just let me rest a bit. It'll be okay."

I can feel him sliding away, but slowly, and I sense that although he's stepping backward, he's still keeping watch over me.

I stare out into space, without focus, at nothing in particular. I look at the vines on the trellis before me. Still, wiry brown branches reach up through the thin metal slats and intertwine with one another. There are small, pretty white flowers scattered throughout. Everything is still.

Then, from a corner of my eye, flies into focus a beautiful hummingbird, green and with a splash of orange on its back, with its bee-like buzz and wings flapping fast—it's a blur. It bounces frantically from white flower to white flower, quickly sapping as much nectar as it can pull, and then moving on. I'm watching it, and my eyes bounce with it. I can actually keep up and almost keep in perfect sync with only a nanosecond needed to react to its new position, but I keep up. It bounces, then zips to another flower. There is no logic to its approach as it zigs from a flower at the upper right corner of the trellis, then zags to the very bottom, then back to the middle, and then back to the bottom again. It does this frenetic back and forth, and I keep up with every move.

It then stops completely, appearing to have come to rest on a branch.

I didn't know they could do that. I have definitely never seen that before, not that I've encountered many hummingbirds here in the city—especially in K-town. For some reason, I just always assumed they were like sharks, who must always keep swimming or die. But this bird remains stopped there, completely stopped, without so much as a flinch, and just sits on the branch in a moment of still peace.

"How?" I say it beneath my breath.

I feel like I'm about to cry. I'd never seen this. *How does he do that?*

He doesn't move as I watch him, my lips quivering and tears filling the lower lids of my eyes, until the water finally leaps to its death and streams down my cheeks. I can feel the waiter's hand rest on my shoulder as I keep mouthing the word, *How*? How?

Then the hummingbird goes back to bouncing and fluttering wildly with wings buzzing at blinding speed, and I cry even harder. He finally buzzes away and flies off as I sit there in a daze.

"How?!?!" I scream. "Just tell me how!"

23

As I arrive at the tenth floor of my apartment building, I lift off my black shirt, stained from sweat, and toss it down the garbage chute. Once inside my place, I immediately take only a small dose of my medicine, as it's already early afternoon. I take a shower, long and cold.

I then perform my ceremony again in order to select another shirt. The one I chose is also completely black. I shake my head, never having owned even one black shirt and yet somehow now pulling a second one. I think about locations and how they're all closing in on me. The furthest was the Observatory, then the Museum was closer, and the bookstore was the nearest of all. *It's closing in.*

And now, a shirt that's all in black. I don't even have time to consider what this might mean when there is a knock at the door.

I don't move or make a sound, hoping if it's the police coming back to arrest me that they'll presume I'm not home and go somewhere else. If it's anyone else, I don't want to see them. Not now.

"Hey Cole, it's Robbie. Open up."

It takes me a minute to register that he said he was coming to visit, and today would be the day. But I can't take him today; I just can't. Still, I can't leave him outside either, so I open the door.

"Hey, Robbie," I say, lacking enthusiasm.

"Dude, what's with the zombie talk? Come on, we got to hug it out!"

He bear-hugs me, and I apologize for my demeanor and say that it's good to see him.

"I hate that shirt though," I add, pointing to his Aztecs T-shirt, which is the team mascot for Robbie's school. I get that many will associate the name with great pride in Mexican heritage, but while the Aztecs may or may not—I don't know—have made some minor advances to civilization—although I doubt they ever had anything on the Mayans, who at least developed a sophisticated calendar even though they got the whole end-of-the-world thing wrong, and I even have a shirt somewhere in my closet that reads, *12/21/2012, I Survived the Mayan Apocalypse*—What really gets me about the Aztecs is that no one seems to know or care that what they are most famous for is—hold on, hold on—*Human Sacrifice!* That's right—slaying innocents to worship some sun god, walking them up stone steps to the top of a tall open-air temple, holding them down, then—while still alive—carving out their beating hearts from their chests.

"Well, now I've got that bad human sacrifice aura all over me," I say. I'm trying to be funny and sound like I'm happy to see him.

"Hey, the world's overpopulated anyway," he responds.

"No. Not true. There are a lot of people, sure, but we need more. I saw it on the news. There's a demographic time bomb ticking where there aren't enough young people to support aging economies around the world, making for catastrophic labor shortage . . ."

"Okay, okay. I meant to say the world's overpopulated with idiots. C'mon, you *gotta* give me that one. And, hey, I thought you didn't watch the news. Changing things up now?"

I shrug.

"Cole, you've gotta lighten up, man," he says, tossing his backpack over to a corner, clearly frustrated. "Dude, I really need a drink."

He's clearly down, and I'm surprised at this because Robbie is always upbeat, always a font of positive energy. He's one of those angels with forty-five wings, and he's more together than anyone I know. When he finishes undergrad, he's going to law school. He'll probably pick one of the best schools in the country because, as he explained to me once, it will matter when he's an attorney to say he graduated from Harvard Law or some such place, and that will impress people, whereas no one asks or cares where you did your undergrad and I know he selected San Diego State—to the disappointment of his parents—because he wanted to stay in SoCal, and San Diego State has the best-looking girls. Besides, after college, he's going to *own* San Diego or Century City or move back to Newport Beach and take over there because that's just the way it is for him. I'd give almost anything to have some of that working for me.

"What's bothering you?" I ask.

"Some lame philosophy professor is riding me hard. Hey, is that Don Julio on top of your fridge?"

"Sure, go ahead. Why are you taking philosophy?"

"I needed one last general education course, and it was the only one offered at the time slot I had open. Hey, where are your shot glasses?"

"Top right cupboard. So what's with the professor? Tough grader?"

"I turn in my paper, and he accuses me of plagiarism!"

"What?!? Did you do it?"

"Hell no! I don't need that. School's easy. I once crammed an entire semester's worth of history into an all-nighter just before the finals—no sleep—and then aced the test the next morning. Anyway, I went around the guy to the department chair. I told him I can't help it if I subconsciously channel some philosopher who's been dead a hundred years. And it's the truth. Dead dude happens to copy *my* philosophy, my way of life, and the way I live every minute of my life because I took it from the universal soul of the human spirit. Right? But this philosopher happens to put it down on paper first and beats me by about a hundred years, and the professor is putting all the weight of his argument on that, essentially favoring the factor of *time*, and everybody knows that time does not exist."

He pours two shots, and I say, "No, no."

"More for me," he laughs, and he downs a shot. "So I told the department chair that it's really all about being authentic and true to ourselves, true to our inner animal, without giving a damn about expectations or conventions—that's the *only* truth. But to do that involves struggle and creativity, and not everyone can or is willing to do that. So we have democracy, which creates complacency and a welfare state. Elitism is the only way to go, and everyone should strive to be an elitist and live to their full potential. We've got to resist being dumbed down into this herd mentality; otherwise, we become strangers to ourselves."

"Wow, that's pretty deep."

"Well, hey, it's a philosophy class. And the department chair liked it! But enough of that. Tonight, we're gonna find some bar with girls and hit it hard."

He then pounds the second shot.

"Listen, tonight's cool for me," I say, "but I have a date tomorrow night, so . . ."

"Nice! So give it up. What's her name?"

There's a knock on the door, gentle, almost a light tap. I hesitate because I've never had a day where there were three knocks on my door.

I open it slowly. It's SteFunny.

"Hey Cole. Sorry to bug you. Listen, I'm sorry about yesterday. I'm really, really sorry. And the things I said were really, really stupid."

"No. No worries. Forget about it."

"Listen, my girlfriends and I are going out to dinner later, and we wanted to see if you wanted to come."

"Oh hey, listen, that's nice of you, but maybe another time. I've got my cousin in town, and we . . ."

"We are in!" Robbie says, peering over my shoulder. "Hi, I'm Robbie, Cole's cousin."

"Oh hi. I'm SteFunny, with an F."

"With an F? That is *so* cool!"

"Thanks! This will be fun! Cole, I'll text you later, okay?"

"Sure," I say.

I feel like things are moving so fast now and not in the direction I want or that I can control. I feel like I don't want to be with Robbie, SteFunny, or her girlfriends, but it's all out of my control because Robbie is here, and I certainly can't ask him to leave, especially when the date is set now with SteFunny and her friends, but none of this is what I should be focusing on.

"So this girl you're going out with is pretty hot, man," Robbie says. "How'd you hook up with her?"

"No, hey, SteFunny is just a neighbor. That's all. I think she likes me, but I'm not sure."

"Dude, she just asked you out."

"Well, sure, but she keeps insulting me, and so that's why she's doing it. I think. I don't know."

"So the girl you're seeing tomorrow is a different girl?"

"Yeah, that's right."

"Dude! You are out of control. What's up with you? Are you possessed by some demon that has taken over the body of Cole Reeves?"

We go on to play some video games and watch some soccer on TV, which Robbie hates because, even though I try to explain to him the tactics of the *beautiful game,* he insists on channel surfing until we find a *real* sport, and we go on for a couple of hours and laugh full, bottom-of-the-gut laughs.

We meet SteFunny and her friends later at a nice restaurant bar at the top level of City Center on 6th, where we talk and eat some fantastic meat that is not prepared like Korean barbecue even though it's a Korean restaurant, and everyone drinks Soju—except for me, because having gotten sick on it once before, there is forever now a traumatic repulsion to the taste, and I'm sure I can never drink it again. I discover that in a group setting like this, there is less pressure on me to say or do anything impressive, but I do get the sense SteFunny is cozying up to me with the way she sits close and occasionally taps my forearm or rubs my bicep when she wants to get my attention. This touching reminds me of the way Julie held me on our walk through the museum grounds the other day, and I start to worry that she might walk in and see me here. So my eyes dart to all corners of the room, watching anyone who walks in. The good news is Robbie is funnier than ever, and it makes for a great distraction; the way everyone is laughing at Robbie being entertained by the buzzer at our table that calls the waiter anytime we want, and though these devices are common in Korean restaurants, he goes on about how he thinks this is possibly the greatest invention ever, and so he keeps buzzing the waiter over constantly for any little thing such as changing his mind on the order or dropping his fork and needing a new one right away or insisting the waiter to tell the chef—right now—that this is the best damn food he has ever tasted, and everyone, except the waiter, is laughing hard. But I at least talk to the waiter away from the table as I'm heading to the restroom and promise him a big tip later, and he seems to be okay with this.

As I return from the restroom, SteFunny waves to me excitedly.

"Cole! Cole! While you were gone, we decided where we're going next," and then she speaks the single most terrifying word in the English language—well, no, I shouldn't exaggerate because that's not who I am anymore with words like *bombings*, *human sacrifice*, or just a simple to-the-point word like *Hate* in circulation—but leading that next tier of words, the best-of-the-rest, I guess you could call it, would be the next activity on our list of fun for the night.

"Karaoke!" she says.

Everyone at the table screams and hoots.

On the walk over to the Karaoke lounge, just down the street, the churning starts up again, and I'm sensing I really can't be here, doing this. I tell Robbie I'm not up for it, but he brushes me off, saying he promises this will be fun. I tell him I can't; I really don't feel I should be here.

"Hey ladies," Robbie says. "Keep walking. We're gonna hang back a bit as I'm just starting up my stock portfolio and Cole is a finance wiz. I just need a little investment advice."

The girls coo, clearly impressed.

"Why did you say that?" I ask. "I don't want them to think I'm some smart guy with money."

"Dude, you at least have a Trust, so that's something. Besides, what, are they going to be pounding on your door asking if they should buy mid-caps or bonds?"

"Okay. Whatever."

"Cole, your problem is that you're way too much in your head and not enough in your heart. This is no way to live a life."

"I know what you're saying, and ninety-nine out of a hundred times that would apply, but tonight, something else is eating at me."

"What?"

"I'm not sure. It's . . . I don't know."

"Listen, you may just be tight about the karaoke. Don't sweat it. It's simple. The most important thing to know is that you need to sing in your natural voice—don't try to sound just like the artist because you can never do it and it will sound bad. Just let go—let it all really come out of you. If you're off, that's okay; it'll be funny. But if you only go halfway, it will sound bad, and not in a funny giving-it-your-all way."

"Robbie, I just don't feel up for any of this."

"Cole!" he shouts, grabbing me by the shoulders and looking at me straight on. The girls stop and turn to see what's going on.

"Sorry," Robbie says to them. "We're just having a small disagreement over putting money into international funds right now because I think it's just way too volatile."

They walk on.

"Cole, you remember that book you lent me a few years ago? The one Grandma loved, and it made this incredible impression on you, so you had me read it?"

"It's called *The Sun Also Rises.*"

"Yeah. That's the one. Well, look, it didn't really hit home with me—not really—I mean, drinking wine from a sack is cool, and the whole running with the bulls challenge is something I'm definitely up for, but overall, it felt a little slow, and the guy doesn't get the girl in the end."

"You want what's called a Hollywood ending. But that's not the way things work out in real life."

"Whatever. But listen, there was one part I liked a lot, one part I vowed I would never forget and would live by every day. It's when the two friends are walking from bar to bar, just like us, and one tells the other that the secret to his success is that he's never been daunted. Not in public. If you're beginning to feel daunted, go away by yourself. Hide. But you have to remember that. Never be daunted."

I say nothing, impressed that Robbie actually read that book and that at least one part really stuck with him. I feel good that I had a little something to do with that. And though apprehension over karaoke isn't what I'm feeling right now, regardless, it's still a good message to carry around.

"Listen, Robbie," I say in a low voice. "I think I . . . I think I may have hurt someone. I don't know, but maybe I. . ." and my voice trails off.

Robbie's back stiffens, and he inhales deeply as he looks hard at me. A minute later, he tells the girls he's really sorry, but he started on the tequila early, and now it's all catching up to him, but hey, it's been great, and there's no way he's letting anyone walk away now without a promise to all get together and do this again soon. Though the girls are disappointed, they understand, and we all give brief hugs. SteFunny rubs my shoulder and smiles, "See you soon, Cole," before they walk on into the night.

"Where's the nearest bar?" Robbie asks.

I look around and point to a place that's on the second story of a strip mall, just across the street, and explain that I think it's a place Ray and I have been to, but it's all Korean, and Robbie says he doesn't care. He grabs me by the arm, and we dash across the street as a car slams its brakes and honks, just barely missing us in the thin fog that has settled in.

We walk in, and everyone looks up, eyeing us with surprise, but just for a moment, then they return to their bourbons and low banter. There are maybe twenty or so people in here, all Korean and mostly men.

"Garçon!" Robbie calls to the bartender, who is in the middle of a conversation with customers at the other end of the bar and making no move to come serve us. "*Dos tequilas, por favor.*"

"Robbie, he's Korean, not Mexican."

"No tequila here," the bartender says, striding over at a leisurely pace. His skin is dark, and I could see him being confused for a Mexican in a dimly lit bar. "Whiskey," he says, and his jaw is hard and set.

"Two shots of Jack," Robbie commands.

I don't even have a chance to complain about hating whiskey before Robbie starts laying into me.

"Cole, why is it that you think you've hurt somebody?"

"There have been strange things happening. I don't know that I really believe I've done something. I'm just confused. But I think the police think I've done something."

"The police? Cole, *why* do they believe you've hurt somebody?"

"There's this kid from the neighborhood, and he's been kidnapped. I'm trying to find him on my own, and I think that's why they think I'm involved."

"You've gotta back off. The police will handle it."

"No. I won't do that."

"Cole, if the police are involved, it's serious. Back off this . . ."

"No. I *can't* do that."

"I thought you were doing better with that defiant diagnosis or whatever it was. This is not the time for that."

"You have to understand. I'm doing this for the boy, but I'm also doing it for myself. I've got to know."

The bartender returns, places the whiskey in front of us, and asks if everything's okay here. I suppose our voices got a bit loud, and he tells us he doesn't want any trouble. I tell him we're fine and there's nothing to worry about. He walks away.

"Cole, you didn't . . ."

"How do you know?"

"I've known you my entire . . ."

"But can you really know? Can you really know what's inside another person?"

The two of us sit quietly for a while. Robbie begins to sip his drink while I just stare at mine.

"I'm scared, Robbie."

He stares at his drink for a while, then rubs his eyes. He seems to be frustrated, and I'm sure it's me he's frustrated with, but I don't know that I can talk to anyone else this way. I've known him all my life, and he's family, and I can say things to him that I can't say to my mother because she would overreact. I don't know; it would just be difficult, and as much as I like Ray and Jamal, we're just not that close. Not enough for me to tell them I may have done something to a kid. Not enough for me to tell them I've never been more scared in my life, and that's saying something given I've spent most of my life scared.

"I've told you," Robbie finally says, "you've got to get out of your head and more into your heart. Fear is in your head. Almost always, what's scaring you is something that's just in your mind. Has it ever happened to you that you were really afraid of something—anything—and then it turned out to be okay? It was nothing at all, or at least nothing nearly as bad as what you were expecting it to be."

I nod.

"Do you know what the most terrifying thing in the world is?" he asks.

I close my eyes. After a moment, I open them and see the way the low light shimmers off the bottles of alcohol and glasses lining the shelves behind the bar. I decide I may as well have a sip of the whiskey. I still hate this, but I have a feeling like it doesn't matter anymore. I think hard about his question—the most terrifying thing in the world.

"It's . . ." I hesitate and take a second sip to hone in on exactly what I want to say. "It's . . . nothing."

I can sense Robbie pulling back on his stool. I'm not looking at him, but I can feel his eyes on me. Maybe I didn't say it in exactly the right way. Maybe Nothingness, or the Void, or something along those lines would have been more precise. Maybe it's Emptiness, a hollow inside so profound that it aches. But whatever—it's still Nothing.

"Yeah," he says quietly. "That's it."

I look around the room, and I notice cigarette smoke—a haze that gives everything an out-of-focus, other-dimension feel. So the bartender lets customers smoke in here. I sense it must be a tight neighborhood bar, the kind of place only regulars come to and no one—no stranger anyway—stumbles across, the kind of place that probably keeps serving drinks past two o'clock. Maybe there are even hostesses here, but it's hard to tell as the smoke gets thick at times, and it almost seems as if all of it—the people, the drinks, and the bar itself—is disappearing.

"You remember, I had a great story I was going to tell you?" Robbie asks.

"Sure," and I think about this for a moment. "It was something about torture."

Robbie finishes his shot and waves to the bartender to bring two more. "My roommate has a cousin who just got out of the military. Special Ops, maybe Navy Seals, since it's San Diego. I can't remember. Anyway, my roommate was telling me what his cousin said about the greatest, most effective torture method ever heard of. He was drinking pretty hard, so I'm not sure he was supposed to say anything about it. I mean, maybe it's a military secret and all that. Seems his cousin was just chatting with some other Special Ops guys, and they were all comparing great torture techniques. I guess that's what Special Ops guys talk about when they're killing down time in some Arab desert."

Robbie goes silent as the bartender returns with the drinks. He waits and watches him walk away until he begins again.

"They take off all of your clothes," Robbie says, " and strip you completely naked. Then they cover your eyes with a mask made of the stuff they make surfing wet suits from. They tape that on tight so it won't come off. Your hands and feet are tied behind you. They place silicone wax ear plugs in your ears. Follow?"

"Yes."

"They give you oxygen through a small tank strapped to your chest and tape the air piece over your mouth and nose. So, you *have* to breathe. The tank also gives you weight, so you sink just a little."

"Sink?"

"Yeah, you see, you're taken to a building with an indoor pool, a very deep swimming pool. Only you *don't know* that. They walk you out there only after you've been blindfolded. At night. So you don't know what's happening. And the pool bottom is painted all black just to make it as dark as possible. Oh, and this is the most important part—the water is exactly *ninety-eight degrees*—the same as the human body."

"Okay," I say, not quite understanding. "What happens next?"

"They push you in."

Robbie takes a sip of the whiskey and looks around, as if checking for eavesdroppers.

"And?" I ask.

"That's it."

"That's all?"

"Well, yes . . . but remember, the pool bottom is completely black. *And*, you're blindfolded. And the water is *precisely* the temperature of your own body."

This makes no sense.

"So what exactly happens?" I ask.

"You spasm and twist, fighting to try to release the rope binding your wrists and ankles. You don't know that you're in water or a pool—everything is the deepest, pitch-blackest you can imagine. Then, you stop fighting, though you're still there beneath and inside the liquid, and you can't feel air around you. In all the wild gyrations of trying to escape, you can't tell now what is up or down. It's completely black, and you're just floating inside there, exhausted. You drift like that, tired, more frightened than you've ever been."

I imagine this and squirm on my bar stool.

"Then," Robbie continues, "panic sinks deep into you as you can no longer feel the water—it's the same temperature as your body. It's as if it has evaporated somehow, and you can't feel it. You just float in pitch-black space. There is no sound or light. No up or down. Only pure, infinite night. You thrash around again but can't really feel anything. And you begin to lose touch with yourself. Your hands and arms grow distant. It's as though they belong to someone else. Your body seems to be outside of itself, then drawn back in, and the cries into your mouthpiece don't help you connect back with yourself. Your soul is floating away outside of your body. You begin to feel less and less of yourself. The blackness around you is closing in, and you have a sense you are disappearing. You're becoming smaller, and then it's as if you are almost nothing at all. The last physical sensation tying you to your body is the slight trickle of air that is seeping into your mouth. That's all.

"*This has to be death*, you're thinking. You are leaving and becoming one with the black nothingness. You are now nothing. Nada. You are ceasing to exist."

I sit on the edge of my stool, and I can't move. I can't even say anything.

"Genius, huh?" Robbie laughs. "My roommate says they even turn out all of the lights in the building—indoor pool and all—and the torturers use night vision goggles. You believe that? Who's sadistic enough to dream up something like that? I think he said it was the Russians."

Robbie shakes his head and drinks.

"What happens to the prisoner?" I ask.

"The guys doing this have to be careful, you know. If they keep the prisoner down there too long and his brain turns to mush, then what good is he? He can't give any information if his mind is completely gone. Think about it. This poor guy is going through crazy hallucinations. He feels an absolute certainty that this is death, although—it's strange—some feel like they're regressing, going back into their mother's womb! Crazy. Like they're going back to their core spirit, whatever that is, wherever they came from. Dying or being born—same thing. It's insane."

24

It's late at night now. Robbie and I have just settled in, having quietly walked home from the bar without saying anything, the low fog providing a fresh, cool mist on our faces. The lights are out. I'm on the sofa, covered in blankets. Robbie's in my bed, occasionally letting out a soft groan, the night's tally of alcohol taking its toll. I don't think he's asleep yet. I'm afraid, as if I'm back as a nine-year-old and just saw a horror movie, my mind still there with the prisoner underwater.

"Robbie," I say softly, on the chance he is just slipping into unconsciousness but not all the way there.

He groans in acknowledgement.

"Why does there have to be darkness?" I ask.

He groans again, and then there is a long silence.

"It's the natural order of things," he finally says, slowly. "The dark has always been there, you know, until God waved his magic wand and said, *Let there be light*. But the blackness, the nothingness, was there before anything. The sun, light bulbs, your loud shirts—they were all splashed on the canvas later, just to break things up."

This worries me.

"So," I say, " black is the norm. It's always there. I guess that makes it the greatest power there is. And we're the ones who add the light, or at least try to."

"Sure."

I can't get the image of the black pool out of my head, and yet, all of it was really nothing. Everything—the real torture—was happening only in the prisoner's mind.

Before Robbie falls asleep, there is something more I need to tell him. I explain how I believe there is someone I am following—the kidnapper—who looks just like me. I tell him it's also possible it may actually *be* me. But I believe, or at least want to believe, that it's just someone else who is somehow similar to me. But I can't catch up to him. I'm just always a half-step slow.

He waits so long to respond that I assume he has fallen asleep, and I'll need to take this up again in the morning.

"Here's the thing," he finally says. "You need to jump in the black pool."

"What?"

"You need to get to your *core*. To who you *really* are."

I think about the whole description of the torture but can't imagine a way to replicate that, and besides, I don't even understand why he's saying any of this or why he thinks this would help me at all.

"What are you talking about?" I ask.

"You need to strip yourself bare of everything. You need to stop the meds."

"What? There's no way I can do that!"

"It's the *only* way. You're too slow with the meds. You're not functioning fast enough. That's why you're always *late*. It's the only way to sync up with this guy. And it's the only way to sync up with yourself."

25

AMAZINGLY, ROBBIE IS UP EARLY WITH BARELY ANY SIGN OF A hangover and shuffles off to Santa Monica to see some friends, which works out great for me because I can now proceed with my T-shirt ceremony and devote a full day to making some progress on finding Juan.

I am especially focused on controlling my breathing, slowing it, and trying to channel some special universal energy that blesses me from time to time, like the zone I achieved in the office of the Columbia interviewer or occasionally experience on the ping pong table, because I need a little something extra today, something special to get me unstuck here. In the closet, lights out, I exhale slowly. I say the word *Tranquility* in my mind, and then I let my fingers gently roam across the shoulders of the hanging shirts. I continue until I feel a jolt of static. I pull out the shirt and lift the light switch. It is another all-black T-shirt.

I pull the shirt over my head and sit at the edge of my bed. I decide I will not let thoughts of negativity fill me today. There is no time—*absolutely no time*. And so, I consider what positive—what small, positive spark of hope I can take from this that will keep me moving forward.

I fairly quickly arrive at a pretty upbeat landing point. With so many black shirts, shirts I do not own, there *has* to be something here, meaning one of the two alternatives I had previously considered—about the shirts maybe meaning nothing or having nothing to do with my search—cannot be an option. This has to mean *something*, and since it's true that this means something, I know that what I have to do is continue on.

The other alternative that continues to haunt me is that the shirt means death, but there's something wrong with this theory as well. Since all of this is being driven by some force that is clearly greater than me, why would this force have me continue to search and waste my time if the boy were now dead? Why not send me a shirt with some depiction of a blank video game screen and an inscription above it saying *Game Over*? I think I'd get that message. So this too perks me up and leads me to believe my goal is achievable and that it's really all up to me.

I walk over to the bathroom and take a look at the pills, my daily meds. I remember Robbie's words from last night and consider that they may have just been the babbling of a drunk—but brilliant, insightful—philosopher. Still, I have nothing to lose. I've been just missing all along, and maybe it's because I've been just a step too slow, and without the meds, I can figure things out more quickly, act or react, and then sync up with the truth. I close the cabinet and leave the pills there.

After an hour of driving around K-town, I feel about as discouraged as I've ever been. "No," I say out loud, and I rake back my hair hard because I can feel the depression sinking in. These are the same streets, apartments, palm trees, and homeless I see every day, and even when I cruise through the parking lot of every strip mall, I come across nothing connecting to a black T-shirt.

By late morning, I decide to stop at a boba shop and have a quick dessert. Boba's are a sweet dessert drink with soft tapioca goo balls resting on the bottom, which you suck out with an oversized straw. It just dawns on me, although I don't know how I could've forgotten, that I need to see Julie later for the tea ceremony. I worry about not having taken my meds on such an important day. Then I tell myself that Julie is as kind and forgiving a person as I know, so I shouldn't feel the pressure of having to be perfect with her—no, she has shown infinite compassion, and so I should just try to relax.

As I'm finishing my boba drink and readying to slurp up the tapioca balls, Jamal calls. He wants a game of pong, but I explain it can't be today. I make the mistake of telling him I really, really need to make some headway on the hunt for Juan Machado, and he fires into a rant so fast I can't keep up with what he's saying, even though my mind has zero dullness from my medication, until I am able to jump in and say, *Listen, Listen*, even if it wasn't *that*, I have a date this afternoon, so it can't happen. Now, even though he lets up on the brutal criticizing of my search for Juan, he grills me with a hundred questions about Julie, and I don't have time for this, but he is on me and won't let up nor let me go, and somehow I need to take control of all of this despite control having always been a problem for me, and I'm feeling so low that it is now sinking into a kind of nausea as I hear him saying how impressed he is with the way I check-mated her by making her first commit that she is sincere, and then took serious leverage over the whole date proposition because she would either have to say *Yes* to the date or essentially, admit that she is an insincere person *and that's what I call check-mate*, but I tell him, "Please, Jamal, I have to go because I really feel like time is running out, and it's not just about the safety of the boy," I say, "it's also that the police are on me." This infuriates him to the point where he's not only ranting at an unbelievably unintelligible speed but also screaming. I say, "Shut up!" But he says now it's important because once the police are involved, it's something serious—serious as a heart attack—and that I absolutely need to be packing a piece now, and I scream, "What the hell are you talking about"? but he says I have to do it because if it ain't the police, I may need it for something else because it's obvious, my *51-50 brutha,* that I have no idea what I'm doing and what I'm getting myself into. And what if I do meet up with this other me, and he's some serious psycho killer, and I need to protect myself? *Not to worry, not to worry,* because he can get me anything I need—small caliber, magnum, automatic, semi-automatic, shotgun—and they will be clean, he promises—no serial numbers, absolutely no way to trace.

"Jamal," I say calmly, but Jamal keeps going until I finally scream, "Jamal!"

He shuts up.

"What does it feel like?" I ask.

"Whatchu mean?"

"The shotgun. What does it feel like?"

"Oh, my brother, you have exquisite taste, because once you feel the weight of a baby like that in yo hands, you have the instantaneous aura of power, and you will not be messed with, and that is *precisely* the perfect piece for someone like you—no experience—and instead of yo hands a-quaking with some skimpy pistol and yo wrists flying and shootin' up the whole place and everything except the mother you want to cap—"

"No. Jamal. Hey, I'm sorry. I mean, what does it feel like to be *shot* with a shotgun?"

"Huh. Well, that'd be a mess you don't want no part of cleaning, know wom saying? Know wom saying? Because it ain't no handgun requiring some precision shot; you just aim the barrel in the general direction of yo soon-to-be-dead amigo, and you deliver a blast that just sprays."

"Yeah, but what does it actually *feel* like, the impact of the shot, when it hits?"

"Man, you don't want to know. Blasted away all at once, just like that. There's some hurtin' fo sho."

"Really? Is that what you really feel?"

"Hmm. Well, maybe not. With all that bullet spray I'm fixin', something's bound to spike the brain—or central nervous system—may be just a flash, a white light, and you greetin' the Almighty."

"No pain?"

"No idea."

I say I have to go and quickly disconnect before he is able to drag on the conversation. I drive downtown, still an hour and a half early for the tea ceremony with Julie, but I just want to be certain I know exactly where her apartment is and the parking situation. I usually do this for big events, like a special date, a job interview, or any new location I've never been to before. I don't park but slow down, just enough to see it is a nice, gated condo complex, and I figure, in addition to her roommate, she must be getting some assistance from her parents because I've heard the girls complain of the low pay at the bar, so I doubt she can be pulling the rent just on her own.

I don't usually travel downtown, other than for clubbing at night, and so, not knowing too many spots to just hang out and relax on an afternoon, I head to The Royal and decide to rest in the lobby area on the comfortable red Art Deco sofas. But, of course, I can't relax. I feel . . . overwhelmed. It's like I can't even distinguish the smothering thoughts any more. It's all just a blanket of white, and that blanket hugs me tighter than ever. I struggle to breathe, and so I just lay back on the sofa, close my eyes, and try not to move.

Robbie's words of jumping into the black pool and getting to my core haunt me because I think there's something to that, but I have no idea how to get there. I try to reach back to my earliest memory, and there are a few candidates, but I think the farthest back I can go is to an incident at our house in the Valley when I was about five years old. My parents had invited a couple of other families, couples who also had young children, and while they left us kids alone to play, the adults went outside to have their own adult discussions and drink wine coolers on a bright summer afternoon. I was playing with a toy—and though I don't remember what exactly the toy was, I do remember it was mine, and I was playing with it—and just as I set it down for a moment to examine another toy within my reach, a little girl, maybe just a few months younger than me, grabbed the toy I had set down. She probably just wanted a look or to play with it for a minute and then leave it, but I thought she was taking the toy from me, and so, as I saw her pulling the toy toward her, my hands leapt for her throat. As they clutched her thin, tender neck, they squeezed. I held her there for only a few seconds before someone yelled, "*Cole!*" and an adult man broke my grip and lifted her up in his arms. My mother then pulled me away, saying, "*Cole, never ever ever do that!*" but what I remember most about that day was the stern voice of the girl's father scolding his wife and saying, "I *told* you to watch her; you can't leave her alone with *him*," and though he tried to say it in a hushed tone, his anger jacked the decibel level of his voice to the point that I think everyone heard it, or at least I did. It was soon after that all the doctor's visits began, and they went on for years and years.

I am tired of memories.

By the time I arrive at Julie's condo, I'm actually ten minutes late, and I don't know if that's a great sin or whether tea ceremonies require the punctuality of a job interview, wedding, or some other special occasion, but I decide it's a first date, so I probably should have been prompt. Then again, it's Julie, and I'm really betting everything in the world that the kind, compassionate, and understanding vibe I've gotten from her is the real thing, because if she's uptight about a ten-minute wait, especially in L.A., where traffic can kill your schedule at any given time of any given day, then in the end, it would never work out between us anyway.

When the door opens, I am greeted by a lady who looks to be in her late-forties and who has the same perfect complexion Julie has and eyes that are just as penetrating, except while Julie's eyes have complexity that makes them seem both happy and sad simultaneously, this woman's eyes are pure happiness. She is dressed in an off-white, full-length kimono with subtle, red flowery flourishes.

"You must be Cole," she says in a humble, demure voice. "I am Julie's mother." She bows deeply.

I bow low as well, assuming this is the proper response, but I don't say anything because I'm sorting through my memory file, trying to remember if Julie ever said anything about her mother joining us. I feel my heart rate increase, and the blood begins to pump harder and faster in my veins.

"Come in," she says, standing back and waving me forward with her hand.

"Hi Cole," Julie says from the other room, but I can't see her. "My mother has studied tea all her life and loves to practice the ceremony with me, so I invited her."

"Great!" I say, thinking about the word *studied* with regards to tea.

When Julie appears, she is carrying bowls of various sizes and wearing a striking kimono of pure white with subtle yellow flowers. She is beautiful.

"Oh, Cole, could you take off your shoes, please?" Julie asks.

I immediately remove them, remembering that was also the custom during the museum's tea ceremony, and how they explained that was the custom in any Japanese house as well.

"Your father was a great man," her mother says to me. "He taught me English."

"You knew my father?"

"Not exactly," she laughs shyly. "When I first came to this country, I did not know English well, but I watched much television to listen to the words and phrases. And your father seemed to always be on the television. I know it is difficult to work in the arts, and so your father was very successful. You must be so proud."

I nod.

"Mother," Julie says from the other room, "Cole has performed the tea ceremony before."

"Only once," I say. "It was a long time ago, and I didn't fully understand it." I am struggling with all my might to keep my end of the conversation short, but I have a building surge of worry because my heart is racing and my mind is trying to take off despite everything I am doing to fight it.

It's clear they have moved around some chairs and a sofa in the living room to make room for the tatami mats they have placed on the floor. There is a single flower vase next to the wall, blue-gray with a splash of yellow, and I mean literally looking as if someone has taken a paint brush and, with a flip of the wrist, splashed a single stroke of yellow paint at it. There is a sole, pink flower rising from the vase. Next to the flower is a long scroll with Japanese writing on it. I step up to take a closer look.

"It says 'Tranquility,'" says Julie's mother.

"I like that," I respond.

It brings to mind the feeling of deep calm and peace I felt that day when I witnessed the tea ceremony at the museum, but today something is wrong because I am not feeling it, and I close my eyes and exhale deeply, trying to find that serenity. I'm sure I took my full meds that last time at the museum, and that, along with the slow, methodical pace of the ceremony and each deliberate gesture and movement, all came together in perfect synchronicity to help me find that one afternoon of true peace. But my lungs are now filling with worry that I will not be able to get there today.

Julie's mother then kneels down onto the tatami mat and shows me, with gestures, how it's done, and I notice Julie is also in the same position, but she is beginning to work, and it's clear her mother and I are the guests, the recipients of her special gift, the tea itself.

Julie pours water into one of the small cups and then takes a small bamboo whisk and quickly whips it inside the cup before pouring the water out into a bowl, which I presume she is cleaning. She gives the cup to her mother, who then inspects it closely, holding it right up to her eyes for a closer look.

As she is doing this, the anxiety is building inside me, and I'm finding it hard to control through relaxed breathing. While Julie executes the whisking at a nice, energetic pace, everything else is moving so slowly that I'm struggling to stay with it, and my knees are shifting beneath me. Julie's mother notices the fidgeting and asks if I'm okay, if I'm comfortable, and I just nod, but I don't open my mouth because I'm fearful that if I start talking, the flow will not stop, and the last ceremony allowed no talking, so perhaps today, if I can avoid conversation until the very end, then maybe I can hold it together.

Julie's mother hands me the small cup she has just been inspecting, and I decide to do the same, although I have no idea what I'm looking for. To watch her mother do it, you would think there was some hidden message there, but to me, it's just a cup, and it's no big deal. I do notice it's thin and porcelain-delicate, and so I decide not to really grab it, but instead I just place it there in the palms of my hands and then lift it to my eyes, palming it.

Julie repeats the same steps again, methodically, and hands this cup to her mother, who takes quite a long time with it before passing it to me with a glorious smile.

"See," she says.

The cup is white with yellow flowers painted on it, and yet I would not say it is beautiful; its surface is uneven.

"This cup has been in my family for one hundred and fifty years," the mother says. "And now, it is Julie's."

I notice a significant chip in the side of the cup, right where the center of the flower should be.

"Oh, so it's probably too late to return it then," I say, pointing to the blemish.

Her mother doesn't laugh, but she doesn't appear to be angry either, so I figure she probably just didn't get the joke—although I admit to myself, it wasn't that funny anyway.

"This cup is very, very special. The most precious of them all," she says. "It is the imperfection that makes it beautiful."

I say nothing. Taking in the words, trying to slow my mind to really understand and appreciate this because something is telling me there is something special here.

"Cole-san," she continues, "this is to remember that we must appreciate who we are, as we are, right now, embracing our true, imperfect selves."

My cynicism antennae go up because the notion is so pure and magnificent that I struggle to believe it can actually apply to the real world, *my* real world, but is rather just something that's said to make you feel good, like the time when I was a teenager and really liked Eileen Flanagan in my sophomore class. Despite my trying to get her attention, she truly never even noticed me, and it was amazing in the sense that, whether she liked me or not, it just seemed unbelievable that she didn't know I was even there, and that was when Robbie told me to not worry, because when a girl is ignoring you, that really means she's interested, and while I have, no doubt, all sorts of issues in my life, I am still the guy who blew through the roof every academic test that's ever been put in front of me and can crush any book-concept ever discussed in a classroom—except, of course, black holes—and so, I pointed out to Robbie that if his theorem were true, that a girl ignoring me means she's actually interested, then that would mean every girl in Los Angeles was madly in love with me, and I need to be careful of sayings that exist only to make you feel good because the temptation for me is to just believe—because I *want* to believe more than anything else in beautiful concepts such as *imperfection is beautiful*, but I'm just not sure.

"Cole-San," she continues, "the reason for this is based on three principles you must never forget. Nothing lasts. Nothing is finished. Nothing is perfect."

For just a second, my pulse slows, and my mind absorbs these words. I sense they have met the test, carrying enough weight that they have sunk below the cynical protective layer of my mind to rest within its warming acceptance of a new concept that is clearly not only pure but also true.

"The cup is beautiful," I say.

Julie is cleaning a third cup, presumably for herself, and this takes quite some time. I'm almost sensing she is *slowing* in her motions, though I realize that cannot even be possible and it probably just *feels* that way. She then takes a small red lacquer container and lifts it briefly, then places it down. She takes a red kerchief from her waist and folds it over a few times and begins to wipe the top of the container in slow, deliberate strokes, and I almost want to scream out, *Will you please get on with this?* and why would she ever be cleaning the outside cover of a container anyway? I begin fidgeting so much that Julie's mother taps me on the thigh as if to say *settle down*, the way you might do to a five-year-old who won't sit still at the dinner table.

Julie takes back our cups and opens the red container and with a long, thin bamboo spoon that resembles a pencil, she takes small scoops of powdered green tea from the container, and places them inside our cups. She then mixes in hot water from a kettle, and each step is taking so damn long that I bend over and grimace because I really want to scream and run and I know if I were to bolt from this room right here right now and run straight from Julie's downtown condo to my K-town apartment approximately five miles away, I know—I just know—I could do it in fifteen minutes.

She hands her mother a cup of tea first, and her mother gives me a long, worried look before finally accepting the cup. Julie whispers to me, "Are you okay?" very low and soft, as if she doesn't want her mother to hear, but this is, of course, absurd because her mother is right there and she's hearing everything. Julie then hands me a cup of tea in the small, thin, fragile summer cup that is, of course, the most beautiful of them all because it is blemished. I'm not sure I believe that, but I take the cup anyway and immediately raise it to my lips and drink, falling back on my previous theory that putting things in my mouth like food or drink will at least keep me quiet, and so now, drinking—no—gulping down the tea, I am angry that after all this time, work, endurance, and yes, *punishment,* this tea doesn't taste good at all, or at least not to me, who I will admit have a bit of a sweet tooth—though I've been doing better at controlling that. But it's just that we've waited so long here, worked so hard, and for what, *this?*

The cup snaps, crushed in my hands.

Julie gasps. The remaining tea and shards of thin porcelain mix with the blood seeping from cuts on my fingers and palms. I close my eyes, and the only words that come to me—in my mind that only moments ago was embracing such dreamy hopeful concepts as *Imperfection is beautiful*—are *No* and *Why?* Julie quickly but gently takes her kerchief to remove the broken cup pieces from my hand and says I've got to run my hands beneath the sink, but I must be saying out loud *No* because Julie says sternly, "*Yes, Cole, you need to run your hands beneath the sink,*" and she places her hand on my bicep to guide me up from the mat, and her hand there reminds me of that magical day—and I mean the word *magical*—when she forgave my wild arm swinging and instead held my arm high, at the bicep, and we walked together as two people do—two people who are a couple, and maybe even in love, and who go on to lead normal lives filled with occasional bumps but also filled with happiness, purpose, and even love.

But that is not my life. No, that is for someone else. *I am the shadow, after all.*

When I rise from the mat, I say, "I'm sorry for everything, but I really have to go now," and Julie is calling me to come wash up, but I say, "No, this time I really have to go." And I mean the word *really*.

26

It's late now—1:30 in the morning. I finally work up the nerve to call Jamal, something I've been thinking about all evening, ever since leaving Julie's. I really wish it could've all worked out, just like I had wished for it to so many times before. But now, I really feel like I'm all out of wishes.

He doesn't pick up, probably clubbing in Hollywood or maybe spending time with his new honey, so I leave a message.

But it's hard to talk; there's a pain in my gut so deep, like everything there has emptied and sunk low. And my whole soul, my entire being, has caved in, collapsed, and fallen through the floor.

This is *Descendo.*

"Jamal, it's Cole. I think I'll need that shotgun after all. Can you hook me up?"

27

It's 9:45 in the morning, and I've slept in. I expect it will be a while for Jamal to call me back if he was out late. I didn't sleep well, but that's okay, and only now is my energy starting to percolate, but I won't go with the meds today. There's no need. I decide I will just get dressed and grab a shirt—no ceremony—and maybe go for some breakfast, really just a little toast and juice, and chat a little with the *That's Life* waitress. I understand her fully now.

I detect the light scent of menthol smoke or whatever it is. But then it's gone. I don't care.

I reach into the dark closet now—no bow or light touch of the fingers across the shoulders of the shirts—and just pull a hanger out. Expecting another all-black shirt. I'm surprised to see it's a navy blue shirt with a gold Aladdin's lamp in the middle—another shirt that isn't mine. The shirt says, *Can't wish for more Wishes? Wish for more Genies!*

I reflect on its message, but, like so many others, it has no meaning to me. I change my mind about swinging by the diner, deciding instead to walk the streets of K-town, which are unusually bright this morning, the typical May gray having taken the day off.

There is something here with this shirt. Though nothing's striking me in terms of meaning, there's a little call inside of me—just a whisper—that seems to be telling me to keep going. The shirt is a call to action. I'm out of wishes, so wish for more genies—which, of course, can grant me more wishes and keep me going. I kick around ideas about the numerous herb shops in my neighborhood and consider whether there is some magic there that might be an answer for me, since a genie's lamp is magical. But after stopping by two different shops, wandering the aisles, and talking with the clerks, who don't resemble genies in any way, I begin to feel that's a dead end.

So I spend all morning walking up and down the perfectly rectangular blocks of apartments, strip malls, and restaurants, and this is all as mind-numbing and futile as the endless parade of black shirts.

I find myself on Wilshire and heading east, back toward my apartment. I'm feeling a bit winded, and it really strikes me that I've changed; something is bearing down on me, whether it's the stress or the frustration of not finding the boy or the worry I could somehow be involved with his disappearance, which is probably it because if something like that is always there, in the background, just gnawing at you, then the spirit has to tire. I notice this now because I can't walk nearly as far as I used to.

Stopping in front of St. Basil's, I lean back against the concrete block, my eyes turned to the sky. I feel like I am breathing a bit easier. When, after a few minutes, I lift away from the block, I see a woman at the top of the stairs leading to the church's entrance. She's wearing a rose-colored dress with lace trim at the neckline and the ends of the long sleeves. Her face is Hispanic. She is absolutely still, just standing there, and her eyes are closed. She is holding what appears to be a white cloth of some sort, folded, and gently rocking it in front of her. Then she tilts her head to the side and slightly downward, as if to look at me. But her eyes are still closed.

She makes a small turn and enters the open doors of the church.

I take the steps two at a time, and at the entrance, pause to look inside. The woman is already in the front pew, sitting quietly, which makes no sense because there's no way she could have moved fast enough to get all the way to the front.

Stepping inside, the church feels strong. I don't know of another way to say it, probably because of its stone walls, interspersed with only small sections of stained glass. There are rows and rows of pews, and in the distance, against the far wall, is a large crucifix, and around it are long, thin wooden slats that run up and down the wall, intertwined the way long, lean muscles look in an anatomy book or like an illustration of a DNA strand. On the cross, Jesus is hanging.

I ease into the last pew at the very back of the church. I breathe easy. I watch the woman at the front, who hasn't moved. We are the only two here. Then I lower the kneeler to the ground, ease my knees down upon it, and make the sign of the cross.

"Our father, who art in heaven," I say softly, "hallowed be thy name. Your kingdom—and will—be done . . ." and I trail off, forgetting the rest of the prayer.

I close my eyes.

"Dear God, this is Cole Reeves. You probably don't remember me. We used to talk all the time, every day, or, to be precise, every night, or at least I would talk, but I'm not sure you were there. I didn't hear you, and I didn't catch any signs like I was asking for. All of that is okay now. I'm not here to ask you why. I don't ask *why* anymore. I'm not here about me. Well, maybe a little bit is about me, because I first want to say I'm sorry—sorry for everything. For the broken cup at Julie's, and for hitting Mr. Sellars, and for the hatred I once had for little Juan, which is hurting me most of all, and though that's all I can think of right now, I'm sure there are other things I've done, and maybe even things I've done that I don't remember. Anyway, I'm sorry for all of that.

"Like I said, I'm not going to ask you *Why* anymore. I'm not saying I'm over that or that I've figured it out; it's just that there's something more important right now. Something more important than me and my problems. I need your help, and if Dad and Mr. Kennedy are there, I really feel like I need their help too. And if Mr. Conrad is there, and he wants to help too and make up for some things, maybe, that he's done in the past—although I don't know him well enough to accuse him of anything—this would be a good thing to do if he feels like he needs this for whatever reason, and I'm hoping it's not too late for him, or for any of us for that matter, because Robbie says time does not exist, and it's a fact according to quantum physics. But I'm not qualified to talk about anything like that because, as I'm sure you know, my scores were off the charts on all the tests, but thank God—uh, thank *you*—for not putting any questions about quantum physics, black holes, or entanglement in there because I just don't understand any of that. But getting back to my main point, I really need your help. And I mean the word *Really*. If you're there, I'm sure I don't even need to tell you the reason I need your help. You know how lost I am. Can you please put me on the right path? Amen."

I make the sign of the cross and sit back. The woman in the front pew is gone. Right next to me—and I mean literally right next to where I'm sitting—is the folded white cloth. I stare at it for a moment and wonder how she could have done it—left it right next to me without my hearing or sensing her movement. I lift it; it has a soft, worn, cottony feel. Unfolding it slowly, I see it is a white T-shirt with a large yellow Happy Face on it. All I can muster in response is a confused, subtle smile.

I walk outside where the brilliant sunlight is blinding, and I think I really should be wearing sunglasses more often, especially living here in L.A. and with all the need I have for anti-aging products given the sun exposure I've punished my skin with over the years.

My mind feels a little different, highly charged and yet more clear. The noise is not overwhelming—it's more like steady traffic on the 405 Freeway, miraculously moving smoothly and keeping everyone on time and in good spirits.

The phone rings, and I see it's Jamal calling me back. I decline the call.

There is something welling up inside of me, and I can almost feel it growing as if a tide is rising. *Keep going.*

And so, I run. Bolting down Wilshire, I dart through the pedestrians, some of whom brush to the side to let me through, and I'm sure they're thinking that this is just some madman running through the streets of L.A.—no big deal—but I'm sprinting hard and don't even stop at the red lights. Though I do have to zig-zag through a few cars at the intersection of Wilshire and Kingsley, and some cars honk, I just give them a polite wave without breaking stride until I burst up the front steps to my apartment building and into the elevator—only because the door happens to be open, being full-on ready to climb ten stories of stairs, if needed.

As I'm stepping into my apartment, I toss the Happy Face shirt on the sofa and pull off my Genie shirt quickly. I rush to the closet to get my next shirt, the one that puts me back on track, and even though I don't know what that shirt will be, I do have a sense of my next step—a little sidestep, I'll call it.

Then, as I'm about to step into the closet, I notice it feels strange. Rather than step into the darkness and feel for the right shirt that calls out to me, I turn on the light.

The shirts are *all* black.

I brush my hand along the rows of shirts, moving them slightly to make sure I'm right in my assessment, but they are—each and every one—completely black. Front and back—black. Gone are the countless—no, not countless—453 shirts I have collected over the years with images of unicorns and Pi and messages of *Je Suis Un Genie*. All of them, gone.

I pull one of the shirts—they're all the same now, after all—and put it on.

"This has to be a *place*," I say. Like the other shirts directing me to a place, this has got to be a place too. *A place close by.* I think of dark places, the bottoms of wells, and other such things, but discard these for the time being because I know there is just one other thing I need to do first, but I've got to run.

28

I WAIT OUTSIDE THE APARTMENT FOR SEVERAL MINUTES, CATCHING my breath. It's an older-style building, ungated and two stories tall, with an outside pathway accessible by stairs—no security here. A little of the old doubt is creeping back, the one that says this move may be dangerous. If she recognizes me and overreacts and doesn't give me a chance to explain, she may call the police. And if they decide it's best to arrest me, even as a precaution, then I won't be able to find Juan. Still, I walk up to the door and knock on the metallic screen. It's noisy as hell—my knocking on the metal—but I don't hear anything from the inside. I wait. I then have to knock again before I hear small footsteps, and finally the door opens. The screen pushes open in a slow, grinding creak.

"Señora Machado?" I say to the woman I recognize as Juan's mother, looking more tired than in my memory of her at the Tofu House, the eyes heavy with bags, the weight of worry, and days of crying and little sleep.

"*Si?*" she responds.

"My name is Cole Reeves," and as I say this, her eyes begin to widen, and I start to worry, but I push ahead and begin to talk faster.

"You probably don't remember me," I say as my voice begins to crack and jump an octave in panic mode, because the look on her face tells me she is definitely, slowly, recognizing me, "but I just wanted to say I'm sorry for some feelings I've had, which are very hard to explain and I'm not sure I'll do a good job of it now," and my feet are inching backward away from the door as she now clasps her hands over her mouth before quickly removing them.

"You!" she exclaims.

I am starting to walk away from the door when she reaches out, arms fully extended, to grab my hand and pull me toward her.

"*Dios mio*, it's you!" she cries.

"I'm sorry."

"Please, please, come in!" she says.

Once she pulls me inside, she hugs me, and it is as tight a hug as I've ever had. She is petite, and so I am surprised by her strength as she holds me there and will not let go.

"*Dios mio*," she says, pulling away slightly but still holding me by my arms. "It is so good to see you."

"So, you remember me then?"

"*Si, si*. That day, eating noodles at the *restaurante* on Wilshire."

"*Si*," I say.

"My little Juanito," she says, and she pulls away now, shaking her head and placing her hand over her mouth as her eyes are on the verge of tears.

"You brought so much joy to Juanito that day," she says.

I wince, trying to find some solace in my own ridiculousness bringing such joy to someone else.

"He laughed so hard and so much," she says.

"That's . . . good."

"He liked your shirt so much!"

"What?"

"The shirt—your shirt—he think it was so, so funny."

My mind flies back in time, trying to remember what shirt it could have possibly been.

"I'm sorry," I say. "I don't remember."

"It was the green monster. The ugly green monster."

"The, uh, Incredible Hulk?"

"And the word, 'Smash!'"

"Yeah, sure. That's it. I remember it now."

"Juanito laughed so much. *So* much. For days, he would make a fist and say, 'Smash!'"

She shakes her head more and cannot hold back the tears now.

"My boy," she says, "my Juanito. He is not like other children."

"Yes, I know."

"It is difficult to say in *Inglés*."

"No. You don't have to explain."

"I don't know why some things bring him joy so much. But he is so pure. He only has love in his heart. Do you know how special that is? To be so special as to have only one thing in your heart? To have only love in your heart?"

"He is very lucky," I say.

"No," she says, shaking her head, crying hard now. "No, Señor Reeves. This is no luck. This world is not a place for this people . . . who have only love. Other children—and I know how children are, Señor Reeves, how they can hurt—they laugh at Juanito. Many times, I don't think he understands, and I thank God for this. But there are so many times I know he does understand. The laughing."

She is shaking now. The tears, the choking, and shaking seem to be overtaking her. I embrace her.

"I'm going to find him," I say softly, but I'm not sure she hears me.

"You make him so happy that day, Señor Reeves. He wants to go back to the *restaurante* for many days to see you again. 'I love the nice man,' he says again and again. 'I love the nice man.'"

I now hold her tighter, not just for her comfort but so that she cannot see *my* tears.

"He loved you, Señor Reeves. He really, really loved you."

29

I GRACEFULLY LEAVE THE APARTMENT AND TELL HER THIS WILL ALL be okay, and though I'm sure I shouldn't say things like that because I really don't know, I do feel as though something is happening. But maybe it's just happening to me, and I shouldn't presume Juan is safe because I am now discovering something deeper about myself, and I want to be sure I'm not mistaking the infinite energy I am feeling now, probably because I am not on my meds, for something that is deeper still. And yet, I am reaching somewhere inside where I don't know if I've ever been before, or if I have, I can't remember because this thing is rising, and I'm sure I'm not explaining it well because it is not a thing but a *knowing*.

I listen to Jamal's voicemail from the call earlier, and he's talking slowly and quietly. He says he's sorry, but he can't really get me a gun, and that was just talk. He says a gun is probably not what I need anyway. I laugh. I knew he wasn't so tough.

I bolt into a hard run down the block, looking everywhere, my eyes darting all around, looking for clues, looking for the mysterious *black*, and somehow I know, that I must be the one to find him. And so I run.

I run through the endless blocks of apartment buildings, then through the strip malls and the boba shops where everyone watches me as I dash by, and the Pilates classes where I can tell they think they recognize me but aren't sure because I'm gone that quickly, and past the homeless, some of whom cheer me on.

I run.

Reaching the massive mural at Normandie and Pico, I look up at the two angels, each with one wing, and I yell out, "Juan!" I then turn to face north and yell out again. People walking through the intersection stop to look at me in wonder. They lean in to talk closely to one another, and I can only imagine they must be asking themselves if that man is drunk, on drugs, or crazy, or maybe they just warn each other to stay as far away as possible, but I yell out again to the east and to the south, "Juan!"

I run and continue through the alleys, past the storefronts,and by the homeless, and in my mind, I am repeating the word *Black*. And what does it mean? It *has* to mean something. There has to be a place. *Black*.

My shirt is soaked through with sweat, and I need to stop. I'm not sure exactly where I am—I'm not paying attention—but I lean against a light pole at an intersection corner. I face west, looking into the dusk sky with a feeling of déjà vu from the first day when I discovered the mural. I close my eyes and try to catch my breath. I can feel the day slipping away, but I don't understand how this is possible because I was so sure—after the feeling from church and having talked to Juan's mother—that this would be the moment to turn the corner and get to that next level.

I throw my head back in exhaustion and hit it against the pole much harder than I expected, and everything turns white. It's only for a moment, and a flash of panic rushes through me, fearing I may have done some damage to my skull or may lose consciousness. Then, in a lazy, sunrise-like way, the world comes into focus again.

Across the street, directly in front of me, is the building that has been undergoing renovation for some weeks now, with scaffolding hiding much of its facade—the building that is all in black. I study it a bit, and after determining that my eyesight is fine and there's no lump on the back of my head, I begin to cross the street. *It was there all along.* I must have passed it a hundred times on my search but never saw beyond that scaffolding, which doesn't even hide all that much of the building—and so it was always there, just right over there.

There is a guy standing in front of where I imagine the door would be, and he has a flannel shirt and an unkempt beard. He's texting someone on a cell phone. He doesn't look familiar. I approach slowly, and he seems to be without care, just leaning against the wall of the alcove, standing right next to what I can now make out is an unmarked door with a simple grasp-handle.

I'm just a few feet away, and he looks up, watching me as I approach. He has a look of anticipation, like he's expecting something from me, as he leans in. I don't know what he wants, but when I reach for the door handle, he places his palm firmly on the door, ensuring it stays closed. He looks right at me with a questioning look in his eye.

"Password?" he says.

"What?"

"What's the password?"

It comes to me slowly that this must be a bar, because I know there are a few of them in L.A. that require passwords to get in. They're not really trying for an elitist vibe like so many places in this city. No, it's more that they only want people who really *want* to be there—people who have put in a little effort to join their family and have a good time at the neighborhood speakeasy.

"Ugh!" I say. "Please, I need to get in. It's an emergency."

"Never heard of an emergency to get into a bar before."

"I'm just . . . I'm just looking for somebody."

"Friend of yours?"

"Yes, that's right. A friend."

"Just call him on his cell. If he's in there, he knows the password."

My pulse begins to pound, and my breathing picks up pace.

"Please," I beg.

He just looks at me straight on, no expression, the look of a guy who's heard it all before and is probably under strict rules from the owner to make sure no exceptions to the password rule are made. It's obvious he's not going to give in, and I'm not sure what to do at first.

Then it's clear I need to turn and run hard back to my apartment, and though I've never been a runner and wouldn't know anything about my speed or how fast I run a mile, I do, at this moment, know I am setting my best time. After getting my bearings, I realize I'm actually very close to my place. When I arrive, I push open the door, throw off my black shirt, no time for a shower, and proceed to the closet.

Bowing before entering, I can tell the shirts have all been restored—the old shirts with all the themes and little sayings that I have used to try to find some meaning for my day, or at least to try to keep my mind still. Sure enough, they have all returned, and the barrage of black shirts is gone. I enter, closing the door behind me, and try to calm myself. I need the *right* shirt. This really has to be the perfect one, and while I try to slow my breathing and say in my mind *Tranquility*, I also think about God, Bobby Kennedy, Dad, and Martin Conrad, and in some quiet, non-verbal way, I ask them to be with me now. I ask that they somehow reach out to me and help.

And then, I touch a shirt that makes my hand go limp with its overpowering energy—a positive energy so strong that it sends a pulse of, I don't know what, but something intensely positive all through my body and deep into my core. I pull the shirt and flip up the light switch.

I laugh.

I laugh so hard that I fall back against the door frame. This was so obvious. I should have been able to select it without even asking for help. But I have no time to stand here and try to understand it all, so I throw it on quickly and burst out the door. I haven't even thought to lock it by the time I am flying down the ten flights of stairs, hitting the pavement, and running hard until I arrive back at the bar.

Slowing just a little before arriving at the bar's door, just enough to get my wind, I can see the doorman look up. His face lights up, and he begins to laugh hard.

"No way!" he says. "How did you do that? You didn't have to—you could've just said—

"Hulk Smash."

Inside, the bar has the charm and homey feel of a guy's large basement—that is, if that guy has decided to decorate it as a pirate ship. There are dark red booths and an ornate cherry red bar with low lighting and smiling bartender girls. They are all pretty.

There are only a handful of patrons. I can't remember what day it is today, and if it's a weekday, then maybe that's the reason it feels slow. There is a couple in their mid-forties talking softly and close in one of the booths, wearing old T-shirts which blare the names of heavy metal bands. Along the bar itself sit two young ladies watching the TV, dressed smartly as if this place is just a warm-up for some more serious clubbing later. There is also an older man by himself, his head slowly sinking then propping up, the alcohol stupor getting the better of him.

"Carlos!" a young bartender calls out to me. She has a pleasant round face and wears one of those flat caps that is similar to a beret that old-time golfers used to wear. As I walk up closer to the bar, she immediately apologizes, saying she thought I looked like someone she knows.

As I pull up a stool, I take another quick look around, but there is no one else here that resembles me. I can feel another headache starting. I'm frustrated as they arrive when I'm most trying to connect what's happening and when I sense I'm getting close. They don't last long, which is nice, and so I'm ruling out migraines, at least based on what I found on the Internet last night. Still, the pain is sharp enough to haze my thinking, and I really don't need this now.

"Hey buddy, you look hot, like you could use a beer," she says.

"Maybe just a shot of tequila, a nice *blanco*."

I take another quick look around, shifting on my stool, but not seeing anything out of the ordinary. She returns a moment later and hands me the shot.

"When I walked in, you called me Carlos," I say.

"Yeah, sorry. I thought for a second that you looked just like this other guy who comes in here. But I don't know. It must have been my eyes playing tricks on me because, as soon as you walked a little closer, you actually look nothing like him."

"He's a regular?"

"Yeah, most nights anyway."

"What's his last name?"

"Have no idea."

"Do you expect him tonight?"

"No. He actually just left. You just missed him."

"Do you know where he lives?"

"Haven't a clue."

I let out a soft groan. I think about the detour I took to see Juan's mother and how maybe if I hadn't, I could've been here in time. But I have no regrets over that. That was important. Mothers are important, and it was a good thing to do. For her and me.

Then something else dawns on me. Had I not taken that detour, then I'm sure I would have been here at the same time as him. Am I—*we*—finally in sync?

"Do you know him?" she asks.

"Sure," I lie. "I just need to catch up with him. Do you think he'll be in tomorrow?"

"Don't know."

A waitress arrives at the bar after serving the couple at the booth their food, and she smiles at me.

"I'm pretty sure he'll be in tomorrow," the waitress says. "Today, he was talking about some big soccer match tomorrow. So yeah, he'll be here."

"That's right!" my bartender exclaims. "We're really not a sports bar. We just keep the TV up there for light entertainment—reality TV shows, you know. When we do karaoke, we put the words up there. But Carlos loves his soccer, so he usually asks us to put it on."

I'm thinking there is a Real Madrid match tomorrow afternoon, though I can't recall who they're playing. I will need to be here for that.

The waitress doesn't seem quite as friendly as the bartender. She's got this stern look, even though she has pretty, gray eyes and pure white skin that contrast perfectly with her jet-black hair. But she's got her brow and forehead all wrinkled up as she studies me closely. I'm thinking she's probably only a few years older than me, and with the pure white skin, she doesn't likely have much sun damage, but if she often bunches up her face like that, she's going to need some serious anti-wrinkle cream soon.

"So you're a friend of Carlos?" she asks.

"Well, yeah," I reply.

"So what's wrong with him?"

"Uh, how do you mean?"

"I mean, most of the time he just sits there and talks to himself. And I don't mean just a little, like most of us do sometimes. He just sits there and talks nonstop. It's like he's saying out loud every thought and every single thing that's running through his head. Out loud. Scary."

"Janice doesn't like Carlos much," the bartender says.

"He's crazy," Janice, the waitress, says.

"I don't know him well," I offer. "It's been awhile, and I just wanted to catch up."

The two are nice and leave me alone to sip my tequila. I watch the young ladies engrossed in the TV show and the older guy next to me at the bar, who will clearly need to be cut off from any more drinks. He growls low and deep, then lets out a throat-clearing cough.

"You said you were a friend of Carlos?" he asks.

"Yeah, um, that's right."

"Carlos has no friends."

"Uh, well. . ." I stammer.

"Why are you looking for him?" he asks.

"I just need to talk to him."

"Hmmm. Don't talk to him. *Kill* him if you want. But don't talk."

"Wha-? Why—why should I kill him?"

"Because that sonofabitch is pure evil. He's insane."

"Why do you say that?"

"The talk. The crazy talk."

"Like what?"

The old drunk just shakes his head.

"Evil moves forward in three steps," he says, a heavy slur in his words. "First, it appears in your mind. Then it moves to your lips. Then it's on your hands."

"I don't understand."

"All sorts of madness might creep into someone's head. That may not be unusual. But if that someone then starts *speaking* it . . . well, it doesn't have to travel much farther to become *action*."

The guy waves to the bartender for another beer. She shakes her head *No*, and he grumbles under his breath.

"And the headaches," he says, "they attack him hard, and they've been coming more often, making him angrier, I think. And crazier. He talks madness and hurt all the time," he says.

"But why?"

"I don't know! The usual kid stuff. His dad would hit him, and then he left when Carlos was young. He was bullied a lot. All of that. . ."

He finally turns to look at me, a look of confusion rising from his bloodshot eyes.

"What's your name, son?"

"Cole Reeves."

"So, Cole, tell me . . . what kind of gun you got?"

"I don't own a gun."

His head sinks, chin fully tucked in, and he's laughing a pitiful laugh.

"By this time tomorrow, young Cole Reeves, you'll be *dead*."

He slides off the bar stool and staggers off. I watch him until he is completely outside the door.

"Don't worry," the waitress says cheerily. "He's not driving."

I sit on my stool for I don't know how long, but I know it's long enough that the bartender swings back twice to ask if I'd like another shot. I say no. The light hits a bottle of Hennessy on a top shelf, and I remember the last time I had Hennessy, I was riding on a train to the Loire Valley, talking to the girl who told me all about Da Vinci.

"But I have a question," I say to the bartender. "Why do we use only ten percent of our brains?"

"Huh? Well, I think that whole thing is a myth. We're using our minds constantly. It's processing *all* the time. Even when you're asleep and dreaming, it's still going."

I sigh. I don't think she understands what I'm really saying.

The two ladies at the bar cheer loudly because it seems the girl on the TV picked the same guy to marry who they were rooting for. I think about all the drinking I've done and the countless hours of video games and watching soccer on television—both live and recorded games—over and over. I wince.

I decide there's no chance Carlos will wander back in here tonight, and so I pay for the shot, bid them all a good evening, and say we'll probably all see each other tomorrow. I ask if the password will be the same, and they say, "Yes, it won't change for another week."

Outside, there is a stillness that scares me. It is not just that the streets are quiet with few cars and empty of people; even more, there is an eerie silence in my mind. I can't explain it. There is almost no current of thought traveling through there, and it is so bizarre that I wonder if I am going to pass out or maybe die, though I don't feel ill in any way. I walk. I pass all the usual places I've grown familiar with in K-town over the months I've lived here, but it feels as though I'm on another planet. If it weren't for the occasional car passing by, I would have thought everyone had left town. And in my mind, the silence is so loud that it echoes.

I walk on and think only of the polar bear, whose wandering, I'm sure, is not limited to utilitarian tasks of food gathering but is truly propelled by an innate freedom to roam. For me, now, the silence is that of freedom. A still, pure freedom from noise, from everything. The silence and the chill in the air make me feel as though I've slipped into someone else's life.

30

I PEER THROUGH THE FRONT DOOR WINDOW OF MRS. KIM'S SHOP. It's dark inside, but I see a light glowing from the back room, so I know she's here. Reaching through the iron security bars, I tap the window. Her silhouette steps out of that room and waves. It's a dismissive wave. A *go-away* wave. I tap again. She then marches forward toward the door in a quick, stern march.

"We are closed," she says. "Come back tomorrow."

"No, Mrs. Kim. It's me, Polar Bear."

She purses her lips and stiffens her neck.

"Polar Bear?" she says.

"Yes, yes, it's me."

She still doesn't move.

"I don't think so," she says.

"Yes, come on. It's me. I just want to talk to you."

She still doesn't move.

"It's me," I say. "Cole Reeves."

She opens the door but begins to slowly backpedal, not turning her back on me. I then step into her shop.

"Please," I say, "don't tell me you don't recognize me either! You can't even *see*! I need to know what's going on."

She stops, sensing she's about to hit the checkout counter. She reaches out with her hand, her palm rising and making small circular motions.

"You say you are Polar Bear?"

"Yes, that's right. That's right."

"Then tell me, why do you roam?"

"What? Huh? Well, I guess polar bears roam looking for food, and—"

"No!" And she then points a finger straight at me. "Why do *you* roam?"

I shake my head.

"Why do *I* roam?"

"Yes!"

"Well, uh . . ." I close my eyes. "I suppose . . . I suppose I just want to connect with people."

"All people?"

"What?"

"*All* people?"

I lean back to rest against a large table.

"No," I say. "Only those that have some good in them. Not like those people on the news."

Mrs. Kim steps forward and gently places both hands on my chest. Her face turns grim. After a while, she begins to walk to the back room and says, "Come with me."

In this room, there is a polished, smooth wood floor, and along the back wall are various small statues, candles, and metallic ornaments, all neatly arranged, like some sort of shrine. She waves me down to sit on a thin pillow placed in the middle of the floor. She then kneels on another one, placed just before the shrine.

"Cole, every being is made up of infinite emotions, memories, impulses, and desires. There are past actions and future intentions. Regrets. Hope. Good. And Evil."

I nod.

Mrs. Kim tilts her head and gives me a sad smile.

"Polar Bear. You have merged with another being. You have connected with someone . . . someone from the news."

I shake my head and start to say something. But nothing comes out.

"It's true," and her face takes on a most sorrowful look, as if she were front row at the funeral of a friend.

"But, why can't I figure it out then?" I say. "Why can't I just see into his mind?"

"Ah, the mind. The mind is like infinite cars on infinite roads, all speeding, stopping, honking horns, turning on headlights, and braking while driving through the dense fog of existence. The mind is blinding noise. But the spirit, the nature . . . not so much."

She goes into the next room and returns wearing a bright red and blue robe with all sorts of gems embedded into the fabric. There is a bright yellow sash as well as an oversized black headpiece. Necklaces of various colors and designs drape her neck, and I'm thinking that this is the gaudiest outfit I've ever seen. It's so distracting that I actually miss the fact that she is carrying large knives in each hand. They have long blades of maybe ten inches and are fixed atop long wooden handles.

"Um, Mrs. Kim . . ."

"I cannot promise you this will work," she says. "I have performed exorcism, but this is something beyond. The bond you have is like nothing I have seen. There is a desire. You *want* to be one."

"No. That's not true."

"There is much desire. You are on another level."

"No."

She then screeches and begins a crazed, twirling dance, chanting to a bizarre melody and cadence. All the while, she is waving the knives to her rhythm, and though I want to dash and just run out of here as fast as I can, I don't dare move. She continues, and her chant grows louder. She makes violent stabbing motions—at *me!* There is a tightening in my chest, and my head feels light. I can't catch air, and my breathing is staggered. It's as if two of me are breathing, and the pulse of our breaths is off and out of sync. And it goes on like this, and everything starts to ache—the muscles in my body and the energy waves of my psyche.

And it goes on.

I find myself curled on the floor, my eyes just opening. At some point, the ritual had stopped, but I don't recall. Mrs. Kim returns from the next room with a blanket, which she unfolds and places over me. She adjusts my head so it fits squarely on the pillow. Her face is more grim than before.

"I don't know if it will work," she says. "I don't know."

She pats me on the head, then turns down the lights. I find I cannot speak.

Soft purplish-blue orbs, translucent and pulsing, begin to appear. They float, slightly pulsing. More begin to appear, just hovering in the air. And then I see more of them until the room begins to fill. In my haze, I don't react, as I'm sure I must be hallucinating. That is, until I see Mrs. Kim's face light up in ecstasy. She throws her arms open, skyward.

"Help him!" she screams. "Help him!"

31

I OPEN MY EYES TO THE STING OF SUNLIGHT. I FEEL ALERT AND rested, as though I've slept for five days. But this isn't how I usually wake up. Right about now, that blue flame pilot light has clicked on, and the energy is starting to burn on high. This is the sweetest change, and I think for a moment if there's some way to bottle this, take it home and have a sip at each sunrise.

"Are you okay?" Mrs. Kim asks.

"Am I?"

She asks if I would like some tea. I ask if I can watch her television. Checking the morning news, Shawna makes no mention of Juan Machado. They've given up—or, if that's too harsh a judgment, in a city as big as Los Angeles, they just have too many news stories, too many other stories of heartbreak or joy, and the news has to cover something that is, well, *new*, and there's nothing new to report with Juan.

Finishing my tea, I excuse myself and say I need to return to my apartment. She walks me to the door, never smiling.

"So, what do you think?" I ask.

She pats my chest gently and lowers her head.

At my apartment, I move to my large window, looking for a long time at the Hollywood Hills—the big sign, the observatory, then down to the lonely pedestrians walking the sidewalks and the light traffic of cars leaving the garages of their apartments and heading out for the day. The palm trees sway in the breeze of a Santa Ana wind that is just picking up, and this means the day will be hot.

The sky is clear and bright. In that sky, a clean slate of blue, I look for the face of my father. I then check for Bobby Kennedy, and though I don't know what Martin Conrad looks like, I scan the sky to see if there is another face up there too. I don't see them, any of them, and yet I wonder, *When I don't make it to the end of this day, is that where I will be? Somewhere up there?*

I head to the closet, and there is a rush through my body, so strong that I'm shaking, and I worry that the shirt will be the right one—it's my *last* one after all, and so it has to be the right one—but even more, I worry I will need to take my meds today because, in spite of the progress I made yesterday, I doubt I can hold it together as I'm shaking already, and so my thoughts might easily become that white blizzard again, where I can't see—think—anything, and so I decide, as soon as I have selected my shirt, I will try just a super small dose, just a quarter of my meds. A quarter should be fine, I hope, and I only have concerns that it may be a bad dosage because I associate it with that ugly day at Cup O' Joe's when I also took only a quarter. But I can't allow myself to be superstitious because it's probably all the caffeine that sent me over the edge that day and not my dosage amount, and even now, I feel my mind racing away. This *cannot* happen today, so despite Robbie's advice, I will need to take something today, and I think just a quarter may be the answer.

I swing the closet door open, but before I even step inside, I realize something is seriously wrong. The closet is *empty*. Well, almost empty. The shirts are all gone except for one. I step in, turn on the light, and check all corners of the closet, but I confirm that there's nothing else here. There is one lonely shirt hanging there.

I stare at the shirt for a long time, then finally smile and whisper, "Thank you." It is a simple white T-shirt with a bright yellow Happy Face in the middle. The shirt the strange lady gave me in the church. I pull it over my head and push my arms through the sleeves, then walk over to the full-length mirror to check myself.

"Looks like it's going to be a special day," I say, sadly.

It feels like a long time until I need to head back to the bar, but I don't know of anything I can do before then. I'm sure the time will fly, and, resigned, I decide to savor my last moments the best I can.

I'm not in the mood for breakfast and will have time for lunch later, so I get out my copy of *The Sun Also Rises* and flip to a page at random, just to relax and think about nothing.

But I get a little unlucky here and land on one of the saddest passages in the book. Jake is alone with his one true love, Lady Brett Ashley, and he wants her to go away with him, to get away from the madness of Paris, to go off into the country. To live together.

But, of course, they can't live together. He has a condition, and because of this, they can never be happy together. There is absolutely nothing they can do. Their emotions don't matter. Words don't matter.

Lady Brett says that it isn't any use telling him she loves him. There isn't any use.

I set the book aside. I pick up my phone, resting there on the small circular coffee table, feeling like making a journal entry but not knowing what to say. I flip through the endless pages of journal notes, amused by the sheer quantity. *Words*. They go on forever. Endless words, taking up most of the storage space on the phone. And yet, all I want is a picture of Julie, just to see her one last time. I wish I had snapped it that day outside the museum, in the eerie in-between glow of the newly-lit lampposts and the sunlight of a fading day. Her perfect white skin. Her smile, non-smile, just like the happiness–sadness of her eyes.

I call my mother, but get her voicemail, so I tell her I just wanted to say hi. I didn't really have much to say to my mother, but I thought I would try, just to hear her voice and, of course, to tell her that I love her. I can't reach Robbie either, but I leave him a message, thanking him for the good time during his stay and all the advice. If the law thing doesn't work out, he should give philosophy a shot, I say.

Jamal and Ray don't answer, and I choose not to leave a message. I think for a long time now about Julie and whether to call her or not, but I don't. There's nothing to say, really, and she's seen enough of me—the real me, the *core* me.

Ray then sends me a text saying, *Let's meet for chapulines! Noon straight up*.

Though it's early, I decide to get going. If I take my time and just walk through the streets of K-town, that might be good. I'll miss this place. It is the most beautiful part of this city—maybe not beautiful in the way most people would define the word, but I truly see it as my home. As I walk, the homeless begin shuffling, the traffic picks up, and people are walking the streets, many with their heads down. I look up to see the palms swaying, and I feel special because I know most people don't look up, way up, and the palm trees are beautiful.

I settle into a chair at the Mexican restaurant and notice the pretty waitress with the curious smile is here. I tell her that I'm expecting my friend, and so she shows me to a table and places two menus down.

My cell phone chimes with a text message, and I see it's Ray.

Sorry. Good fare came up. Heading to LAX. Talk tonight.

I look at the people at the other tables. A couple exchange bites of their respective dishes. A family at a table behind me is celebrating the birthday of an elderly woman, probably their grandma. I think about leaving and heading over to Yellow House for a light snack since there's no way I'd be here if it weren't for Ray.

The waitress returns and places chips and salsa on the table, along with two waters.

"It's good to see you again," she smiles. It is the same smile as last time, and even though I know it's not a special smile just for me, I accept that there is beauty in a smile just for a smile's sake.

"Thanks; it's good to see you too," I reply, and I mean it.

"You want to order or wait for your friend?"

"My friend's not coming, so it's just me."

"Okay. Are you ready?"

"Is it true you have the best mezcal in Los Angeles?"

"Yes, this is true."

"I'll take a shot."

"What kind? We have many."

"Do you like mezcal?"

"Yes, very much."

"Then pick your favorite, and I'll try that. And bring two."

She gives a wry smile.

"I'll have the chapulines too."

"Very nice! The small dish, or the lunch meal."

"Lunch meal."

She walks away, and, again, I love the sway of her skirt as she leaves—the smooth, side-to-side rhythm.

I try to remember the words to the Our Father, but I can't reach back to them. I can remember choking a kid when I was five years old, but I can't remember a prayer I said just about every night before I gave up at twelve. I try to remember the Hail Mary, but struggle even more here.

Turning around, I watch the family celebrate Grandma's birthday. A small dessert is placed before her with a single lit candle, and they all sing Happy Birthday in thick Mexican accents. The grandma holds her little granddaughter tightly, gazing only into her big, smiling eyes. She looks happy.

The waitress returns shortly with my *chapulines* and two shots of mezcal. She makes her eyes big in anticipation, and I can tell that she will stay a moment to watch, probably questioning my nerve.

"Mezcal first," I say. I raise my glass and extend the other to her.

"No. I cannot. I'm working."

It hits me that this is a normal restaurant, unlike the Q Bar, and so the waitresses, I'm sure, are not allowed to drink on the job.

"Listen," I say softly. "Drink with me, just a little. I won't say anything."

"No. I can't."

"Just a little. You don't have to finish. It's important to me. I don't want to drink alone."

"You are a little crazy today, no?"

She looks over her shoulder to the main register, where I'm sure the assistant manager must be lurking. I don't see anyone there, and so I presume she thinks it's safe, and she takes the glass from my hand.

Her smile is now very naughty, as if saying *you're a bad boy and we shouldn't be doing this, but you're a little crazy today, and I respect that.* We clink glasses.

"Never be daunted," I say.

We both just take a quick sip, then place our glasses down. The mezcal is good. She points to the plate of *chapulines.* I take one of the soft flour tortillas and scoop up a tablespoonful of dead grasshoppers onto the tortilla, then add some salsa and hot sauce. I don't think about it. I just take a bite. My eyes get big—the chapulines are *delicious.* The waitress gives a quick clap of her hands and says that she must get back to work, but she'll return in a little while.

I take another flour tortilla and scoop more chapulines into it, place a hefty serving of salsa and hot sauce, and can't believe that not only is it nothing special in the sense that there was never anything to be afraid of, but even more, it actually tastes great. Ray was right.

I lift a half-eaten tortilla full of them up close to my mouth as I take my cell phone in my other hand to snap a picture to send to Ray. I want him to remember me. As I lift the tortilla up, looking into the camera and not at the tortilla, I tilt my head back as if about to bite into it. I snap the picture. However, I feel a quick nudge at my elbow and spill hot sauce onto my shirt. I jerk around to see if Ray had shown up and was trying to be funny. But no one is there. And yet, I'm sure I felt something. I look down at my shirt and see that it's only a small amount of sauce, but when I quickly dab and brush at it with my thumb, it only smudges.

I close my eyes. There is a sour feeling in my gut. I feel as if I'm losing my balance, and I place both palms on the table to steady myself. The palms are sweaty. I am given a beautiful and miraculous shirt—a shirt I've always wanted—and I stain it with hot sauce. I feel scared and low, knowing this must be a bad omen. *I can't mess this up now.* I need to hold it together; so much depends on this.

I rise and go to the restroom to see in the mirror how bad it looks, and while it's not a huge stain, it is right in the middle of the Happy Face, and the way the stain angles to one side from my thumb smudging it sideways, it looks exactly like the face has a nose.

I ask the pretty waitress for my check and sip a little more of the mezcal since I still have a little time. I *know* this is dangerous, but just like the whole search for Juan from the beginning, it's something I have to do. I think of my grandpa and what he said about Bobby Kennedy, and how if I get the chance to put myself out there, way out there on a limb for something good, something bigger than me, I have to do it. I just *have* to.

About a block away from the bar, I say to God, "I'm sorry for not remembering the Our Father, and I'm sorry for everything else I've done," but I can't focus just right now. I wish I could remember more of the stuff I really am sorry for. I've heard that just before you die, you're supposed to ask forgiveness for everything you've done wrong. I suppose it wraps up everything from this life nice and neat—going into whatever's next with a clean slate and all that. I think, *Dad, if you're there, maybe I'll be seeing you soon.*

As I get closer to the door, I see the same doorman as yesterday. Someone else darts out and begins to walk quickly away. I don't get a good look at him, but from the side and back, he looks to have big James Dean hair, styled up and uneven.

"What? No Hulk T-shirt today?" says the doorman.

"Hulk smash," I say, then rush through the door and head straight for the bar.

"Oh, hey, you just missed him," the cute bartender with the flat cap says.

"What?"

"Yeah, I told him an old friend was coming to see him, and he just took off."

I turn to leave but hear someone call, *Wait!* I see it's the same old man as last night, frantically waving me over.

"What?" I say.

"Don't go!" He grabs me by the arm. "I saw the receipt! He showed me the receipt. He just bought ammunition this morning."

I bolt outside and can still see him about a block away. I speed-walk behind him, making slow but steady progress in catching up until I'm just close enough to keep a safe distance. From there, I watch him closely. As soon as he even starts to turn to look back, which he does every twenty feet or so, I stop. There is a decent crowd on the street today, making it easy to dodge his view. We continue this dance for what feels like a half mile, and I'm cursing myself all the way for being so stupid to not tell the bartender to keep quiet and that I want to surprise him—or some excuse like that.

He turns off onto a less-congested residential street with apartments and houses all around. I stay way back now, just enough to keep him in my sight, but he's about a full block away again. Plus, he's turning back to look now after every few steps, and so I pull back even further, afraid he may have seen me or that he suspects he's being followed. I lean against the wall of a building, just around the corner from the street he's on and out of sight. I hang back, uncertain of my next move. I wait. When I slowly poke my head around the corner, he's gone.

Gone.

A throbbing ache weighs on my gut. I lean against the wall for support. I turn to watch the street for a long while, looking for signs of movement—a bustle of bushes he may have ducked into, a swinging screen door left ajar from sudden entry. But there's nothing.

Gone.

I begin to walk down the street, fully exposed now. I've got to hope he didn't recognize me earlier, so that now, even if he were to see me, I wouldn't necessarily raise suspicion. I'm just a guy walking down a street. My walk is at a casual but steady pace, and I try to keep my head forward and not turn side to side as if I'm looking for someone. I allow my eyes to glance over to the right, studying the doors and windows of the apartment buildings—some old and with big names cast on the walls like *The Stratford* and *Venetian*, or some more modern and taller structures with beige California stucco designs, and the single-story houses whose glory years were decades ago. This would be so much easier if I had sunglasses. I'd be able to shift my eyes to the side while still keeping my head pointed straight ahead, and there would be no way anyone could tell what I was doing.

Reaching the end of the block, I walk across the street, continuing forward, but I'm sensing this can't be right. I hadn't ducked behind that wall so long that he could have gotten this far. I'm slowing, rubbing my temples. This isn't working.

I turn around and look back at the block I've traveled. *Where are you?*

I begin walking back but decide to go down the other side of the street, and it hits me to take my cell phone out and stare at it as I'm walking, then look up at each residence I pass, pretending to be lost, as if looking for an address. Doing this gives me a much better view of the buildings because I'm turning my head now and looking directly at them, their facades, the cars parked in the driveways, the landscaping, and the address numbers by the entrances. I'm focused more on this side of the street, but occasionally glance across to the buildings I checked earlier.

I come to an old house with dark green paint chipping off the wood, and it has a slightly different look from the others, maybe just a little more run down. As I pass, I can't seem to look away. I slow down, pulling my view down to the phone so as not to seem too obvious, but then can't resist looking up again to the door. The address reads 314.

Inching ahead, I start to walk past the house, but there's something holding me back. *314.*

The barrage of stars begins shooting through me now, but I've got to find that one star that matters, because if this keeps on, it will all become white, the overload of memory, thought, emotion, all of it. Closing my eyes, I exhale long and slowly. I need to empty my mind and find that zone, the zone where everything flows naturally and easily, where I can answer any question from an interviewer or hit ping pong balls with precision, and it is all flowing and focused, yet unfocused. Exhale. Everything means something.

Sure. That's it.

Pi.

As I approach the house, I do not consider checking for alternate entrances or planning what I might do or say. I slowly and quietly walk up the steps. At the door, I grasp the knob as softly as I can and then turn. It's unlocked.

For a millisecond, my stomach feels heavy, and my mind tries to process why the door would be unlocked, but I reject these feelings and thoughts, then exhale once again. I turn the knob all the way and then push inward. There is no creaking or telltale sound, but there is a darkness that is so dark that I know I have clearly exposed myself in the doorway. This is not a normal darkness. It is deeper than dark. What little light that filters in from behind me from the open door reveals that this house appears to be empty, but no other ambient light seeps into this place. So it must be altered by some form of special drapes or screen that blocks out all sunlight. I take slow, deliberate steps into the house but can't make out anything because of the darkness. It appears to be a large house, or at least this first room is large or deep.

And then the door slams shut behind me.

I don't know if someone has closed it or if it just shut on its own in the way some doors have a hydraulic that brings it back to a closed position, and I can't see anything—not a solitary thing—and it is pitch black. On reflex, I shrug my shoulders up, expecting a gunshot to my back or head, as if that's the sort of thing a shoulder shrug could help you brace for.

There's a long silence, and I'm listening as hard as I can because I can't see. I allow my shoulders to gradually fall. I can sense that there is someone here, and I feel this person is in front of me, not close, but from a direction ahead of me—the slightest shuffling of nearly-still clothes, the faint wisp of breath coming from the nostrils, the tempo of nerves.

Just exhale, I tell myself.

I'm unarmed and deep into a darkness, where being weak will not help me in any way.

Relax.

Exhale.

"Who *are* you?" A male voice asks, young and with a Hispanic accent.

"I've come for the boy," I say, and I'm satisfied with the way it comes out determined and strong.

"You *can't* be real," he says, in a tone of disbelief. "Who *are* you?"

I can't see him in the absolute darkness, but he must be able to see me somehow, maybe with some night-vision goggles or something. It hits me that I must appear like a mirror to him—someone who looks a lot like him.

"Listen," I say. "I don't know how any of this works. But . . . but we've crossed somehow, like our energy waves have overlapped. I've connected to you. Maybe there was a small, better part of you that existed once, was still out there in the universe, and never fully went away. And you can have it back. You can *really* have that back, but, you just have to give me the boy."

"I will save the boy. I will set him free."

I pause, not sure I heard him right.

"Really?" I ask.

"I will set him free of everything wicked in this life. The suffering. Set him free . . . to a better place."

"No, hey, don't do that!"

"I have seen the teasing and the laughing. I have known this too."

"Hey, hey. I've dealt with this myself. *All my life!* But this isn't the way!"

"You're not *real*!"

"You're not *rational*! Get out of your head. You have to find that place in your heart. You know you don't want to do this. There has to be something inside of you that realizes this. Right? You would have done it already. Think about that. You would have done it already. But you have to find it. This isn't you."

He doesn't say anything. He seems to be waiting me out.

"I'm not afraid of you," he finally says, but there is something wrong with it—the inflection, an almost imperceptible quake in his voice at the very end like a doubt. I pick it up only because my ears are attuned; my sense of hearing is heightened due to my blindness. I feel sure.

"I have a gun pointed at you right now," he says.

"Listen to me!" I shout. "I am NOT afraid of dying, and the absolute worst thing you could ever do is kill me because then I will be with you forever. You're mistaken if you think it's just me, because it's not. I have help, and it's from forces unseen and people—some you might even know—that are no longer part of this world, but they're here now—in this room—and so I am not alone. You can kill me if you want, but then I would just join the others, and I will hunt you down and never let you rest. I will be the ghost that lives with you in your head every single moment, when you're awake and in your nightmares. You will never *ever* be free . . . unless you let the little boy go."

There is a longer pause now, and in this precise time-space realm where I am not thinking, thoughts come to me in a natural and relaxed way. I determine that this is good. He wants to talk. He is weak.

But then, something changes, and the silence extends and becomes more profound, as if a vacuum is sucking out all particles of even the slightest noise, and the darkness is now thicker, deeper, darkening still, and seeping into me. How can this even be possible? Everything is shifting and loosening beneath me as my stomach seems to become weightless and float. I'm changing. I'm leaving him.

A metallic click echoes, the gun hammer cocking back, and I sense I'm losing it now, whatever energy I had with me, propelling me forward. I'm alone, after all.

A bolt of light suddenly floods the room. I recoil and cover my hands over my eyes. My shoulders shrug up fully—high—so high that they almost touch my ears as I brace once again. And yet, I don't hear anything. There is no gunshot blast. I don't feel anything or any pain.

I realize it is only light—a light that is immensely bright and blinding. Still struggling to see, I can barely make out the outline of a figure. A man.

There is a short silence, and then I hear a gasp.

I don't know what's happening—the man and the light—and I still feel unsteady. I'm scared because I know this will never work, and I'll never get out of here with Juan unless I can find it again—that perfect zone.

I can make out that the figure is slowly lowering the gun, a long gun, with one hand. He lifts the other hand to point straight at me.

"Did she . . . did my . . . *mother* . . . send you?" he asks, and his voice is shaking.

I close my eyes. I try to clear my mind. I exhale. I can hear the word *Yes* escape my lips. I don't understand this. But this is what I hear.

"*Mi mamá?*" the voice asks, and he is weeping.

I don't know what's happening, but there is now an altered state. For him and me.

"*Si, su mamá,*" I say softly.

My eyes are adjusting more to the brightness of the floodlights bearing down upon me, and I can make out the man is now down on his knees, in the same position as the tea ceremony, except his upper body is lowered fully to the ground. His arms and face are on the floor in front of him. He's crying.

Exhale.

There is a shotgun next to him, and I tiptoe over to take it. I then turn to the side and begin to walk down a dark corridor, my hand feeling its way against the wall. At the end of the corridor, there is a sliver of light seeping out from underneath a closed door.

With each step, I feel immensely lighter; the weight of Carlos that was inside of me is now gone.

I lean against this door and hear a soft, happy humming coming from the other side. I open the door, and there is Juan. He is sitting sideways on the floor, coloring in a book. We look at each other for a moment, and then he recognizes me. He rises and rushes over to give me a strong hug. Then he pulls away, makes a fist, and hits me as hard as he can in the chest and says, "Smash!" I pull back, coughing, amazed at how hard a ten-year-old can hit, but then shoosh him to be quiet, and he nods. I put my arm around him, and we walk out the bedroom door.

As we approach the main living room, I tuck Juan behind me and peer into the room, where I see Carlos sitting upright and leaning against the corner wall closest to where I left him kneeling just moments before. He is sobbing and saying softly, *Mamá*. He pulls his knees tighter against his chest, and he pushes his back hard against the wall, as if wanting to disappear into it.

I pull Juan out to join me, placing my arm around his shoulder as we walk out of the house.

On the sidewalk, police officers rush up to me and grab the boy as I hand another officer the gun. *Where have they come from?* Things move fast now; it's all a blur, and I am leaving whatever quiet ethereal domain I had entered that allowed me to capture for a short period of time a certain relaxed focus. Detective Harrison rushes up to me and asks if the kidnapper is still inside, and if he is armed.

"He's there, and I don't think he's armed anymore," I hear myself saying.

Another officer pulls me away briskly while others still charge the house, along with Detective Harrison, all with guns drawn. I watch one of the officers talk to Juan, and I can't hear what he says, but his gestures and the expression on his face tell me he is speaking to Juan in a kind and gentle way. He is probably doing a quick check to see if he has any obvious injuries, but I'm sure they'll take him away to a hospital to be examined thoroughly any moment now. Officer Smith takes my arm, walks me over to a police car, and says he needs to ask me questions. He doesn't appear as mean as he did in my apartment, and though I wouldn't say he was smiling, he has a look of contentment, or satisfaction, maybe. He says to me, "Way to go."

When Carlos is led out of the house, head down, hands cuffed behind his back, an officer on each side holding an arm, my eyes bore into him. He's dark-skinned and muscular, like he lifts weights every day, with big biceps bulging from the long white shirt sleeves. His hair is straight, long, and black. *I don't look anything like him.* At least, not anymore.

I lose sight of him in a crowd of officers.

I spy Juan as he's placed in the back seat of a police car. He sees me and waves enthusiastically with the biggest, over-the-top smile on his face. I can hear his crazy, wild, and beautiful hyena laugh even through the locked doors of the car. As the squad car starts to pull away, I make a fist and then throw a punch into the air and yell, "Smash!" He claps his hands quickly and laughs even louder.

32

It's 1:30 in the morning. I arrive at my apartment following a long walk in the cool mist of the evening. My face is damp. Cool and damp. I unlock the door to my apartment and step in, but before I can close it, I stop hard, freezing up, as I see the silhouette of a man, back turned to me, standing at my large window, looking out to the hills. The shape is of a purplish-blue tone. I blink fast, then squint hard, questioning my sight. Though the apartment is dark, lit only by the glow of the city lights outside, the man—this man-figure—appears to be *shimmering.* It's the shimmer of a person or thing that is out in the blazing desert sun, where the heat melts the hard figure of life into a sizzling pulse of something that is only half there, more real than a mirage, but just barely.

A smoke arises from the opposite side, the front side of this being, and I recognize the menthol scent.

"You can close the door," the shimmering man says in a soft but gravelly voice. "It's okay."

But I can't move, astonished now that the thing speaks.

"No, really," he says. "It's okay."

I slowly close the door but do not take my eyes off him. He doesn't turn his back; he just stares out at the city lights and the Hollywood Hills beyond.

"God, I miss this place," he says. "I didn't used to. But, you know, hindsight's everything."

I take small, slow steps into the apartment, angling toward the side and bending in an effort to get a look at his face, but he does me the favor of turning. His eyes are dark and calm but hard-focused on me. He's got a short, cropped beard and medium-length black gelled hair. His clothes are all dark, and it's hard to make out any detail in the unlit room and with the shimmering. He takes the cigarette from his lips and blows out a thin wisp of smoke.

"Sorry for my appearance," he says. "I'm not as still as I'd like to be, but I'm getting closer, I think. Trying, anyway. Have a seat."

I ease onto the edge of a dinette chair, but I'm not placing much weight on it, just in case I need to bolt into a hard dash out of here at any moment. He strides to the sofa and sits, fully reclined, apparently relaxed, despite the shimmering and all.

He's got a thin smile, and we look at each other for a long time before he flips his wrist up off the arm rest.

"You probably have a lot of questions," he says.

I do, and yet, because there is a stillness to the thought flow streaming through me at the moment, it doesn't feel all anxious and frazzled. So I feel a focus, which is something I'm not used to.

"Let me first tell you," he says, raising his hand, "I won't have all the answers. I'm only a conduit. I'm here to help. I want to help. We're all on different paths, Cole, and if you're really lucky, then a little bit of it will make sense. But no one can ever fully understand it—not all of it. You've got to accept this and just keep moving forward."

"So, your path is to help me?" I ask.

"We're a lot alike."

He coughs, more like he's clearing his throat than choking on the cigarette.

"I'm just," he pauses to think about his words, "I'm just trying to make up for some things. From my past."

"Did you do something bad? In your past, I mean."

"I didn't actually *do* anything—take action that is—but the thinking, my thoughts . . ." He closes his eyes and shakes his head. "My thoughts were not good. Not letting go of a slight, allowing it to fester . . . I grew tired and bitter. And the real sin was the time lost and how it affected me—to be all ensnared in horrific thoughts."

I think about the word *ensnared* and how that is such a perfect word and how I have never used it before, even though that could apply to me at any given moment of any given day.

"It's so hard to control thoughts," I offer.

"Ain't that the truth."

"Is that why . . . the shotgun, I mean."

"Oh, that. Yeah, see, that was all about *Anger*—a terrible, terrible thing. The madness of the world smothers you, and you lose who you are. You lose it in the darkness, where it's impossible to see the fine lines between sanity and madness, the madness and evil. All of it running through my head, I didn't want to just 'quiet' those voices—I wanted to *obliterate* them."

"I understand."

"But it's okay. It's okay now. There's no anger now. I just wish I could've figured that out before."

He shakes his head, eyes closed, and presses hard.

"The time lost . . ." he continues. "There's a point in a person's life when he looks back more than he looks forward. And looking back on the true purpose of it all, the question that rises to the surface is, *Why?* If there is no answer, then the trigger gets pulled."

Though I settle back onto the chair, placing my full weight there now, I fidget as I struggle to get out the next question.

"So, *you* sent me the shirts."

"Well, I helped with that. Placing them here, in this place I have some synergy with. But your dad was really driving this."

"My dad? My *dad*? Then why isn't he here?"

"He's just on a different path. He wanted to, but . . . it's hard to explain."

I shift around on the chair as I feel the calmness leaving me now. I feel pressed to get as much in—as many questions in—before I lose this state and he leaves. And then I don't know when I can ask again, or whether I'll ever see him again, or if there's a way to just call him, like putting him on speed dial on my cellphone, but I'm pretty sure that's not the case because if any of this were as easy as that, he probably would have just shown himself earlier and just calmly explained it all to me, but while I can, at any time, be completely flooded by the inner workings of my mind, he—on the other hand—seems as calm as the night mist.

"Wait—," I say, a bit too loudly. "I need to know more."

"Okay."

"Are things going to change for me?" I rub my temples, not sure that makes any sense, but the wanting to do more, be better, and all of it—am I going to make it? Will I get it to turn around, or will I be ensnared in this trap forever until I can't take it, and the anger builds, and then—

"I know what you're saying," he says, "but I'm sorry. It's just hard to say. I don't make any of the rules. I'm just a conduit."

I shake my head. *Why does it have to be so hard?*

"It's okay," I say. I can feel the revving in my spirit now. "Thanks for answering my questions," I say. "I think—maybe—it's helped."

"Hold on now; we're not finished. It takes a special energy for me to get here. Smart as you are, you could never understand how this works. So this ain't something I can just pull off whenever I want. But the reason I'm here is about your dad. He and I—we want you to know you've done something special here. You're a special force, Cole. Sure, you're not perfect—*nobody* is. But you're still special. The way you empathize with others, slipping into the lives of strangers and losing yourself so deeply, leaving you with a spiritual amnesia. And putting yourself out there like that . . . way, way out there."

"Huh."

"You have a *gift*. And your dad, he really wants me to tell you that you were always good enough—actually, *more* than good enough."

"No! Don't say that."

He pulls back, maybe a bit surprised, or maybe I just said it a bit too loud and abruptly.

"He says he's sorry too," the shimmering man adds.

I start to say something, a sentiment of thanks, but I just choke up on the words.

He nods in understanding, then continues. "He was happy you didn't veto the I YELL shirt again because that's what started all of this, really. It was a message from him. He also held you back there at the crime scene. He just wanted to set all of this in motion to get things moving. It's not good to use the veto—*everything* has some meaning."

"Okay," I say, but I'm struggling through the connection of it all. "So, you really know my dad?"

"Now I do. Sure."

"And what about Mr. Kennedy?"

"I'm proud to say I do. He's a *very* special spirit."

I study him, wrinkling up my face. "But," I start, "how is that possible? There must be so many . . ."

"Well, sure. But we have plenty of what you call *Time*, because here that doesn't exist."

"Huh. That sounds great. You just go around connecting with others."

"It's so, so beautiful here, Cole. And yeah, we just . . . roam."

The shimmering, the vibration itself, slows, and I can see his figure starting to fade, and my mind begins to speed up because I'm trying to capture any other questions or ideas I want to discuss with him, but I can't, and the next thing I know, Martin Conrad is gone.

33

I DIDN'T WAKE UP UNTIL 10:00 TODAY. I SLEPT LONG AND DEEP LAST night. I took a full dosage of my meds this morning because I wanted the numbness and quiet to fill me. My mother returned my call earlier this morning and wanted to see me today. I said I would like that very much. I didn't tell her about anything that happened yesterday, and I'm not sure I will. But I took my meds for her because that's what she wants, and it will at least make me appear as normal as I can. For her.

I spend a lot of time now, this morning at the diner with the Latina waitress, who once studied math and science but is now stuck here. I am grateful she allows me to take up a table for such a long time, even though I have barely touched my toast and am now just sipping my watered-down orange juice. I need the time to catch up with my journal, thumbs typing, though not as fast as they usually do, and putting as much into my phone as I can remember. A lot of this is hard to describe, and so if someone is reading this someday, I hope you'll forgive me.

"You are very quiet today, honey," she says to me. "Everything okay?"

"Yes, I'm fine. Some days I'm just quiet."

"You sure? Just don't let any troubles get you down. Don't give up. Anything can happen."

This makes me smile, because I sense now that her *That's Life* comment didn't really mean that this is the end of her life, as I had feared. It just means the usual *life is crazy and never what you expect*.

"Believe me," I say, "the one thing I know for absolute certain is that anything can happen."

Shawna Cleary calls me and says she heard from Detective Harrison that I was involved in helping to find Juan. She says she wants to know more and would like to do an interview as well. I say maybe someday I'll tell her more, but there's no way I'll do an interview. I don't want the attention. She says she's proud of me, and I thank her.

I finally finish my toast and sit here for a while, uncertain that I'm capturing everything I need to in my journal, and maybe it would have been better not to attempt this on full meds. I do want to try to get in as much as I can while it's still fresh, but I may need to just check all of this tomorrow and add some more if something comes to me.

I decide to go over to The Line hotel and sit by their pool, maybe order a sparkling water. The weather's warm, but the sky is overcast, the May gray hanging in a little longer than usual into the early afternoon. I take a seat at a table close to the same trellis as last time, facing away from the other diners. I wear some sport sunglasses with rose-tinted lenses that actually make the day look brighter. I decide to wear them more often since there is no point attacking the festering underlying skin cancer and my prematurely aging skin if I let the sun force me to squint and develop crow's feet around my eyes. Besides, it's better to cover up because on days when the numbness fully sets in, I imagine my eyes carry a dull, sleepy appearance, like I'm on meds or something.

I stare straight on at the trellis and see a hummingbird come into view. I can't tell if it's the same one as last time, but it doesn't matter. It darts from flower to flower, and this time I can't keep up, and this frustrates me. I try, but now I'm fully aware—as if I ever needed to be made aware—of how much my spirit slows when I'm drugged like this. And yet, there is no other way. And what's more, I know that if this were a day when I could sync with the bird's every move, its every bounce to a new flower, I would be filled with such profound sadness that I would search every corner of my soul for a way to escape. Where is the balance, the right setting? There is no answer, no escape. I try to think of a word

I once created to capture the absolute greatest feeling you could feel in this life. I want to linger on that word now, maybe to give me a little hope. But it won't come. That word is a quadrillion miles away.

I sip my sparkling water and see from the corners of my eyes the people that walk past me, behind me, on their way to the pool area, and I have no doubt they're wondering about me. A guy turned to face the wall instead, staring at the boring trellis of vines. I then hear a familiar voice.

"Mr. Reeves?" Detective Harrison asks.

"That's me. How are you, Detective?"

"Fine, fine. I didn't recognize you behind the sunglasses and that nice polo shirt."

I look down at my shirt, contemplating the word *nice*.

"It was a gift from my mother for my last birthday," I say. "I'm seeing her later tonight, so I thought it would be nice to wear it."

"Looks good. Mind if I join you?"

"Okay."

He pulls out a chair and takes a seat. I now angle my chair a bit sideways out of courtesy to see him better.

"Did Shawna Cleary tell you I was here?" I ask.

"Yes, she did. She mentioned that you're a little shy about TV interviews. I don't blame you." He waves to the waiter to bring him an iced tea. "I would like to talk to you a bit, though, if that's okay."

"I answered the questions Officer Smith had yesterday."

"Sure, sure. Although some of the answers were a little . . . incomplete." He stops to pull out his sunglasses and put them on. "It's overcast, but my eyes are still a little sensitive."

"You should protect yourself from the sun," I say.

"Listen, first, I want to thank you for your help. I'm not exaggerating when I say we couldn't have done it without you. We've got a lot of good officers, good tactics, and great technology, but sometimes first-time offenders are impossible to catch. No trace in our system. No DNA to compare."

"Is Juan going to be okay?"

"The doctors say he wasn't touched. They're still examining him, but they think he will be fine."

I nod.

"I also wanted to say I was sorry when we interviewed you the first time."

"It's okay. I'm sure it's just your job."

"That's right. And we had nothing to go on at the time, you know."

"Did you really think I did it?"

"Actually... no. Not really. The way Ms. Cleary described your meeting . . . it was definitely different. But it just didn't feel right to me. And then the call came about your DNA not matching the samples from the boy's apartment."

I mull this over, trying to recall where they would have gotten a sample of my DNA.

"It was from the shirt you gave Ms. Cleary, if you're wondering."

"Oh, sure," was all I could muster. If I wasn't on full meds I would have something clever to say—maybe a joke that I deserve some of Ms. Cleary's DNA as a reward. I think he would laugh at something like that. Jamal or Ray sure would.

"We'd like to give you a commendation—a medal," he says. "The city does that for citizens that—"

"No."

"—put themselves out there for others. You know . . . heroes."

"No, thank you."

The waiter brings us menus. We flip them open, studying the selections.

"The guy who kidnapped the boy," I start, "was his name Carlos?"

"That's right. Carlos Rivera. He's being evaluated. Honestly, I think he wanted to be caught—cry for help and all that. He says he saw the child being taunted in the park one day and wanted to 'save' him. Definitely crazy."

"A 51-50?"

"Now how would you know something like that?"

I shrug.

"He says . . ." and the detective shakes his head, smirking. "He says *you* are an angel."

"An angel?"

"That's right. An angel, sent by his mother. His *deceased* mother."

My eyes narrow.

"He says you had on a shirt yesterday. A shirt that belonged to him."

"What? It was just a Happy Face T-shirt."

"Yeah, well, he says he had that same shirt when he was a child. His mother had given it to him, and it was his favorite shirt. Wore it all the time. He said it even had a stain on the face, right where the nose should be. That's how he knows it's his."

The menu slips from my fingers.

The waiter returns, and the detective orders a Cobb salad, and I order the clam chowder. Oh, and more water.

"How long had you known Carlos?" Detective Harrison asks.

"What? I didn't *know* him. I just tracked him down."

Harrison stares at me.

"Is that the truth?" he says.

"What do you mean? Of course it's the truth."

"Well, then this is some strange coincidence the likes of which I've never seen. The two of you are connected."

I sit straight up in my chair, thinking maybe he knows, and if he really does know, then maybe he can explain some of it to me.

"It's still not coming to you?" he asks.

I shake my head.

"He was the one at Cup O'Joes that day—"

"No. No, you're mistaken. I see that monster at night, in my dreams. I will never forget his face. The way he sneered—"

"No, not him. Not the guy you assaulted. There was a customer there quietly taking a video of the whole incident. Rivera was the one who shot the video that backed up your story and got you off."

I shut my eyes tight, trying to shake off the meds and really get through to some deeper layer where the fog isn't so thick and I can make some sense of this.

"I'll tell ya," Harrison says, "there's a fine line... there's a fine line..."

I nod.

"Cole," the detective starts, "oh, and may I call you Cole?"

"Sure."

"Cole, Ms. Cleary thinks very highly of you, and she shared with me everything from your conversation together. It sounded like the two of you had a pretty good talk. I feel like I know you, like I have a sense of where you are right now."

My cellphone rings. I check the screen and see that it's Julie. I close my eyes. I'm torn, just like everything else tears at me, because though I would like to hear her voice again, I can't, because I'm all out of wishes here and I can never win the never-ending battle to thread that needle and line things up perfectly so that they are the right time and the right day, when I'm at my best, just-right equilibrium and focus, and it's just so hard to manage and I can't do it—I *really* can't—and I'd much rather be sent out on the next trek to find the future Dalai Lama because that would just be so much easier.

"You can take that call if you need to," Detective Harrison says.

There isn't any use. . . I shake my head before hitting the Off button.

He struggles for a moment to get back on his train of thought. "Listen, can you forget for a moment that I'm a detective, and can we just talk? Just two guys talking?"

"Sure."

"So, you have some great instincts, Cole. Approaching Ms. Cleary to see the news team's videotape of the scene that afternoon. Of course, we did that first, but we didn't know who we were looking for. I checked it again last night, and sure enough, Carlos Rivera was right there."

I nod, uncertain as to whether he's asking a question. The tone in his voice sounds like a question.

"So, I guess what I'm asking," he says, "is how did you do it? What led you to him?"

This was a question Officer Smith asked yesterday. I can't remember my exact response, but I know it was vague. Now, my mind feels slow and yet surprisingly light and empty.

"My . . . shirts."

"Your shirts?"

I shake my head. I stare at the trellis and try to follow just one vine, but it gets intertwined and connects to another, and they all just snake in and out and over on themselves. They really all become one.

"Everything," I say, "is entangled."

The detective purses his lips and looks at me sideways. He seems to be waiting me out, as if wanting more, but I stay silent. He doesn't follow up.

Our food arrives, and we thank the waiter, who asks if everything looks okay before he moves on.

"You know, in your first conversation with Ms. Cleary, you said you were a psychic," he says.

"Oh, that was just talk."

He takes a bite of his salad, and I taste my chowder, which is tasty but a little hot still, so I place my spoon down next to the plate to wait until it cools. Though I am on a full dosage right now, there is a churning inside and an anxiety that's building, and while my meds control the emotion from spilling out and all the wild ranting and my making a scene, they can't always keep it all down inside. I can still feel it there. I am only halfway to a mannequin, but not all the way.

"I want to tell you a story," Detective Harrison says. He dabs at the corners of his mouth with the napkin. "When I first started with PD as a rookie beat cop, I was assigned to South Central. Bad turf back in the day. Still no picnic now. My partner and I were sent to check on a domestic violence call. But hell, there were drugs running through that neighborhood and gangs, so we knew it could be anything. They sent a backup just in case.

"We go up the stairs and approach the apartment where the domestic dispute is supposed to be. As we walk down the hall, I hear my father's voice."

"Your father was there, at the apartment?"

"Oh no," Detective Harrison says, shaking his head. "My father had died of cancer five years earlier. Never saw me graduate from the academy or grow into a man. Broke my mama's heart. But it was his voice—definitely his voice—and he says softly, 'This way!' The direction his voice was coming from was at the opposite end of the hall, away from the apartment we're supposed to check out. So I said, 'Johnny'—that was my partner—'hold up!' He ignores me, points to the apartment door ahead, and keeps moving forward, and so I follow too. But then I hear my father's voice again, like a strong whisper, louder than before, saying 'No! *This* way!' and this time I turn and slowly head in that direction. It's like I was pulled there; I wasn't even thinking. I mean, you hear your dead father's voice calling you, and you lose sight of where you are and what you're supposed to be doing.

"But Johnny keeps walking on, and I don't know what to do, so I run hard at him, grab him by the arm, and yank him back. The next thing I hear is gun blasts blowing out the door ahead of us, and we take cover, return fire, and then the backup shows up and we get into a long, crazy gun battle until finally the shooters give up."

I take my spoon and swirl the soup. "So, your father—your dead father—saved you."

He nods.

"Of course," he says, "I couldn't put any of that in the police report. I'm a one hundred percent straight-up honest cop, but there are some things you just can't put in a report."

I nod my head, then try the soup, which has cooled to the perfect temperature now.

"Cole, do you know that in any given month, we get nearly three hundred missing person calls in Los Angeles?"

I know, of course, L.A.'s a big city, but this number still surprises me.

"Many are found pretty quickly," he goes on. "Maybe just a miscommunication. Maybe a kid runs away from home, then regrets it and comes back. But some become true disappearances—kidnapping, murder, all of that ugliness."

I set my spoon down, trying to think hard—even though it's really difficult now—where he's going with this.

"So. . ." and the detective pauses for a long time now, really hesitating. "You know, at the start of this talk, I said this is just you and me talking? Forget I'm a detective, and we're just two guys talking here."

"Sure."

"So . . . the policy of the LAPD—and I mean the hard, stone-cold policy of the department—is we don't use psychics to help us find people. The reasons are pretty obvious. Most people who say they are psychics are not. Those that may have some limited power—and I'm not even saying I believe one hundred percent in any of this, mind you—don't provide much help. There's also the image of the department to keep up, you know. You use outsiders for help in this way, and it's basically the department saying we believe in this stuff. Like I said, I don't even know if I fully believe. I'm just a guy who's seen some things and tries to keep an open mind."

"Huh."

The detective goes back to his salad.

"You know," he says with a mouthful, "I feel like I'm doing all the talking here."

"Sorry," I say. "Yesterday was a long day."

"Understood. Listen, I'm just saying that from time to time, we could really use your help. It would all be quiet. No publicity. Nothing in the police report. I can't pay you anything. It would be just between the two of us. Just two guys talking."

"I . . . I don't know."

I look around to see the hotel guests pass before me—mostly younger, hipper clientele that the hotel tends to attract. They look a lot like me or Robbie, and there are plenty of hipsters like Ray or Jamal. And there are families too, and I see a brother and sister in their swim suits dash by on their way to the pool, and the sister has a round inflatable tube around her waist, and she's chasing her brother, and they both jump in, laughing and cheering, and I try to count the people here on the deck and in the pool, but there's too much movement, and my mind is dull, but I try to imagine three hundred of them, every month, just vanishing, and they're not just numbers, but they have names, and they are each real people who have countless other people who love them.

"I have to ask you something," Detective Harrison says. "With Juan . . . why did you do it? Why did you feel you had to help him?"

My mind begins to shut down, because I really want to answer but wouldn't know if I could even explain it, the feeling that if everyone tries to be a little better, a little better than the ten percent the world is putting out right now and to stand up for an ideal or act in some way to improve the lives of others, then that would grow, exponentially grow and overlap on itself and become like compound interest that Einstein said was the most powerful force in the universe or that Bobby Kennedy said would create a great current which could sweep down the mightiest walls of oppression and resistance, helping people make for a better life, or that I once said could take life from being a bitch to being a beach, but I would struggle to articulate any of that on a good day, and so I have *no* chance of saying it now.

"Listen," the detective says, "that day when I questioned you in your apartment, at the end, once I knew it wasn't you, I told you to stay away from this case. We would handle it. Remember?"

"Sure."

"But you had this look—this wild, defiant with a capital D look—and I just knew there was no way you were going to back down. And so we tailed you from that point on since we had nothing else to go on, and you led us to the boy. But what I'm saying is that that look you had that day was a look of, *I have to do this.* I didn't understand why—and still don't—but you had to keep going and not stop. It's what you were *meant* to do."

I swirl my soup some more, then take another sip.

"This is really delicious," I say, "you should try it sometime." I hope it's enough to change the subject. I really want to change the subject, and I can feel the energy *really* building up inside now.

"You know," he says, "it may be just the thing you need. Something to make you feel, I don't know, fulfilled in life?"

I rub my temples.

"I really think it could help you become . . ." he shrugs, "happy."

I watch the lone hummingbird frantically flying from one flower to the next with an incessant buzz, wings flapping in a dizzying blur. I feel a pang in my heart. My breathing becomes hard and fast.

"Cole, are you okay?"

I narrow my eyes, teeth clenching, then throw my head back to the beautiful azure sky, and scream, "*EVERYBODY'S GOING TO BE OKAY!*"